THE MARRIAGE OF
TIME & CONVENIENCE

Also by Robert Winder

NO ADMISSION

THE MARRIAGE OF TIME & CONVENIENCE

Robert Winder

Robert Winder.

HARVILL
An Imprint of HarperCollinsPublishers

First published in 1994 by Harvill
An Imprint of HarperCollins*Publishers*
77–85 Fulham Palace Road,
Hammersmith, London W6 8JB

1 3 5 7 9 8 6 4 2

© Robert Winder 1994

A CIP catalogue record for this title is
available from the British Library.

ISBN 0 00 271360 8

Photoset in Linotron Galliard by
Rowland Phototypesetting Ltd, Bury St Edmunds, Suffolk

Printed and bound in Great Britain by
HarperCollinsManufacturing Glasgow

TO HERMIONE

"Examine for a moment an ordinary mind on an ordinary day"

VIRGINIA WOOLF

PRELUDE

Luke must have been dreaming, because one minute he was leaving the office at the usual time and in the usual way, and the next he was lying in the road in front of a large red bus. Actually, he was just wondering why seconds were called seconds when he stepped off the pavement, but before he had time to run through the possible explanations the bus hit him. The driver was quick with the brakes, and somehow he managed to swerve a fraction towards the centre of the road. So although Luke didn't know exactly what had happened, it was the flashing orange indicator that tapped him on the shoulder and knocked him backwards on to a patch of wet leaves.

He was lucky, everyone agreed. It could have been . . . well, anything could have happened.

A few passers-by were standing around, waiting to see how bad things were. Luke heard the doors of the bus flip open with their whiplash gasping noise, and was aware of feet thudding on the tarmac. For a minute or two he did nothing but blink up at the pale faces of the onlookers.

I'm sorry, he said. I just didn't see it, I can't think why.

There was a strong smell of oil fumes, and Luke thought he could hear birdsong – sparrow, with a touch of blackbird and pigeon thrown in.

Are you all right?

Yes, I'm fine, I think.

Luke thought about standing up, but decided to stay lying down a bit longer. Far above him a mass of dirty clouds, darkened by the dusk and pushed about by the March wind, seemed to be swooping down for a closer look. Then a face loomed in and blotted out the view.

Don't try to move.

A hand touched Luke's elbow.

Really, Luke said, forcing himself into a sitting position. It's nothing. His arm felt heavy and he rubbed his shoulder.

No one seemed to know what to do.

Really, Luke said. It was the only word that sprang to his mind, even though he had a sharp sense that the situation was anything but real. And why was it up to him to reassure these people? He leaned back and then forward and the rocking motion helped him to his feet. I appreciate your help, he said in a clear voice, but I'm fine. It was my fault completely.

You're telling me. Jesus, I thought I was going to hit you for sure. If you hadn't jumped back . . .

Jumped back?

At the last minute. Christ, I couldn't believe it when you stepped out. What the hell were you doing?

I wasn't doing anything.

Well. You seem to be okay.

Don't know what I was thinking of.

Afterwards, he would decide that it was because the bus had been so close. It must have been right on top of him, blocking out the sky, the edges too high and wide to make an impression – how else could he have missed it? Okay, he hadn't been paying attention, but even so . . .

The driver climbed back on board, and so did the passengers who had hopped down to see what was going on. Luke felt a sudden shiver of embarrassment, but forced himself to stand back and even managed a friendly, laughing-it-off sort of wave as the bus pulled away from the kerb, wipers swatting to and fro across the big windscreen even though it wasn't raining. He took a couple of deep breaths, moved his shoulder up and down a few times to test the pain, and began to walk towards the tube.

He stopped when he realised he was walking south instead of north, and that's when he noticed that his hands were shaking. He tried clenching them into fists, but this only encouraged the ache in his shoulder, so he shoved them into his pockets. As he walked back the other way, he inhaled for the first time since last summer the green fragrance of freshly mown grass.

Almost without thinking, he stopped when he came to an amber light, and it was then that he realised he would not be able to face travelling underground. He wanted to be here where the air was, even if, apart from the odd grassy whiff, it was only dull city air, full of chemicals and grime. An exceptional thing had happened to him, and he decided to mark the occasion by riding home in a taxi, for once.

When he touched his shoulder, he jumped at the almost tangible jolt. When he closed his eyes for a second, all he could see was a flashing orange light.

He watched the cars go by for a while, each with a little aerial jabbing the sky. They were like fishing rods, he thought. People these days weren't happy unless they were throwing baited hooks into the shimmering pool of electronic signals, hoping to net something that would make them feel better.

Was it possible that there were things so big you couldn't see them coming? For some reason, the idea bothered him a good deal.

At home he ate two fried cheese sandwiches with some red wine, and fell asleep in front of the television. He woke up twice in the night, quite a novelty for someone who normally, according to his girlfriend Carmen anyway, slept like a log. And the following morning he was an hour late for work, another first.

For a day or two he felt a kind of euphoria. The bruise on his shoulder came up nicely: plum-coloured with a very dark centre and an impressive yellow surround, just the way bruises were supposed to be. Luke was happy to let anyone who wanted have a look, and after a while even started showing it to people who didn't mind whether they saw it or not. The world was divided, he said with a laugh, into people who had been hit by a bus and people who had not. He now belonged to much the more exclusive group. It struck him that he was living an interesting life, a life in which anything could happen.

If he had seen Carmen, he would have been only too glad to let her inspect his wound. But they didn't often meet in the week, and once the swelling had gone and the colours had faded there didn't seem much point going on about it. Carmen phoned one evening and they talked for quite a long time, but somehow the opportunity to describe what had happened never presented itself. And in their subsequent conversations Luke realised that it would be odd to mention it now: he would have to explain why he hadn't said anything before, and he couldn't think of a single reason.

By the end of the week, in any case, Luke's high spirits had dissolved. The idea that there were things too big to see nagged away at the back of his mind, and sometimes at the front. More than once he found himself calculating how close he had come. Several times he rewound his memory back to the moment of impact, and on each occasion he flinched at the shock, which in retrospect was even more intense and painful than it had seemed at the time.

What if he had taken one more stride? What if the bus had been going a quarter of a mile an hour faster? Luke started to have visions of himself crumpled in the road, feet up on the kerb, his head beneath a giant metal hood, the blue glare of an ambulance spinning round like a lighthouse, or like the hands of a clock out of control, faster and brighter with every revolution.

Bit by bit, the scene became so clear and so frightening that Luke grew reluctant to close his eyes, and began to fall asleep in front of the television almost every night.

Something had to give, he told himself. Something had to change.

But what could he do, trapped in a godforsaken dead-end of a job, with never a spare minute to mull things over?

A dead-end job – what was he saying? He liked his work fine, and was good at it. Besides, what about Carmen . . . Surely he wasn't going to let a farcical little traffic accident shake everything loose?

But no matter how hard he tried, he wasn't able to shut down whatever part of himself was generating these unwelcome doubts.

One evening, a few weeks later, he was leaving the office at the usual time and in the usual way when he found himself standing on the very same spot where he had been bowled over. It wasn't much of a spot. There was a drain below the kerb with cigarette ends stamped around the edge, and a drift of leaves and newspaper was gumming up the flow and creating a shallow pool of greasy water.

Luke let a few cars go past and waited until he could see a bus come lurching up the road. He stood on the edge of the pavement until the bus was just a few yards away, watching it grow and grow until it blanked out the colourful advertising hoardings and the rooftops of the buildings. He took one pace forward, and for a second it was as though he was going to let the bus hit him again, but at the last minute he pulled back and felt a sudden, shocking wind ruffle his hair. The warm exhaust tickled his shins, and a cold bubble of petrol-filled air slapped him in the face.

He rubbed his shoulder and watched the bus topple down to the roundabout. Two sharp red flashes lit up the evening when the driver touched the brakes, but the road must have been clear, because the bus didn't seem to slow down at all as it swung left and fell away down the hill on the other side.

Luke was working, while all this was going on, for a small computer outfit. He'd wandered into this field after a long devotion to computer games, and although he started out by working in a stereo shop, high fidelity let him down in the end. He was surprised when he discovered that his computer knack made him sought after, because he could not see what was so hard about it. But he wasn't going to complain if people paid him to tinker with expensive machines.

His desk was a trestle table in a cavernous office – formerly a ballroom – criss-crossed by head-high partitions. This, too, was fine by him: he enjoyed working on his own. So long as he kept his head down it was private enough, though it was never quite possible to ignore the constant tapping and beeping on the far side of the flimsy screens that surrounded him.

At the moment, Luke was working on a system for controlling traffic lights. He enjoyed thinking of all those motorists idling at junctions, cursing the way the lights always seemed to be red. How could they know that their journey home was governed by the suppleness and fluency of his own invisible design? They might zip through an amber light and think they'd been lucky, but Luke would know that good fortune had nothing to do with it. Those commuters racing down the wide highways, the lights turning green in front of them as if they had seen someone coming and were politely raising the gates – don't tell me, a coincidence, right?

The aim was to replace the old system of remote timers with a more fluid, brainy approach. Luke was busy developing a network of lights that would take their cues from the cars, and it involved all the new tricks of artificial intelligence – or fuzzy logic, as the buffs called it. Nothing made Luke tremble more than the thought of fast cars stranded at a red light when nothing was coming the other way. In theory, it was now possible to scan the roads automatically and tailor the signals to the weight of traffic. The only problem was speed: everything had to happen instantaneously. Real time, they called it – real, human time. The computers had to be as fast as thought, as slippery as a conditioned reflex.

Luke had scored an eye-catching success with his latest toy, a computerised model – essentially a game – which allowed the controller to drive an entire system. You could sit there, staring at a magnificent view of the slow-moving cars, and switch the lights around as you pleased. It was great fun to play, but people weren't clever enough: they always lost track somewhere. So Luke had programmed the system to drive itself. There were some underlying rules: plenty of green in built-up areas, swathes of red if nothing was waiting, and so on. But otherwise the computerised brain watched the cars like a patient sheepdog, nudging them into new pastures with quick, soft benevolence.

A vast amount of work on the actual roads was needed to make it work, but the system made quite a splash when Luke exhibited it at a trade fair. Noisy crowds heaved around the booth to watch him nurse cars through the grid of streets. Luke became something of a celebrity in routing and signalling circles, though he was alarmed to hear that the police were taking an interest as well (for entrapment reasons).

His private ambition was to reduce the amount of time a city might spend on amber. Hundreds of car hours were wasted in that idle grey area between red and green, stop and go. People hardly ever noticed this, the way they didn't see that the moon was half-full twice a month. But Luke was making a big point of squeezing amber out of the system as far as the safety regulations would allow.

It was partly a philosophical question. The whole beauty of computers was that they saw the world in black and white. They responded to only two signals – a high voltage and a low voltage; and could never see more than two sides to a question. So these traffic lights, which had three alternatives (four, if you included red-and-orange together) gave Luke quite a headache. If you weren't careful you could get trapped in amber, like a fly.

It was amazing how much you could do, though, with a straightforward binary intelligence, and it delighted Luke that astonishing effects could be achieved merely by the accomplishment of a thousand simple tasks.

This was useful knowledge: a big decision, he figured, was just a confused group of easy decisions piled up together.

Sometimes Luke tried, in a playful, experimental spirit, to imagine his own intelligence computerised (he was capable, in his bad moments, of being an out-and-out electronic junkie). People were right, he thought, when they referred to human brains as grey matter: they had a murky quality which made the bolshy, one-step-at-a-time single-mindedness of micro-thought even more seductive. The human memory was fallible, whereas computers had total recall. It was an uphill struggle – he was the first to admit that. But the idea of holding a mirror up to science, of turning the tables on the goals of artificial intelligence, impressed him no end. He was sure it would lead to something refined and new, because no matter how elaborate the intelligence he fabricated, he always came back to one basic truth: computers were nothing more than decisive, high-speed choosers.

To tell the truth, Luke had always been a bit shaky in that area. His first year up in the big city had been dreamy to the point of disaster. Metropolitan life, which he was not used to, ran him over. For months he wallowed in a deep rut of solitary self-absorption. But then Carmen reached out a hand and pulled him up towards her, and made him feel as if he were a normal person, just like anybody else.

This is why his accident, which in truth was a collision of the most pedestrian sort, gave him such a jolt. His faith in the power of binary calculations, which usually helped him to make sense of things, took a nasty bruising. He explored the incident on his computer at home, itemising as many individual factors as possible. But though it was easy enough to unravel the web of circumstances that led the bus to be at that precise place at that precise time – the number of passengers, the time-consuming fumbles for change, the way the driver had shot the lights further up the road, the unexpected moment of generosity when he pulled away and then paused to let one more person run panting up the steps – there was no accounting for the fact that Luke, though he had his eyes open and was not remotely short-sighted, never saw it coming.

It was too damn close, too damn big. It was right on top of him. That's all there was to it.

Another thing bothered him: when he began to imagine the spanner he had thrown into the bus timetable, he felt weak all over. It was the same when a traffic light jammed. The ripples from a blow like that could set in motion waves strong enough to drown the entire city.

The more he processed the data, the more he turned up stray facts that didn't make sense. The way the bus had its wipers on, for instance, even though it wasn't raining. Maybe the driver was dazed; maybe he meant to hit the indicator and put his finger on the wrong toggle. Perhaps it was the first time anything like this had ever happened to him – for all Luke knew, he might have been well known around the depot as a man of extreme caution, who in twenty years had never hurt a sparrow.

Or maybe there was a smear of dirt on his windscreen.

Maybe, maybe, maybe: it didn't look as though the steady sifting of yes/no options was going to help at all.

It shocked Luke to realise that the accident hadn't happened to him alone, that there were others involved who perhaps saw themselves as central characters in the drama. It all provoked in him a restless urge to get away, to see things from a new angle.

Something had to change, he began to tell himself. Something had to give.

*   *   *

A month passed, and outwardly Luke seemed fine. His bruise flowered and died with dismaying speed. He cracked the usual jokes at the office and spent the weekends with Carmen, watching films and eating afterwards as if nothing had happened.

But inwardly he was experiencing a mini-crisis. All he ever did, a voice inside him pointed out, was stare at screens. He spent his long office hours gazing at a monitor, and then most of the evening, too.

And they weren't called screens for nothing, he thought, growing sombre. Salesmen called them display units, and talked about windows, but in fact they were designed to cut things off, to give you a partition to hide behind. More and more, Luke wanted to find out what was on the other side.

If anyone had asked, Luke would have claimed that his disposition was sunny; but as Carmen had once told him, he was also prone to cloudy spells, some of them prolonged. For several weeks he struggled to see blue sky, but he couldn't find a way through the gloom that had settled over him.

Even his work suffered. He started to think of computers as blunt. He'd devoted years of thought to the idea of artificial brain power, but hell, they couldn't even ride a bike without calculating the effects of centrifugal force and the physics of gravity, and by the time they'd worked that lot out they'd have fallen off for sure. They'd be rubbing their scuffed elbows and saying they didn't want to ride a bike anyway, what was wrong with walking.

Maybe human memories weren't so much fallible as selective. Perhaps they edited life as if it were a manuscript, hanging on to the crucial things and discarding the rest.

One evening Luke went with Carmen to a Chinese restaurant. They fiddled with their chopsticks and were talking in a relaxed way about summer holidays, when suddenly Luke stabbed a piece of spring roll and said the thing was, it was pointless just going abroad for a week or two, you had to live there. Carmen agreed: she'd always wanted to work overseas. So they spent an hour talking about where they'd most like to go. Carmen said Spain. Luke said California. But then he added that it wasn't so much the country, the real issue was whether you lived in a city or not. Carmen shrugged, and said that people from cities always dreamed of thatched cottages, wisteria over the porch and so on, while rural folk had visions of terraced houses and late-night taxis home after the concert. Believe me, she said, I know what I'm talking about.

It was just a conversation: neither of them expected it to amount to anything. But a week or two later Luke received a letter from an Italian company which had heard about his new system. Might he be interested in joining them, heading up a new team? The package would be attractive, if he wanted to talk further. The language was no problem, they said. He spoke computer, and that was what counted.

Well, it felt like an omen. Italy, though? He liked the food, sure, didn't everyone? But he was happy where he was, wasn't he?

And then one day Brian, his boss, invited him to lunch. It was bad timing, with Luke in the mood he was in. And he didn't think much of Brian at the best of times. He was taken aback, all the same, when he heard himself murmur that he needed a change and was thinking of accepting a job in Italy.

It was a fib, little more than a boast. But lies, as everyone knows, can return to haunt us. Maybe because it was improvised, Luke felt he had to be more resolute than usual, so he made it sound as if his mind was made up. By the time the coffee arrived it was pretty much official: Luke was going to Rome. Brian accepted it with humiliating good humour. Traffic lights in Italy, eh? he said. That's a good one.

After that, well, it was too embarrassing to explain that there was nothing to it. If something had gone wrong at the interview, Luke might have had to crawl back and stammer on about second thoughts, about the package not being quite up to snuff. But everything went like clockwork. They wanted him to start as soon as possible.

Which is why, on one particular morning in late March (a Friday), Luke woke up at twenty past seven exactly. He knew the time was dead on, because he had taken particular trouble to set two alarm clocks. He had a plane to catch at 11.15, and there was plenty to do between now and then. More than he knew, in fact.

Three months divided Luke's bus adventure from the morning he was supposed to jet off to Italy. Three months – and yet it took only a few pages, only a few minutes of reading time, for us to catch up. This is one of literature's advantages over life: it can make time fly. Books are full of breezy fast-forwards such as this: days, months and years can expire in, almost literally, the blink of an eye.

That's about to change. From now on we'll be following Luke's life at more or less the right speed. There are three hours to go before the plane leaves, and this book will take three hours to read.

It is, in other words, a story set in what Luke would call real time. He knows that this is a fiction, that things only ever seem simultaneous. Radio signals travel faster than television waves: sharp-eared listeners can discover the winner of the hundred-metres dash, or some great horse race, a fraction sooner than viewers. But these are minor quibbles. As the minutes pass on the page, so the hands on our wrists will flicker on in their endless circuits, for all the world as if they had their fingers on our pulse. If printed letters can leap up to our eyes at the speed of light, why shouldn't we read, once in a while, at the speed of life?

Much will depend on how quickly you turn the pages. Reading is like any journey: there can be delays, hold-ups, leaves on the line. Skim along fast, and Luke's morning will go by just like that. Take it easy, and three hours will feel like for ever. To be absolutely accurate, we need to assume an average reading speed of seventy pages per hour. Obviously this is right up against the speed limit, so it might be better to clamp down right now and settle for a steady sixty pph – this would have a certain aesthetic coherence, would imply a variety of *interesting equations between speed and time, and might even lead us to address the latest games of continuum warp and collapse. But you have to be realistic – and if things do slide, well, it's not the end of the world.*

Anyway: if you're travelling by train from Liverpool to London, or by plane from Glasgow to Athens, or by bus from the outskirts of York to the town centre, you'll be turning the last few pages, hurrying, as the platforms slide past on either side at Euston station and the train plugs into the capital, or as the plane sinks towards the classical smog beneath the Acropolis, or as the grey buttresses of the Minster shimmer out of the soggy Yorkshire sky. If you're sitting at home when the Nine O'Clock News comes on, and you decide not to watch and start reading this instead, then you'll complete the journey, rubbing your eyes and cursing yourself for staying up so late, on the dead stroke of midnight.

The sad thing is, books aren't like planes or trains – you don't cruise at a steady speed. Reading is lumpy, like life. There are times when you slow down or stop altogether, times when you replay something in your mind or pause for a closer look, times when you rush ahead, thinking you'll nip back later to see what you missed. Truth be told, time is about the most slippery, the most easily convertible and the most plastic of all our modern currencies. You can make it, save it, waste it and spend it. You can keep, lose, find, run out of, borrow, and ask for a bit more of it. You can have a hard one, an easy one, a good one, a bad one, a great one, even a wild one. You can check it, take it, be ahead of or behind it; you can be in it or out of it. Time will let itself be pushed around by almost any verb: you can even, as the saying goes, do it. You can race against it, though you'll hardly ever win. And if you're lazy, like most of us, you can kill it.

It might be that our willingness to treat time as a noun is what makes it seem so concrete. As soon as we depict it as something we can measure, we lend it the solid attributes of a mountain, or a river, or a piece of string. We speak of our allotted span, our threescore years and ten, as if our lives had an identifiable length. Possibly the only truthful version of time is when it is a verb, when we ourselves hold the stopwatch, when we do the timing. Only then does it sound like what it is: our own idea, a way of making the untraceable gap between events seem palpable. We do the same thing with life, of course, detaching ourselves from the verb as if our lives have their own shape, as if it's just a stroke of luck that we happen to be living them.

We can fool around with definitions all we like – in the end, no matter how much time we borrow, we have to give it back. Somewhere there must be a big safe where all the time-bullion is stored, but no one has ever picked the lock. We flutter into the unknown, but time's careless wings just go on beating, beating.

More vexing still: as time goes by, it speeds up. When you are ten years old, a year is a tenth of your life – a chunk worth worrying about. But when you're fifty, a year is . . . are you having me on? What's a year, between friends? At such moments life can seem like an old clock that's running ahead of itself: suddenly you find yourself wishing you'd splashed out on an expensive one, instead of making do with these cheap imitations.

Only when there's a bomb about to go off, and the hero has just seconds to work out how to trip the fuse and save the world – only then does the narrative clock run true, and it is odd how drawn-out these moments can seem. More often, characters turn grey, grow mournful and fall out of love in the time it takes us to turn a few pages. Or a single swing of the pendulum, a passing thought, is spread out over chapter after chapter.

It's only natural: some times are more crowded than others. Either the days are hurtling past and last weekend is already hard to recall, or the minutes are trudging along one by one, with heavy steps. Yet the passage of time in which nothing unusual cropped up always seems, in retrospect, to have lasted no longer than a split second. To make time, all you have to do is slow down.

I'm aware of this. I know that it's taken a minute or so to read even the last page, and can well imagine all the other things you could have done. You could have run a quarter of a mile, or walked about a hundred yards – just to name two things well worth doing. You could, according to the record books, have drunk nine pints of beer by now. You could have toasted a slice of bread – or two slices, while you were about it – and in the meantime the kettle could have been boiling; and while that was happening you could have phoned friends and left messages on their answering machines. You could have booked a flight to the far side of the world, or decided to change your life by asking someone to marry you. It only takes a moment to do these things, though usually we're too busy to get round to them.

If you were a particle of light, you could have travelled about ten million miles, assuming you kept your foot down. If you were a fly, or one of those bugs that only lives for a few hours, you would be growing up fast, your youth perhaps squandered – already you'd be full of regrets about opportunities missed, crumbs not taken. If you were a whale, you wouldn't even have taken a breath.

Maybe you've had several cups of coffee, too many cigarettes, or a high-achieving day, and you're gliding along more easily than usual. The next three hours will pass by in a flash. It'll seem amazing that so much could have been crammed in. Perhaps you're lying in a bath, and the water's growing cool, and you don't know why but you feel like finishing the book before you get out, and even though you're shivering you want to get this over and done with – well, if that's the case you could probably do it in an hour.

But it will take Luke three hours to get to the end of the book: it is one of the few matters in which he has no choice. When he woke up it was twenty past seven. And his flight number was already on the television screens at the airport, winking on and off as it worked its way towards the head of the queue.

The idea that anything unexpected might happen to him this morning was just about the last thing on his mind.

Twenty past eight

Actually, it wasn't the clocks; something else woke Luke, but afterwards he couldn't remember what it was. A gurgle in the pipes, possibly, as the nervous system of the house warmed the radiators and filtered heat behind the taps. It could have been his thoughts, some small turbulence in his dreams. It might have been the phone ringing. Or maybe it was just some stray noise from outside, a car horn or the rattle of junk being tossed into a skip.

Luke's bed was underneath a window which looked out over some gardens, and he'd left the curtains open on purpose, so that the sunshine would wake him if the clocks failed. He squinted at the sky, but couldn't see much, just a grey filtered light that didn't seem to begin anywhere and splashed a special urban glare across the room. Now that he looked, he could see that it was wet outside; not raining exactly, just grey air full of water. It was supposed to be spring, but this looked like one of those days when you felt like giving the sky a good squeeze just to drain the moisture out of it.

Through the half-open window he could hear speeded-up pop songs. It was a habit they had, the children who lived in the houses over there. The voices went all high-pitched and squeaky, and the guitars sounded like harpsichords. Every now and then they would hit on a song they couldn't get enough of, and play it over and over again. Yes, there it was. Luke let his eyelids fall and tried not to listen. They might be saving time, but they were sure as hell killing music.

Further away he could hear the roar and clang of the

car-wreckers by the main road. You could see it from the train – an enormous graveyard piled high with dead vehicles. Someone had spray-painted in large white lettering on the hoardings outside: RUST IN PEACE. But there was a fat chance of that – what a racket. Didn't they know what time it was?

Luke rolled over to his left with a sudden jerk when it occurred to him that it might be late; but he had to relax half-way when he felt a muscle in his right arm crease and stretch. One of the clocks, the digital one, said 07:19:15 in red digits, the colons flashing on and off, on and off. The hands on the other stood at just after twenty past seven.

The digital alarm went off the second Luke touched it. It was like stepping on a mine. Luke snatched his hand back fast. But the clock soon settled down and started making its little bleating noise, with those rhythmic gaps which could fool anyone who didn't know into thinking that it had stopped. Luke let it go for a while, then pushed the small black slide away from al:on and back to al:set. It was a red plastic cube with a company logo printed in white on the sides, beneath a crown pattern. On the top it had a dial which showed the time in about thirty cities across the world. Right now, for instance, in Hawaii, it was about . . . Luke tried to turn the disc, but it was a long time since he'd used it, and his fingers were still a bit fat and sleepy.

He decided to wait for the other alarm. It was odd, this waking just before the bell. Usually it pleased him, made him feel well-regulated. But this morning the pleasure was fringed with shadows. Was he so enslaved to the routines of the day that even when he was unconscious he noticed the seconds ticking past?

It was as if the clock, unwinding through the dark hours, had somehow turned a small key in his back and released him with a jangle into the morning. For a moment he was tempted to let himself slither towards sleep again, just to let everyone know who was the boss around here.

It didn't dismay him that the two clocks hadn't kept up with each other, though he was the kind of person who was sometimes bothered by such things. He would even wonder, now and then, whether putting one clock on the floor and the other on the table made any difference. Would the higher one, tugged by weaker gravity, go faster, as the experts claimed?

To tell the truth, the mechanical clock was past its best. It wheezed a bit in the early hours and dropped off the pace. But Luke had a soft spot for it. He enjoyed swivelling the tense golden pin to the chosen time, much as he had always liked making circles with compasses when he was young. You always had to perform this motion anti-clockwise, as if you wanted to get up hours ago, and this gave Luke a few uneasy moments; but it was still better than these digital clocks, which stole the narrative out of time, cut across the slow rotation of the hands as they wheeled round the black illuminated circle through the night, and annulled the astronomical associations, the curve of the sun across the sky, the movement of the stars, the rotation of the earth. If you took that away, severed the previous connection with original science, what were you left with? Nothing but cold, numb data. Numbers.

It was even worse with radios. With the new sort, you had to know how many kilohertz you felt like; it wasn't enough to remember that the station you wanted was over to the left some-where. Luke didn't listen to the radio as often as he used to, and sometimes thought that this was the only reason.

Nor did it occur to him that this sentimental fondness for the old order did not tally with his enthusiasm for high-speed binary precision, parallel processing and all that. There were contradic-tions in there that Luke perhaps didn't want to think about too often. Even the artificial intelligentsia had a few blind spots.

At least he didn't have to rush. He could spend the next few hours inhaling the implications of what he was about to do.

These big decisions, he thought; you never really made them. The small ones always pushed to the head of the queue, and the big ones had to wait their turn. Sugar in your coffee? Milk? Full English or Continental? Red or white? You want that hot? With baked potato or fried? Extra cheese? French, Thousand Island, Italian? Smoking or non-smoking? Single or return (the return's cheaper)? Leaded or unleaded? Diamond service or regular? Superseal wash and wax or just wash? Straight glass or mug? First class or standard? Greasy or normal? Spring, dawn, dew or

23

autumn mist? Decaffeinated? Sparkling or still? English or French? This or that? That or this? Sometimes life seemed like one big multiple-choice exam, forcing you to take decisions all the time. Or was it a series of forked paths? Either way, it was against the rules to retrace your steps to the last turn-off, and what's more it was all one-way up ahead – there were no handy cross routes if you found yourself on the wrong track.

It was only recently that Luke had started to mind about any of this – since that business with the bus, in fact. For years he had gone on relishing the different options, the breadth of choice. He would linger with his head in the icy fumes over the frozen-food cabinet in the corner shop, wondering whether he felt like Tiger Prawns in Oriental-style Ginger Sauce or just some simple Chicken Croquettes alla Milanese. But these days he resented the effort required to choose. Man could not live, he said to himself, by breadth alone.

And the trouble was, while you dithered in front of the cartons, the really big changes just came sneaking up on you. They seemed no different from the tiny choices you were busy making, and then wham! – you found yourself with a new job or a new partner, or in a new place. By the time you started to unpack them into the pyramid of smaller options on which they rested it was usually too late. It was like, Luke thought, being smacked without warning by a bus: one of those things that came out of nowhere and landed on top of you before you knew it. Why was he going to Italy, for instance? Why not Sri Lanka? Why not Saudi Arabia?

No one had asked him, that was why.

It was never possible to admit this. He was fed up with England, so what the hell, he was going to Rome – that was how Luke put it, laughingly, to his friends. They all thought it was great, or so they told him. If they thought it was *that* great, he said to himself once or twice, it was funny that none of them thought of doing the same thing themselves. But he never had time to think about this for long. There was always something to do, another round to buy, some appointment he was late for; or perhaps the subject changed to last night's television pro-gramme: Did you see it? – It was incredible, I just turned on and happened to catch it. No, I was watching the England match. Yeah, I caught the end of the highlights, too. Tragic.

And by then it no longer mattered what anyone thought.

Oh well, he said to himself. Time to log on.

He made a few mental notes. The flight was scheduled to leave at 11.15 – a little under four hours from now. He never knew whether this was the time the plane was supposed to leave the ground or just the time it was meant to pull away from the gate; but he'd have to assume the worst. He'd need to be there by, say, 10.30, so to be on the safe side he had to be away by quarter to ten – though ten would do.

He still wasn't sure whether to call in on Carmen now or later. Now would be easier – they could have a nice breakfast, relax, maybe go for a little walk if the sky brightened. But perhaps it would be better to get everything cleared up here first. That's what Carmen would do: she was a great one for getting the boring stuff out of the way so you could enjoy yourself in peace. Luke, he had to admit, was the opposite.

And if he went later he could take her a present, pick up some flowers or a plant (more permanent).

He should have thought of this before, but there it was.

Another reason to leave it till later, he almost realised, was that he had no idea what he was going to say.

What was this? Cold feet? Did he wish he wasn't going? It wasn't a nice feeling, whatever it was. It made Luke want to pull his legs up under his chin and stay beneath those warm blankets for ever. But there could be no backing out now. He'd already said goodbye to everyone at his farewell drinks party. Even if he wanted to, he couldn't just go back and say, Hi, guess what, changed my mind, what's new?

It had all happened so fast. When he accepted the Italian job he wasn't certain that he would actually go. It was almost like a dare. If anyone had objected he might have had second thoughts, but most people seemed to think it was a terrific idea, Carmen especially. They'd gone back to that same Chinese restaurant and spent the entire evening eating bamboo and seaweed and talking about Italy, about sunshine and mountains and wine, things which naturally had nothing to do with the job at all.

With a move like this, you needed a breathing space. That was why he was going on a Friday, so that he'd have the weekend to get acclimatised. Ideally he would have gone a week ago, with Carmen. But there hadn't been time for anything like that.

They hadn't even had much of a chance to talk it through. Luke couldn't help feeling that something was missing. What did Carmen really think? Was she upset? Luke had been expecting – maybe he'd been hoping – for at least a gesture of sadness, the lifting of a finger to dab the corner of an eye. It was odd that he should harbour the slightest desire to make her unhappy, but we all know how these things are. He would have liked it, to be quite honest, if she'd burst into tears there and then.

That evening in the Chinese place: it seemed ages ago. But Luke could remember – he was still lying in bed, by the way – looking around at the empty platters of shredded beef and abalone and whatever else they had ordered, and waiting for something a bit more . . . dramatic. If Carmen had raised even one of her smooth eyebrows . . . well, it's possible that the whole idea, which was only a momentary flourish in a discussion about something else entirely, would have gone up in smoke. But she hadn't voiced any doubts at all. Why not? she agreed. You had to get out before you got sucked in for good.

What did she mean by that, exactly?

The idea that this whole Italian business was part of a conversation with Carmen, a conversation they weren't even having, made Luke frown and rub his eyes. He nibbled away at this thought until there was very little of it left. Almost mechanically, as if there were no alternative, he forced himself to check the clocks again. In looking forward to the final hours before his departure, he had never been able to get past the point where he was getting out of bed on a sunny morning, all set.

But it was raining, and he didn't know what was supposed to happen from now on. He had four hours, just under, to find out. He lay back into the pillow, and closed his eyes. Four last hours at home. It seemed like plenty of time, and he wanted to appreciate every moment.

*   *   *

You'd think that little white spaces like the above would be unnecessary in a novel that observes real time. You're thinking: what's wrong with an ordinary paragraph break? I mean, we know that Luke woke up at seven twenty, and it can't even be half past yet. You're probably wondering why, given that he has a whole book ahead of him, he didn't spring from bed refreshed and eager, or why he didn't get up even earlier. Well, that's Luke for you. But maybe, to be fair to him, he stayed up late last night, till two or three in the morning, packing clothes into suitcases and wrapping glasses in newspaper before stacking them in a cardboard box for storage.

Or it could be that he was drinking with friends, having one last fare-well party. That would be only natural. For all we know he might have intended to spend the evening packing and getting ready when they dropped round, eight or nine of them, old friends with bottles. He couldn't have thrown them out, could he? Anyway, he'd have been pleased to see them. What a nice surprise! One of the points of leaving home is to give people a chance to say how much they'll miss you. And you get a chance, your heart swelling with emotion, to return the compli-ment, though presumably you wouldn't be going if you really meant it.

It's more likely, in fact, that Luke spent last night with Carmen, eat-ing and talking, wondering if this whole trip was not so much a fresh start as an ending of some kind. She would have been cool, a little within herself. They would have talked about when she might come out to see him, whether he'd be back for her birthday (July) and so on. She would have reminded him to set an alarm clock, and he would have laughed and said, Don't be stupid, what do you take me for? All the time he would have had an uneasy feeling that he was not saying enough. He would have pretended to be more excited about going than he really was; she would have pretended to mind his leaving less than she really did. It was, they would have agreed, a chance not to be missed. But their conversation would have been punctuated by longer pauses than usual, little white spaces that both of them found uncomfortable.

And that's what this is. It often happens that the gap between one second and the next requires something larger and more definite than a punctuation mark. One minute you can be lying in bed, thoughts running through your mind like water through the pipes of the house, preparing yourself for the day, warming up. The next, you could have clambered to your feet – clambered, at any rate, if you're as tall as

Luke – and pulled a dressing gown over your arms, ducking your head to make sure the collar falls properly. That's if you have a dressing gown: maybe you've just pulled on a sweater draped over the back of a chair. You could already be dressed for all I know. Anyway, between those acts there's a gap, a caesura, which a thin sliver of white space understates, if anything.

It isn't always easy to say how long these white spaces last. You shut your eyes for one final whiff of sleep, and bang, that's the morning gone. That's how it was with Luke. There he was, a lump beneath his ancient blue duvet. It seemed ridiculous to hurry. All he did was shut his eyes for a second and then, an unguessable period of time later, he rose from the warm nest of cotton and down and unfolded his long white limbs into the day.

For the record, he lay there brooding for less than seven minutes after the clocks crowed; not much of an indulgence. If it took more than seven minutes to read about it, you'll want to take into account that beginnings take longer to read than endings – everything's new, and you have to find your bearings. So if those early pages dragged, well, it was only a few minutes.

Come to that, it might have been better if Luke had brooded a bit longer. You can save time, as he well knows, by organising it in advance. A little more planning, and he might have been able to make fewer trips between the bathroom and the bedroom, each of which ate up valuable seconds. But how could he have predicted what was about to happen? I mean, he was aware that there was this screen of unspoken feelings between himself and Carmen right now, but that was inevitable at a time like this. He couldn't have guessed that Carmen was preparing, even as he lay in bed thinking idle thoughts about clocks, to punch a hole through it.

But we're getting ahead of ourselves. Luke's feet have only just hit the floor.

The phone rang, and Luke opened his eyes. He smiled, and thought about not answering – he didn't have all day – but you never knew: it could be Carmen. They'd sort of said goodbye the night before, but not with any great conviction. Luke had tried to concentrate on having deep feelings of a memorable sort, but in the end it was just two people in a taxi, him saying he had his packing to do, her saying, fine, him fumbling for some money, her saying she had plenty, don't worry.

Even Luke's daydreams didn't always go according to plan. Several times this very morning he'd caught himself behaving as if Carmen was watching, or as if she would, later on, play back the film. It was like when the bus whacked him on the shoulder, and he went home with his head full of his lucky escape, imagining how people would react to the news of his death. What . . . Luke? You're kidding! Holy Cow! God, I hardly knew him, but he always seemed like the nicest . . . But then he had not been able to help imagining other people saying, Luke? What, the tall guy? That's terrible, but listen, I'm a bit tied up right now, could I get back to you.

When he asked himself whether he would miss Carmen he found it hard to reply. It took some effort to imagine not aiming his life in her direction. Once or twice he had created minor fantasies set in Rome. He would run into some olive-skinned, jet-haired beauty at a gallery or a swimming pool and escort her to a café for a drink. But invariably Carmen would be sitting at one of the tables, sunglasses pushed up into her hair, drinking a cold beer, a thing she loved to do. When he made an effort to block her out and concentrate on his imaginary companion, he could not prevent himself glancing across the sunny terrace to see what she was up to.

The phone was still ringing. Luke yawned and reached out an arm.

Hello?

Luke? It's Emma. Hope I didn't wake you.

Oh, right. Course not.

You probably don't remember. We've been sitting in the same room for the last two years.

Oh, now you mention it. Hi, Em.

How's it going?

Christ, you're in early.

Special occasion. Guy just left, we're all celebrating. Actually – her voice dropped a bit – you're well out of it. Brian's in one of his moods.

That's a surprise.

Luckily he's leaving in a minute.

Well . . . how's my desk? Anyone sitting there?

Oh, there is someone, yes.

Anyone I know? Don't tell me. Looks a *bit* like Cary Grant, but when he smiles it's more Tom Cruise . . .

No, he's coming in later. This one's a she. Tallish, auburn hair. Friends say she's slim but she doesn't agree. She'd look a bit like Goldie Hawn if she had blonde hair and that gap between her teeth. She's wearing . . .

So I've heard.

Thank *you*. Well, I've been through your drawers. I know all your secrets now.

Name your price.

Actually, it does look like this'll be my desk from now on.

How come?

I've been moved.

Since when?

About five minutes ago. It's good news, actually. I'm going to be working on Japlish, you know, the translation thing.

Since when did you know anything about Japanese?

Didn't I tell you? I used to be a geisha girl.

Oh, I remember. People ate lunch off you.

It's going to be fun. Did you know Japanese hasn't got a word for I?

No, I . . .

Anyway, I think the real reason was to move me further away. Brian said he couldn't stand me shouting down the phone.

Specially not in Japanese, Luke said.

Good old Brian, he thought. No one liked him. He was used to bigger companies, and more obedient staff. He liked people who wore suits and turned up on time and stopped talking when he came into the room. And he hated it when the computer kids started talking about log-switching into the centrex nodelinks, downbooting the perceptrons and inverting the analogue three hundreds. Was he aware that his staff sent joke messages about him through their computers, knowing he wasn't smart enough to read them even if he wanted to? Now that he was safely out of there, Luke felt a twinge of sympathy.

Actually, Emma was saying, it's fine by me, so long as I don't

30

have to work with Sam on anything. Don't know how you stood it.

Oh, he's all right. Speaks *very* highly of you.

That's what I mean.

Well, it could be worse. Least it won't be Keith.

Talking of Brian, you want to be careful you don't run into him at the airport. He's going off this morning somewhere. Lunchtime, I don't know.

What for?

Convention of some kind, I think. Least, that's the official line. Don't ask me why he got Cathy to book two tickets.

Really?

Cross my heart.

I almost hope I do run into him. That's amazing.

When are you leaving? All set?

In about . . . what did you say the time was?

Hang on. She must be twisting to look at the clock in Brian's office. Luke could visualise her slim legs – they *were* slim, whatever she said – resting on the pile of phone directories, the pale denim of her jeans drawn against the inside of her thigh. Coming up to half eight, she said.

Half eight?

Told you I was in early. That reminds me, the clocks go forward this weekend. God, it was funny last year. I remember my sister . . .

Jesus Christ!

What?

I must have . . . I thought it was half seven.

It was, an hour ago.

Thanks a bunch. Luke gave a snort. Oh well . . . What was so funny?

Oh, it was nothing. It was when the birds started clustering in the trees outside, and my sister said – she's amazing sometimes – she said how come the birds know the clocks have changed. I mean . . . nobody realised for a minute.

Well I feel like the clocks have changed this morning. It was half seven a minute ago. I must have gone back to sleep. Jesus, I've lost an hour, just like that.

31

Funny, isn't it? An hour. Just flew away in the night.

Hilarious, yeah. Still, it'll be nice next week. Long evenings and all that. You won't believe it's time to go home. It'll be too light.

I think it's time to go home now.

A whole hour. I can't believe it.

My heart bleeds. While you were dozing I was on the tube. Wish I hadn't bothered, I must say. Didn't realise Brian would be here already, and I didn't get a seat, as per usual. But I'd better let you go. I just got a coffee out of the machine, thought I'd ring to say bye.

Ah, the coffee machine. Luke would miss that, for sure. You fired in a coin and got a light saying: Machine Ready to Vend. One of the chaps had unscrewed the processor and rejigged the program so that you could get two cups for the price of one. The maintenance men couldn't work out how come it kept running out of coffee powder and whitener.

Yeah, well, thanks. Things are a bit hectic round here, as you can imagine. Freshly squeezed orange juice, the paper, rain seeping in the window, you know. Make sure I've got plenty of sun oil.

God, poor you.

I know. But someone's got to do it.

Thank you for Friday, by the way. That was fun.

Friday? What, the drinks?

First Caroline, now you. I'm starting to feel like the only one who hasn't left.

I should be thanking *you*. For coming.

Well . . . That was it, really. Maybe I'll see you. In Rome.

Great. Do. Call my secretary, make an appointment. Might be able to squeeze you in.

You don't say. Well actually I *will* be taking a holiday soon, I'm owed enough. And I think I'd . . . I wouldn't mind being . . . squeezed in.

Luke was glad Emma couldn't see him blush. Come on out, then, he said. We could go to a football match.

Brilliant. Can hardly wait.

No, it'd be different. He hesitated. Carmen, er, I don't know if you've . . . she might come out at some point.

Oh. Right.

But really, it'd be lovely to see you. I mean, I know it sounds . . . but probably I'll just spend a fortune on English papers and wish I was back here. If you came . . .

Okay. I'll let you know. Have you got a phone number?

No, I . . . I'll send it to you. I've got your address, haven't I? 27 Coventry Road.

By the cinema.

That's the one.

Yes.

Well, if you really mean that, about me coming out.

Yes, any time. I'll let you know where I am.

Great.

So . . .

Oh, I nearly forgot. There's some post for you. That was partly why I . . . What shall we do about letters?

Save them for posterity. Give them to the National Gallery.

Seriously. I'd better send them somewhere.

Er, well, here, I suppose.

Okay.

Only if they look nice, though. Pools wins, job offers, ones with pink envelopes. Anything perfumed. Burn the rest.

Okay.

Honestly, do come to Rome. It'd be fun.

I know.

Bye, Emma. Good luck with the translation.

Sayonara, Emma laughed. Bye then.

Luke carried on holding the receiver in his hand after they'd stopped talking, as if he wanted to keep the line open. Emma. Em. Emergency, they called her sometimes. Luke didn't know why: it was one of those names that just stuck, implying various things which perhaps weren't true at all. He'd never been anything but Luke – monosyllables had their advantages. For a while he tried to suggest that people call him Cool, after the Paul Newman film, and also because it was Luke backwards; it never caught on. His friend Jonathan called him Lucozade sometimes, though Luke pretended not to hear.

But never mind that: how on earth had he let himself go back to sleep? He had been feeling great a moment ago; now he was in a daze. What a way to start.

He wished he hadn't mentioned Carmen. It would be a shame if Emma didn't come . . . She was so easy-going: you could say, Let's catch a train up to Florence or to the coast, and she'd say, Great, okay, yeah, let's go. And she was – Luke tried to see her in holiday clothes, with warm light on her face and her hair glittering in the sun . . . I mean, if she wanted to come all that way it must have crossed her mind that they might . . . They could be lying on the beach, face down in the sand, and he would see her honey-coloured arms and those tiny wrists of hers, with the bangles, and he'd lean sideways and there'd be this skimpy band of turquoise cotton across her . . . and she would open her eyes and move a bit closer, and they'd . . .

But what was he saying?

God, an hour gone, out of nowhere. Maybe if he went high up, up to where time stood still, he could get it back. Or he could just get a move on.

He rolled on to his side, swung his legs over, and got out of bed.

It was rare that Luke could do much before a cup of coffee, so his first manoeuvre of the day was to sidle into the kitchen, yawning. Come to think of it, his first move, since we're being strictly accurate, was to go to the loo. He started off by aiming at the sides, moving his hips to keep the jet, which was a surprisingly rich colour this morning, away from the water. He even tried to hoover off a fleck of dirt at the back. But after a bit he realised that there was nobody around, so he went for the bull's eye.

Then he went into the kitchen and switched the kettle on. He kept one hand on the lid while it grew warm, and listened to the steamy gurgle gathering inside. A minute passed, just like that.

Some people were spooners, but Luke was a shaker. He waved the granules over the mug to control the flow and poured hot water on them. He had spilled a few too many out of the jar, so black clusters of coffee freckled the surface and hung there like weed. He added some milk from an open carton, thought for a moment, then tipped the rest of the milk into the sink. A perverse gesture, he could see – but he knew what he was like. Only if he chucked it away could he be sure that he wouldn't persuade himself to have another cup. And getting rid of the milk made him feel that he was taking a firm grip on things.

These cartons, some of his friends went into raptures about them; but given the choice Luke still went for bottles. Washing them out was supposed to be the hard part, but Luke quite enjoyed filling them with hot water and shaking the suds out like a firefighter or, if he used both hands, like a road-repair man with a boisterous drill.

The trouble with cartons was that you couldn't see what the milk was like until a rash of tiny yellow clots rose to the surface of the coffee like swept mines. Plus he knew someone who worked for one of the country's great paper makers, who told him about the chemistry that went into finding the balance between firmness and low conductivity of heat and about ten other things. Want to drink your milk out of a laboratory experiment? It was bad enough that it came, these days, from cows with no legs, just seven stomachs and a handful of udders mounted on a computerised milker. No thank you. Nice glass that smashed when you dropped it, that's what Luke liked.

He reached into the cupboard for some sugar but remembered, just in time, that there was none left. Instead he found an almost empty jar of honey, coated with butter and crumbs of burnt toast. A dash of wild flowers and bees legs to go with the roasted Brazilian beans and the rich, fresh-from-the-churn cow's milk . . . what luxury.

Did they *have* battery bees? Could you rely on the honey to be natural? On the jar it said Mexican Orange Blossom Honey, but that could mean anything. His coffee had been ground, sprayed, steamed, frozen, dried, and probably manicured as well; the milk had been sterilised, pasteurised, vitamin-enriched, skimmed, heated, cooled, and almost certainly inoculated against the major viruses. And the honey: for all he knew it was just a stew of ultra-refined sugar, with some bizarre sulphate or oxide that produced a honey effect, and some high-tech anti-plaque agent, boiled up with vanilla and cinnammon and maybe just a hint of Mexican orange blossom to give it that piquant, fresh-from-the-campo taste.

35

But the coffee smelled good. Luke took a sip. It tasted good, too.

Now, where were we?

He opened the paper – yesterday's – and turned it over. There was a large picture of a swimmer, arms high, head lost in the splash, neck and shoulders plunging, which he ignored. Instead he scanned the weather report. It was sixty-one degrees in Rome, but look at that – ninety-two degrees in Riyadh. Jesus, that's where he should be going – though probably it wouldn't be as interesting from the traffic angle.

He'd better ring Carmen now, to make sure she was still there.

Carmen, he said when she answered.

Luke. I was trying to call you a few minutes ago.

Oh, I was talking to someone.

How are you getting on?

Disaster. I overslept, would you believe? But I could . . . when are you off?

That's what I was going to ask. Come round for breakfast. Come now. I can be a bit late for once. Please say yes.

I'll just finish up here, then I'll be round.

I know all about you finishing up. Don't even start. There's something . . . I've got something to tell you.

Tell me now.

No, it'll wait. Be a surprise. How do you want your eggs?

What is it? What sort of thing?

You'll see.

Is it black tie, or what?

No, nobody died. Carmen laughed. Dress casual. Dress ready for action.

You make it sound . . . well, okay. I'm on my way.

Don't worry. Just come. Don't even think . . . no quick baths or anything, okay?

Right, well. I'll leave in a few minutes then. One last check.

I'll be here.

Before you go . . . Do they have battery bees?

What, like chickens?

Yes, strapped in long lines of pollen extract or something. To make honey.

What do you want to know that for?

Just occurred to me.

Actually, it's about the only thing they can't fake. They've tried, but they can't do it without the bees. And the bees can't do it without the flowers. Anyway, it's cheap, so what's the point.

Good.

I didn't know you were into natural food.

Well, I'm not. But I just ate some. Or drank some.

Drank?

It's a long story. Tell you later.

Great.

See you in a minute, then. Bye.

Ready for action? Whatever could she mean? He was about to ask again, but thought better of it.

But when he put the phone down, he frowned. Bang went his idea of surprising her with a present. Still, it was good that she wanted to see him one last time.

One last time? What was he saying? Was that what this was all about?

He took a gulp of coffee and walked over to the window. You could hear from the noise that the world was going about its morning business. Milk vans were sliding between the commuter hatchbacks, bakers were heaving fresh loaves out of lorries and lugging them into warm doorways, people were gathering at bus stops and railway platforms. Miles away, in huge out-of-town warehouses, cold rooms filled with high technology kept an unblinking eye on the flow of traffic.

He put his coffee down. It was – there was no other word for it – lukewarm. Still, it was nice to relax up here and watch the daily rush down below. Not that you could see a great deal: the view had never been one of the flat's best features.

He bent down and picked at a toe. There was a sharp snag, but as soon as he started tugging it felt as if the whole nail might come away in his fingers. So he pressed it back again.

Come on, come on. He felt . . . how did he feel? These days, he never knew. It was mostly grey – or amber – and he preferred life when it was black and white (at least he thought he did). But there wasn't much chance of that, not with Carmen around. She'd been keeping him guessing ever since . . . well, ever since they'd met.

He turned on the radio which was in its usual place, on the chest of drawers beside his bed. There were spots of yellow paint all over the top, which made it almost impossible to see the wavebands. But Luke didn't mind: you could feel your way across the frequencies. He spun the dial – anti-clockwise, of course – looking for a voice, and tangled himself in several hissing knots of static on the way. For a moment he hooked into a well-bred announcer introducing, with a sorrowful tone, some piece of music – the concerto in A was written when the composer was nineteen, and shows him experimenting for the first time with symphonic . . . – but he scrolled on through. Eventually – all of this took only a few seconds – he found a news programme. He turned the volume up loud and carried the radio with him into the bathroom.

He was wearing only a pair of shorts – he must have slipped them on when no one was looking – but even after standing in the kitchen talking on the phone he wasn't cold. The place had an empty feeling, though, which made him shiver. There were white patches on the walls where pictures used to hang, and little bits of rubble – wire coathangers, newspapers, torn envelopes, diskettes, ties, a golf tee – on the floor. The bathroom in particular looked abandoned, all white tiles with chipped edges, and higher up some yellow paintwork which had flaked off because of the steam. Luke remembered doing the painting himself: it took four coats to cover up the rich beetroot shade he had inherited. There were no towels, and most of the bottles and sprays and combs that had accumulated over the years had been chucked out.

On the radio they were saying that Lake Chad was losing all its water, thanks to the hordes of refugees huddled around the shore. Then they changed the subject. A giant pharmaceuticals company had been bought by the Japanese.

Luke listened with half an ear. He brushed his teeth and tried to steal a glance at himself in the mirror while he wasn't looking. One thing was for certain: he wasn't going to have much luck passing himself off as a local. He was tall, with very blond hair which he kept cropped hard in above his ears because when it grew it went curly, and for some reason he hated that. They'd almost certainly think he was German or Swedish. Maybe it was these Northern looks that made him insist on his love for the sunny nonchalant south. For a pale person he tanned okay, though, and in summer, once he'd gone brown from tennis, he wore shorts all the time.

Luke still tended to think of himself as slim, but you couldn't fool the mirror. At the office people kept coming round with straw baskets full of sandwiches and chocolate, and it was hard to resist the odd snack. Okay, more than odd. Luke wheezed when he ran up the stairs these days. One of the plus points about Italy was the prospect of a better diet. He lifted his shoulders and breathed in. No one could say he was trim, but there was still hope.

He bounced his eyebrows a few times as if that would be enough to rub out the wrinkles on his forehead. He had never imagined himself a frowner until one of the girls at the office, Emma probably, imitated him during some game or other by screwing up her face tight, like a baby about to cry. He had flinched at the time, but the evidence was there all right: three vertical grooves between his eyebrows and a deep pucker away from his lip on one side. He opened his eyes wide and bent forward. All his life he'd been worried that a dark fleck in his brown eyes was growing larger, but every time he looked he couldn't tell if it was bigger than last time. He often imagined the fleck growing into a spot and then turning into a stain that would gradually blind him, but so far it was still hardly visible.

Rescue workers are still searching, the radio said, for five miners who were trapped when a roof collapsed earlier this morning . . .

Christ, Luke thought. They must start work early. Then, ashamed of his reaction, he tried to imagine being buried in a mound of black, wet coal half a mile underground.

Pleaded for calm . . . believed to have been triggered by a gas explosion . . . no sign of life . . . rescue workers struggled to gain access . . . families braced themselves . . .

Luke sighed, and rinsed out his toothbrush. He twisted his head and tried to look at a filling he'd had done a fortnight ago.

39

He had once devised a new sort of looking glass. People talked about mirrors as if they were dead accurate and hardly ever suffered from interference, unless you counted steam. Luke thought the opposite. All those people who were praised for holding mirrors up to nature – what, they got everything back to front? So he spent quite a bit of time making a mirror that kept things straight. It wasn't too complicated, though it was more difficult than you would have thought. But a few simple laws of optics, a couple of wasted visits to the glaziers, and a special trip to a photographic suppliers did the trick.

Luke mounted his new toy in a black frame and put it over the basin. It was fun, at first. When you lifted your right hand, with a razor or a toothbrush, so did the figure in the screen. At last, Luke thought: he could see himself as others saw him. He tried frowning. God, he could see what they meant.

But it was hard to synchronise your own movements with the ones you saw. You'd grown used to the old reverse methods. If you wanted to look at your left cheek it was only natural to turn your head to the right, and when the chap in the mirror did the same thing it looked as if his left hand didn't know what his right was up to.

It was as if there was a different person in there. In the end it gave Luke a queasy feeling that he was about to fall over. Combined with the fact that the image, because of a slight lack of flexibility in the focal length, was always blurred, it was enough to make him abandon the experiment. He still had the mirror somewhere: probably stashed up in the loft with everything else.

The radio was still going. A callous disregard for the safety of workers . . . doctors standing by . . . survived by building a makeshift shelter . . .

Luke tried to change stations, but they were all telling the same story. The dead man has been named as . . . a community in shock . . . an inquiry under way as soon as possible . . .

Different voices, same words. And Luke was not keen to let this news into his life this morning: he had enough on his plate as it was.

He thought about having a bath, but Carmen was right. If he

lay back and let the hot water run up under his chin he'd find plenty of reasons to stay there for a while. He'd already let a whole hour skip away without so much as a hand raised in protest. Still, his hair was messy.

The shower hose was in a storage crate (surprise, surprise), but he thought, yes, he was pretty sure . . . He hurried back into the bedroom and leaned over a pile of boxes with GOOD TEA FROM INDIA stencilled on the plywood. He tried to lift off the top chest, but it was heavy: he had to slide his thumbs under the rim, feeling for nails, and drag the box towards him. It resisted for an instant – probably the tin hammered into the edges had buckled – and then came free with a jolt.

But his right hand slipped a centimetre as he adjusted the angle of his elbows to let the box down, and he felt a sharp metallic edge nip at the base of his thumb. He held his hand up to his face, fingers towards his eyes, for all the world as if he was about to spit something out into his palm. Blood was spilling out fast, and he could see a neat crescent of white flesh further down.

He never should have bothered. But what with the inadvertent lie-in and the phone ringing all the time, he needed to wake himself up. He bent down and rummaged in the tea chest; but blood began to fall onto one of his sweaters. He hurried to the lavatory, tore away a few arm-length strips of tissue paper and wrapped them round his thumb. By this time he'd given up any thought of finding the shower attachment.

But he was feeling obstinate. It was too early in the day to start taking no for an answer. He went into the kitchen and found a mug – white, with a ring of yellow primroses round the side. A big red stain, quite dark in the middle, was spreading through the tissue on his hand, so he held the mug in his fingers while he sat on the edge of the bath, waiting for warm water.

The news was talking about a dockyard now. Hard-edged voices went on about productivity and community. Luke had once been invited to represent his fellow workers on some kind of employee council. He'd allowed himself some grandiose visions in which he played the part of a peacemaker with calm and irresistible dignity. But in the end they all sat round the polished boardroom table voting about things like whether they should shut down the cigarette machine, and Luke (a smoker in those days) got out of it as fast as he could.

He paid attention again when they switched to the weather. It was going to be wet. Luke bent low over the bath, gathered water in the mug and tipped it over his head. Reaching for more water, he stared at the familiar scratch-patterns on the tap. These domestic signatures – you hardly noticed them until you were about to leave them behind – had been giving him trouble for the last few days. He even thought of taking a photograph, but only for a second.

He didn't have a camera, for one thing.

He must be going mad, dreaming away like this. He poured water over his hair, shook his head like a dog, and reached, with his eyes shut, for the towel rail.

Oh, that's what he'd done: the towel was on the radiator in the bedroom. It wasn't very clever to get it wet at this stage, but what choice did he have? He nodded sharply a couple of times and moved back across the corridor, his sound hand up to his hair as if he could stop it dripping, his head craned out in front so he didn't soak himself on the way.

With his face under the warm towel he heard a voice on the radio say, with a strange sing-song emphasis: And the time: it's eight thirty-eight *exactly*. This was getting serious.

Where was his watch, by the way? It wasn't by his bed. It wasn't by the kettle. It wasn't by the phone. He didn't really need it this minute, but once again he had the uncomfortable sensation that the day was slipping out of control.

Some eager environmentalist was telling everyone about the new thing for kitchens: instead of rubbish bins, you had a worm-ery. Luke stood by the radio for a moment, interested to hear how it worked. It was basically a can of worms, the man said with a chuckle. You stuffed your rubbish in, sprinkled garden earth on top, and the worms would do the rest. Luke was not squeamish, but ugh! The idea of having an enormous mutating worm curled up beside the fridge was, well, it would never catch on, would it?

They could escape if they wanted, the man said. But why would they ever feel like making a break for it? It was worm paradise in there.

Luke searched in the drawers and cupboards. Nothing. Or worse than nothing – clumps of wire, old keyboards, golf balls, one or two playing cards, bits of circuitry, pens . . . He'd have to clear them out at some point (though it didn't really matter: the agency would be sending cleaners round before anyone rented the place). There were plugs, a couple of blunt pencils, postcards . . . Some were of beaches, some showed cities. He picked up a blue and white picture of the Alps and turned it over. The note was in green ink, with big scrawly lettering.

Actually, it's not a bit like this, he read. It's cloudy, and why doesn't anyone tell you how cold it is! I haven't exactly got the hang of it. Pascal our instructor insists that if I don't bend the knees I don't can do it(!) In fact I've been bending them so much that I have a new name. Lots of love, Amen! xxx

Luke gave up worrying about the watch and sat down.

It must have been two, no three winters ago. Carmen was the estate agent when he bought this flat. He could remember the way she led him up the dark stairs, explaining over her shoulder, her face full of hair, that the residents had some sort of fund going which was going to pay for redecoration. He remembered her opening and closing all the cupboard doors, just as he was doing now, and telling him, as if he couldn't see for himself, how light it was with those big windows, and how quiet it was at the back, where the gardens were. He followed her from room to room trying to imagine living there, but he was happy just to say yes, if that was what she wanted. When he was supposed to be admiring the view he couldn't help glancing sideways at her maple-coloured hair and the classic line of her throat; when she led him up the stairs he couldn't help noticing her magazine-standard legs and slim waist.

Afterwards, back at her office, she gave him a cup of coffee and sat quite close while she explained about the lease, the fees for the upkeep of the gardens and the communal boiler. The details were spread across her lap: Luke gazed past them to the silk join between her pressed-together knees. She was smartly dressed but there was a touch of scandal in her blown-about hair, and something careless about the way she wore these trim salesman's clothes. Was he just imagining the poised suggestiveness with which she drew his attention to the lovely big bedroom, and said, See, you could happily spend all day in here? (Yes, he discovered later.)

But after he moved in, she came round one day. To see how he was getting on, she said, and to deliver the spare keys as well. They walked round the flat – the bathroom had an unconvincing yellow wash over the beetroot by now – with Carmen nodding and smiling all the way. Luke offered her a glass of wine, and they ended up drinking the whole bottle. When she saw that he didn't have a cooker yet she said there was a place round the corner, walking distance; so they ended up having dinner too.

She had plenty of funny stories about clients: there were the ones who had to see a flat ten times before they could make up their minds, the ones who had to bring their mothers, fathers, uncles, aunts, cats and dogs to see what they thought of it; then there were the ones who took one casual squint through the letter box and said, Where do I sign? There were the people who backed out or accepted higher offers at the last minute, there were those who, you gradually realised, didn't want to sell at all, they just liked having people around, showing off their new tiles and their neat grouting, which they had done themselves in fact. By the same token, there were plenty of property nuts who visited places as a hobby. They were the worst: they were always late, they poked around for ages and of course it never came to anything. Propertography, Carmen called it. Sometimes, she said, you wondered if they weren't criminals, checking for burglar alarms and so on.

And yes, she went on (Luke not sure what kind of a face to pull), there were clients who tried it on, invited her out, gave her things and all that. Look, she said, this lighter. I was taking someone round, a ghastly little place, we'd been trying to sell it for ages. And this guy, he was so quiet, hardly said a word all through. I mean, it was awful, a real dump. Most people could see straight off it was too small and dark. But he didn't say anything, so I had my hopes up and talked away, trying to be cheerful, and then I made the mistake of mentioning that it was my birthday. Rule one, never tell them anything about yourself. Anyway, that evening he came past the office, put in an offer, and gave me this. I could tell he was going to ask me out or something – you should have seen him, huge and silent, awful – so I kind of hurried everything through, thanking him in that busy way, the way you have to.

Yeah, said Luke, trying not to appear huge or silent.

Next thing I knew, he rang up. Said could I have dinner, he was free every night except Tuesday.

So you suggested Tuesday, I hope.

Wish I had. No, I did a terrible thing. I said yes, and stood him up.

That's not so terrible, Luke said. Anyway, he got the message.

If only. I started getting these letters.

What, you know . . .

No, not like that. Quite sweet, in their way. But I didn't reply.

Oh well. Hence rule one, Luke said. It seemed that in his case she might already have broken it, but he didn't say anything.

Nor did he spend much time talking about what he did, though he would have liked to. He mentioned that he worked in artificial intelligence, which wasn't strictly true, and if he thought it would impress her, he was wrong. Carmen said that if he had any spare he could let her have, she'd be delighted. But as soon as he began to explain, she just laughed and said she preferred the real sort, by the sound of it.

Carmen had a grandmother in the town where Luke had grown up, and had even spent a year or so there herself on the army base nearby; so she knew all the haunts he mentioned, and some he didn't. She was a great reader of novels, and Luke was delighted because – he didn't mind admitting it – he was an honest-to-goodness bookworm himself. She played the piano too, she said, but Luke couldn't keep up with her there.

Their childhoods were what you could call similar, if you wanted to make a point of it – as Luke did. Carmen was an army daughter, so she'd moved around all over the place, dropping in on different bases for a year or two, never at home in any of them. And Luke – well, his parents had bought the roomy old guesthouse on the coast when he was eleven, and from then on . . . put it this way, it was odd feeling like a visitor in your own house. You couldn't move without tripping over leaflets advertising the beauties of the many spectacular rambles and historic country houses within easy reach.

The way Carmen said goodnight that evening, nibbling him on the corner of his lips, made him edgy for days. And when, at Luke's house-warming party a couple of weeks later, she stayed after everyone else had gone and started helping with the clearing up, he knew he couldn't be imagining it. She was wearing clothes so simple it was as if she was wearing nothing at all: just a roomy white shirt and pale jeans. He tried to hide his excitement as they jostled against each other, picking up glasses and setting them down again. Back in the living room she pressed her toes behind her heels until the shoes flicked off, and underneath her feet were tanned.

Even then, maybe nothing would have happened if Carmen hadn't smoothed the hair over her shoulders, tilted her neck and put a hand on Luke's arm, saying it was late, perhaps she could stay.

What happened to rule one? he asked, holding his breath.

This is rule two, she said.

After that, Luke left messages for her, which she didn't answer. One morning he bought a spray of irises and roses and took them to her office. But when he saw himself in the plate-glass windows he remembered the lighter, so he took the flowers home and put them in a plastic mineral water bottle with the top sliced off, and left them there for weeks, until the smell of dead stalks and rotten water forced him to ditch them once and for all.

When she did ring back it was only to ask him if he fancied a drink. But then it turned out she felt like making pasta, so they sat on the balcony in the sun and guzzled food and drank wine, and at last moved indoors onto the sofa as if they had both known all along that this is what would happen.

For a year Luke was dazzled and confused. They played tennis when the weather was fine (Carmen making jokes about Luke's convoluted service action) and went to films on wet afternoons. But she declined most of his advances: she didn't like the sound of his dad's boat – quite a nice one: you could take it out to sea, lie in the sun; and she made excuses, in a busy way that made Luke gulp, when he invited her to an opera. So he became cautious. But every now and then they would meet and the time would come when she began to undo the buttons of her shirt or slip her shoes off, and Luke would feel so bemused and glad that he didn't care about anything else.

He spent a few late nights writing a program for her computer at work. It was called HOES, he explained: the Home Evaluation System. Here, he said, it's houseware. You put in the variables – location, rooms, size of kitchen, storage, outlook, view, noise, and anything else you liked – and look, the computer came up with an instant calculation of the price. Luke couldn't see what was wrong with it, but Carmen, though she was terribly grateful, really, said that selling houses was more of an art than a science – a question of feel more than anything.

He tried not to think about her, but failed. She had invaded his thoughts and set up camp in the heart of his mind. Sometimes he loitered outside her office, hoping – hello, what a coincidence – to bump into her; wherever he went he looked for her car, and once he saw it, parked in a mews. When he peered in at the back seat – the umbrella, the lipstick, the road atlas, the empty bag of mints, a red scarf – he felt his scalp tingle and a strange kind of ache in his chest. The car – a perfectly ordinary hatchback – seemed fragrant with her perfume and character. He let his hand fall onto the wing, and stroked it a couple of times until it occurred to him that people might be watching.

At home, if he closed his eyes, he would see her with her head arched back, laughing. She had a bright laugh which always made Luke think of splashing water in a fountain. He saved up things to tell her, like a boy collecting conkers. In the amusement arcades he always went for the two-player option, just in case she turned up. And in a deliberate homage to the old habit of carving the sweetheart's name on a tree, he left her initials on the scoreboards of computer games all over the city.

Luke couldn't believe how quick Carmen was. He wasn't used to people with sharp tongues, and without even trying she man-aged to make him feel slow and heavy-footed. Once, he was making some point about his work and she said, I get it:

electricity is like life, or a mountain stream – it follows the path of least resistance. Civilisation, she said another time, when they were watching a television programme about cultural decline, is a habit. A habit everyone seems to want to kick.

To his astonishment, when he said he might go to a football match, Carmen insisted on going with him. I only said might, he said. But off they went. Men should be banned, she said as they pushed through the turnstiles, unless they were accompanied by women – to stop them fighting. You could abolish hooliganism at a stroke, she declared. As it turned out, there was no hint of violence at the match. No goals either, a fact for which Luke found himself apologising more than was necessary.

One time, he was saying something about what most people believed, and Carmen interrupted. Oh, beliefs, she said with a smile. Whenever you hear someone express general opinions about what people think, you know it's only a puffed-up version of a private prejudice. That shut him up for days.

Sometimes Luke couldn't sleep for wondering what it would be like to have Carmen's special vitality beaming at him, only at him. Just out of range of his vocabulary, a single word tapped against the window: love. He kept the window closed. He quite enjoyed being lovelorn, but wasn't willing to imagine what being in love might be like. And he certainly was not going to mention the word himself – it would sound greedy, an invitation to have it batted back to him.

In the high winds of his vexed enthusiasm he had a single prevailing worry: it was a mistake, it couldn't last. There was something about her: she was reserved for someone else. He was only a stand-in.

But sometimes, at night, he allowed himself to forget all this, to push his face into her endless hair and imagine that it might go on for ever.

Only once was there anything like an argument. Luke asked her to go skiing. A bunch of people from the office, he said. It'd be fun. She was sorry, she said, it was an awful shame, but the fact was, she laughed, she was snowed under. But then she went off to the mountains anyway, with some friends Luke had never even heard of. Luke tried to show his displeasure by turning up late for dinner a week later, as if he had better things to do, when really he had killed an hour in the pub on the corner, making sure he timed it just right.

I'm sorry, he said later. I was embarrassed, that's all.

Embarrassed? Carmen said. You think everyone's interested in what you're thinking, but they're too busy thinking about themselves. So you can stop worrying.

If Luke had been a different sort of person, he might have been stung by these remarks. But he was too impressed to be wounded. He was always giving her things – flowers, records, books, bottles: he was never a man to turn up empty-handed. And a few times he did wonder why he rarely received gifts in return. Then one evening they were sitting round playing one of those embarrassing parlour games which required you to name the quality you most admired in your loved one. You had to write it down, to make sure you didn't switch at the last minute. Luke remembered blushing when Carmen (in a moment of candour which the game didn't really call for) wrote that the thing she most liked about Luke was his generosity. He was the Man who Couldn't Say No, she said. Luke had to shake his head and grin, but then he had to reveal what he most admired about her: her forehand topspin lob. Everyone laughed, though Luke would never forget the flash of disappointment on Carmen's face when it was read out.

Was it true that he couldn't say no?

The postcard had come on a cold, bright morning, Luke recalled. He gazed at Carmen's jaunty green script, and for the second time that day he shivered. A dab of blood from his hand coloured the tops of the mountains red, like a sunset.

On the radio someone – a woman – was being interviewed about a journey to the South Pole. She was saying that she didn't actually enjoy the trip, don't be stupid. It was bloody freezing and you were hungry and tired most of the time. It was just one of those things that when you weren't doing it you wished you were, she couldn't be more precise than that. You find out, she said, what you're made of when you're alone out there. You didn't even have dogs for company any more, you had these motorised sledges. But you became attentive to the smallest motions of the ice, that was the thing. And you never saw such sky.

She was just starting to say that no, she didn't find it at all unusual that a woman should want to risk her life, when Luke switched off. Carmen would go crazy if he didn't leave now. And he really ought to pick something up on the way. Some fresh coffee or croissants. Somewhere would be open.

But what would he say? A couple of times in recent weeks he had glimpsed what he thought was a sorrowful look on her face and put his arm round her. But then he feared that she wasn't feeling sorrowful after all and took his arm away again. Anyway, she could come out, couldn't she? As soon as he found a place – he was going to stay in a cheap hotel at first, while he looked – she could come for a weekend; or she could take some holiday, stay a whole week. They could get a car, drive around with the roof down, hair blowing in the warm wind.

But what did she think, deep down? That it would be just a few months and then he'd be back? Or that this was it, over, and it was fine to drift apart without saying anything? I mean, he hadn't included her in his plan, hadn't suggested they elope or anything. But she hadn't said a word either.

Amen, he said to himself. For ever and ever, Amen.

The phone was ringing again. Carmen, almost certainly, wondering whether he had left yet. He looked around for somewhere to put the card, dropped it back in its drawer and padded down the corridor. Without thinking he picked up the receiver with the wrong hand and smeared blood onto the white plastic.

Hello?

Thank God. I've been trying to get you for days.

Oh. Dad. Er, how are things? I tried to phone you yesterday. How's your leg?

Oh, I saw the specialist again. He said it would be a couple of weeks.

Well, that's . . .

And that's only when they take the plaster off. I'll have to be extra careful after that. When are you off? We don't have your address, not even a number.

Don't have one myself. I'm leaving in a minute.

When, today?

The flight's at . . . Luke paused. Eleven. I'm just . . .

God, well . . . I'm glad I caught you.

Yes, I'll . . . what is the time, exactly?

Now? It's . . . nearly ten to nine. Almost lunchtime.

Of course. No problem. I'm about ready. How's business?

Oh, still quiet. But it's picking up. We're booked solid over Easter.

Good.

The thing is, I was going to ask if you could do something for me. But it sounds as if you won't have time.

You never know.

No, I know what it's like. You must have lots to do.

Well, it is sort of a rush.

I was going to ask you to pick up some things for me and drop them off at Mrs Granville's. Mainly breakfast things. We're running a bit low. Your mother can pick them up on her way home. She's in London today. Flower show.

How come you didn't go too?

Well, my leg, for one thing. And there's someone coming round to see the boat. I didn't want to risk going out.

The boat?

Yes. Finally decided to sell it. It just sits there.

In the winter, maybe. In the summer, though . . .

I would ask Mrs Granville, but she does so much for us already.

Yeah, yeah, Luke thought. Sure, what do you need? he said. The honest answer was no, of course he didn't have time, even though Mrs Granville did live only a couple of streets away . . .

You're sure you have time?

It'll be tight. But I need to go to the supermarket anyway. He tried to snatch the words back, but was too slow. Why on earth . . . ? Was he hoping to make his father feel better about it, or did he want to deny him the satisfaction of having a favour granted, make it sound casual, no big deal? Whatever the reason, it was foolishness.

It would be such a help. Have you got a pen?

Go ahead.

Well, the basics, you know: bacon, eggs, tomatoes, cereals. Get plenty. Then a few other bits and pieces. Mince, about four pounds, and some lamb chops for the freezer. Then, two tins – I think that says tins, can't read your mother's writing – yes, two tins of tomatoes and two of sweetcorn, actually, better make that three of tomatoes; then brown sugar, demerara, single cream, not double; coffee for the machine, mustard, English mustard, you know the sort, and horseradish if they have it. Am I going too fast?

Luke was holding the phone in his fingertips about a foot from his ear and reaching out to the bookshelves where there was a pen. He realised now that his father was just being, well . . . And it crossed his mind that there was no way, no way in the world, he was going to be able to fit this in. If it had been just a couple of things . . . But this lot: it was hardly worth writing it all down. He'd have to phone later and apologise – no sense arguing about it now.

No, that's fine, he said. Beef, chops, tomatoes, sweetcorn, cream, mustard . . . Christ, would this pen please work. Luke scribbled on the floor.

Demarara, don't forget, and horseradish.

I thought you made your own.

Would you believe we've run out? You should see how much people take, how much they leave. Your mother doesn't like me scraping it back into the jar.

Is that it?

No. A bag of peas, frozen is fine, loo rolls, don't mind what colour, oh, and some shortcrust pastry, one of those packets. They might have pie cases ready made up, in which case get two instead of the packet. A lemon, a bottle of washing-up liquid, and some new rubber gloves would be nice. Oh, and some Brillo Pads.

Is that all? *Is that all*!

Custard powder, cheese, any sort. Fruit, apples or pears, plums if they're ripe. Anything else you see, I'm just reading this. And two packets of cigarettes, menthol.

Cigarettes?

For Lawrence – the new gardener. I like to keep some around.

Luke felt dizzy. His hand was starting to sting again. He pressed the phone hard to his ear. Another cup of coffee would help, but when he gave the kettle a shake there was an empty, slushy sound, the noise the sea makes when it drags pebbles down the beach. Besides, he'd thrown the milk away.

I think I've got all that, he said. But I'm going to have to get a move on. I'm supposed to be . . .

I *hate* having to ask you. I would have done it myself, but the doctor said I mustn't put weight . . .

Yes, well, I'd better get on.

Oh, a few tins of dog food wouldn't go amiss, while you're there. Amazing how they get through it. Ring me before you go, will you? Then I can stop worrying.

Yeah, sure.

What's happening about your flat?

I'm . . . It's rented to someone. He switched hands and dabbed at the blood on the phone with his tongue. It'll be all right, he said.

It's a good job I rang.

Pity about the weather, Luke said. I'll probably get soaked lugging my bags around.

I haven't been able to get out for days. And did I tell you about the car?

The car?

I bashed it. Went to the market late, as usual. You know, when they start selling everything off.

Oh, you did tell me. The van.

I was furious. I was just backing out and literally never saw it. Dad . . .

You must go.

Yes.

You are lucky. Swanning off to Italy. I'll ring Mrs Granville. Don't forget how deaf she is; lean on the bell.

I'm not swanning off. I'll be . . .

She's been *so* kind. Did I mention horseradish?

There was nothing else for it: he'd have to lie. Dad, hang on, he said. There's someone at the door.

You're okay for getting to the airport? I wish you'd let me come up and help. I could have given you a lift.

Oh, I'll probably get a taxi.

A taxi?

Well, the rain and everything. Love to Mum.

What about that girl of yours. Can't she drive?

Dad . . .

It's your mother's birthday soon, don't forget. How long does the post take?

I won't forget.

Right, I'd better let you go. Terrible about those miners, isn't it?

Awful. I'll ring you later, okay?

Thank you, Luke. Take care, all right?

Bye.

Luke unwrapped the tissue and looked at his cut. It was still bleeding, but was beginning to scab around the edges. He fetched some clean tissue, and this time tried to tie it into a rough knot; but it kept breaking.

With great care, he took the shopping list in both hands and tore it in half. But then he felt a twist of shame and wondered whether, if he hurried . . . It would be good to depart on a high note.

If only he'd left five minutes ago. He would have missed the phone call. Damn. As it was, Carmen was going to be furious.

How much blood had he lost, he wondered. And how long would it take for his body to replace it? Would he be full-blooded again by the time he caught the plane? Assuming he did catch it. At this rate . . . Well, he wasn't getting anywhere.

Come to think of it, what *was* he going to wear? Ready for action, Carmen had said. What did she mean by that? Flak jacket?

He'd packed all his decent clothes (of course) but on the bedroom floor there were some jeans. He never wore jeans, but he'd come upon this old pair while he was emptying his drawers. If he wore them to travel in, everyone would assume he was a denim sort of guy, part of the jean pool – which was far from the truth. But the Italians would mark him down as a jeans-wearer, and that would be that. Oh well.

Maybe he could get away with that shirt, too: the red-and-white stripe he wore to the office. And he supposed he'd have to wear yesterday's boxers and socks. It seemed silly to pack them dirty – and he couldn't just leave them under the basin in the bathroom as he usually did . . .

That was a point. He went into the bathroom and opened the

cupboard. A familiar story: sweaters, tea-towels, a sheet, an anorak. At the back – he had to grope to reach it – there was a sleeping bag and a tent.

God, what was he going to do with all these? He thought he'd finished packing except for a few last things, but there were an awful lot of few last things.

The newsagent would have a box or two. He could pick up a paper while he was at it.

Or better – if he did make it to the supermarket after seeing Carmen, he could collect some boxes then.

What the hell. He'd have a quick bath. He wasn't going to get anything done unless he had a few minutes to think. Five minutes wouldn't hurt: he could be quick, for once.

On the radio there was a phone-in – or a moan-in, as Carmen sometimes called them. He nudged up the volume, turned the taps and dropped the plug in the tub. He always meant to put it in first, but usually forgot. By now he was quite expert at slipping his hand through the gap in the streams of water, holding the chain of silver-coloured beads high up, and dropping the black puck into its hole. The water that was swirling down there just seemed to drag it into position. But Luke was more dextrous with his right hand; this time, the plug hooked itself on the rim and stuck at an angle. He had to wrench it out hard and try again.

It reminded him of those games at fairgrounds where you had to steer a set of claws over a tray full of goodies – sweets, bottles of beer, sets of dice, packs of cards – and grab what you wanted. Luke was good at games like this, and had even tried to get his computers on to it. But this was a forlorn task: artificial intelligence was pretty thick when it came to simple human movements. Microchips couldn't catch. Even a soft lob was a nightmare for a one-step-at-a-time brain that had to consult the relevant law of ballistics every time, and it was tough keeping an eye on the ball with all that going on.

How come, when they were so good at tricky problems, they were so dumb when it came to seeing what was staring them in the face? As hot water swirled and splashed into the tub, Luke had a vision of a brilliant orange flash, and felt an odd twinge, the echo of a bruise, in his shoulder.

According to the radio, the weight of all the ants in the world was greater than the weight of all the people. Pull the other one.

What would Rome be like? Luke didn't know much about the place, though he had learned in the interview that the ancient road system groaned under the strain of modern traffic. There was a lot of one-way, and the historic parts were closed to cars altogether. He wasn't sure he had ever seen an Italian traffic light, though presumably they worked on the same principle. Come to think of it, there was that adventure film – a crime gang turned all the lights green to create a diversion and block the roads. It worked, but it was only half a good idea. If they had really wanted to produce a jam they should have gone for amber.

The bath was nearly full. Luke climbed in while the taps were still gushing, taking care to keep his feet on the cooler side. He leaned back with a certain amount of care, bracing himself against the moment when his shoulders hit the cold iron, then sank down until he was underwater.

Not that he could ever submerge himself entirely. He was too tall. Either his shoulders were out of the bath, or his knees were doubled up so that his legs froze. He'd experimented with various systems for keeping the water away from the overflow, most of them involving the top of a shaving foam canister. But they never worked unless you took away that pearly rope to the plug, and even then you had to keep your foot against it – there wasn't enough suction.

When he turned off the taps he could hear the radio: politicians' voices roaring and groaning. They kept going on about the community, and seemed to assume that everyone belonged to one, but there were so many: a farming community, a black community, a teaching community, an Asian community, a health community, a financial community, a world community, and hundreds of others. There were small communities, lots of them, and sometimes even the whole community got a look in. Luke had never been sure which community he was supposed to be part of, so it didn't mean much to him. Communications, ah, now we were talking.

There was no soap within range, but there were bottles of shampoo on the basin, and if he stretched . . . He had to put one hand on the floor – his bad one, which he'd been careful not to get wet: it still had white lavatory paper strapped round it – and he could just tease the fingers of his other hand . . . yep, got it.

But his good hand slipped and his stomach whacked quite hard into the side of the bath, throwing water onto the carpet. He kept his head up and managed to suck himself back into the water, but the pain made him furious.

He read the label on the shampoo: Coconut and Rhubarb Fragrance. Come to think of it . . . there were some bottles of bubble bath over there as well. He stood and picked them up: revitalising foam bath, he read, with forest herbs. The other one was called Wild Lagoon – a glorious deep blue. Luke remembered buying it now: it was a toss up between this and Coral Reef, a reddish-pink extract with added frangipani for that authentic island paradise feeling. He paused, then emptied both bottles into the bath.

Without saying a word, he rubbed foam and shampoo over all the parts of him that were above water, holding up his feet so that he could get at them too. The room filled with steamy tropical scents and subtle rainforest overtones. Luke lay back in a pile of suds and imagined palm trees with a hot sun beating down. He thought about whistling, but decided not to bother.

He pulled the plug out by tugging at the leash with his toes, and for some reason – probably because he had glimpsed his own pale heel, the cord drawn tight like a bow – he thought of Achilles and the tortoise. The clock had an Achilles' heel, too, and it was this: the minute hand could never overtake the hour hand because every time it caught up, the hour hand moved on a bit. So time could never move on: it kept running, but it stood still. There was one about an arrow too, which went . . .

As the water lapped around his feet in little waves, Luke heard a voice with an American accent say that there were more gun shops in the United States than there were gas stations. He chuckled. Morning, Biff. Fill her up, would ya? Yeah, the usual – nine millimetre fully automatic. Nickel-plated, sure, why not? Long as they're not lead-free. Plus I'll take a coupla clips of oil.

He started to imagine what kind of a postcard he'd send from Rome. But just then the phone rang again.

Oh dear. That would definitely be Carmen.

He couldn't believe it: he'd left the towel on the bed. By the time he reached the phone he'd left a trail of splashes across the corridor and wet footprints on the wooden floor of the kitchen. The phone was still ringing when he picked it up, but by the time he got it to his ear it was too late.

Hello, he said, just in case, picking up the phone with his good hand. The heat from the bath was making his thumb bleed.

He should have synchronised his watch when he phoned the speaking clock: he realised that now. Still, while he had the phone in his hand . . . He dialled the number again and made a note of the time. Eight fifty-seven, and twenty seconds. Then he went back into the bedroom and checked his clocks. One of them said 08:58:08. The other showed the hands a whisker before nine. Losing an hour had been bad enough: losing a minute as well was too much to bear.

He was dry now and dressing fast. A woman was making a lot of good points about the plight of hill-farmers in Wales. Something to do with the agricultural community, perhaps.

He'd better check his tickets. They were in the briefcase, with the rest of the luggage in the living room; his wallet and passport should be there too. He was certain they were all right, but you never knew.

Was there some deep reason, he wondered, why he was refusing to leave? Or only shallow reasons – everyday stuff. Something to tell you, Carmen had said. Maybe he should just phone her, say he was really sorry, he had too much to do, he'd phone her later from – hey! – Italy.

Was it worth attacking the supermarket early, to beat the rush?

What rush? It was Friday.

How come he was willing to consider almost anything that would prevent him from going to see Carmen, when that was the one thing – or so he believed – that he really wanted to do this morning?

There was still that last bit of packing. He could leave most of the books on the shelves in there – but he was hoping to take the ones he'd been meaning to read for a long time: classics, important history, significant science, plus the language tapes.

The Origin of Species was there. Luke had never read it – hadn't met anyone who had. It would be interesting to see what all the fuss was about; though it wasn't easy, when you were rushing around, to think that things that had happened millions of years ago had anything to tell you that couldn't wait a while.

One book was already in his briefcase: a colourful and comprehensive guide to Rome. It was a leaving present from everyone at the office, and it came with a big card filled with silly messages, some from people Luke didn't really know. Best wishes, Roger. All luck, Alan – who the hell were they? But some of the scribbles meant something. Emma had written: Missing you already – forever amber! love M. Then there was: Go for it! – Brian; No hands make lights work!! All the best – Cathy; Give my love to Gazza – David; and many more. About five people had put: Ciao! And one wag wrote: So they made you an offer you couldn't refuse!

Of course Luke had to laugh and pretend it was all good fun, but actually he was touched. He'd never thought of these people as especially close – no one mingled much outside office hours. But when he saw all the different bits of handwriting, sloping this way and that, he couldn't hold back a surge of warm feelings. He almost wished he wasn't going anywhere.

The guidebook was nice – thoughtful, aimed at his future rather than his past. Luke hadn't planned to take it with him – he wasn't a tourist, after all; but when he put it on the shelf a funny feeling crept down his back and behind his eyes, and he ended up packing it.

He remembered other office departures, and no one had made a fuss like this. It was a shock to discover that he was, in his own way, popular. He had spent a long time thinking of himself as a loner. But now he looked back on the office banter – the jokes round the coffee machine, the fried lunches in the cheap grill over the road, the late nights trying to push software further than it had been designed to go – and sighed. He should have realised when he had it made. He wasn't sure he felt like starting all over again.

But he forced himself to wake up. On the coffee table – now that he was in here, he couldn't stop glancing about – was a folder from the estate agent. Another thing he had to do this morning: drop off a bunch of papers and keys with Martin, the chap who was going to handle the letting. He'd have to do that later, though it would be a bore, with his luggage and everything.

He had started, once, to ask Carmen about renting the flat.

Oh, about the flat, he said.

Yeah, things are pretty dry for long leases, she said, still watching the television. But a good agent should be able to keep it full of short stays.

Or something like that. It was always hard to tell what Carmen would come up with. Sometimes they would go out to eat and she would drop the menu onto the tablecloth and say, Oh, I'm not so hungry. I'll just have a tomato juice. But once, when Luke tried the same gambit, Carmen laughed and said, Well, suit yourself, I'm ravenous. And Luke had to sit there sipping coffee while she ate three huge courses, all of which smelt delicious.

He opened a window to let in some air. He could hear the rain tapping through the trees and onto windowsills. The groans of the lorries changing gears up the hill were muffled, but the sticky whop-whop noise of tyres on the road made his head ring. Further away, out of sight in the low mist, some kind of aircraft droned over the rooftops. A helicopter. It clattered angrily for a few seconds, then was gone.

He should have driven to Rome. He could have loaded up, all in his own good time, and then sauntered down to the Channel and cruised across France. Flying – it was the digital clock all over again: one moment you were here, and the next you were somewhere else. You couldn't feel the wheels under your feet, see the landscape scrolling past your window, measure the space that you were crossing. Travelling too fast – Einstein had proved it – disrupted not just the clock, but time itself. Real time existed, but if you disobeyed it the frozen minutes would trip you up. Flying was wild time.

But he'd better get cracking. It was like his mum always said: there weren't enough hours in the day.

If it's true that there aren't enough hours in the day, then there aren't enough days in the week, either.

The basic astronomical logic can hardly be tampered with. But why didn't they decimalise time, like money? At a stroke, we'd have thirty-six-and-a-half ten-day weeks. Three new names for days would have to be found, and it would be interesting to see how these were devised — probably some bureaucratic think-tank would grind its caterpillar tracks and lay down terms based on adaptable modern alloys with letters that most words didn't use. But look on the bright side: the new system would almost certainly mean seven working days followed by a three-day weekend. If Luke had been able to count on one of those, he'd have been able to prepare for his trip with plenty up his sleeve.

It is odd how fixed and unalterable the calendar seems, when we know perfectly well that we made it up ourselves. Julius Caesar responded to complaints from his astronomers that life kept slipping out of kilter with the movements of the heavenly bodies by adding five days and naming a month after himself. Charles IX of France decided to change the date of the new year from March to January. And Pope Gregory XIII suppressed ten October days in 1582 to rescue Easter, which was in danger of sliding back into the winter.

In those days, of course, people looked up to nature: the natural world was alert to the passage of time in ways they could only envy. Trees knew when to burst into leaf, and the entire animal kingdom obeyed a reliable inner clock. Only humans needed timepieces, because only humans didn't know what day it was. No wonder they conferred a special wisdom on green things; no wonder they imagined a god in *every bush, a spirit in every stream. This might have been connected with the extreme feebleness of human life – those frail, timid babies unable to fend for themselves. But above all it was to do with the accuracy of nature's clock, which you could set your watch by.*

Talking of timepieces, Luke has cashed in forty minutes so far. Are you managing to keep up? Probably you noticed, a while ago, the line: He was dry now and dressing fast. That was a minute going by, right there. And you might have thought that it took Luke less time to have a bath than it took him to talk to his father on the phone. In fact, the reverse was true. Yet that conversation, fleshed out by echoes of an emotional history we can only guess at, seemed to take much longer, especially to Luke.

But it is never a question of how long things take – the key aspect is the to-and-fro wandering of our attention. It's possible to lag behind for a while and then make up ground in a sprint finish; just as a bus, stuck in a queue at the lights, can accelerate past the stop on the other side to catch up with the timetable. If you are falling behind, spare a thought for Luke. He took a giant step backwards before he even started, so don't look for any sympathy from him.

If we are going to be precise, we might as well point out that according to the latest theories, we are permanently behind the times no matter what we do. It takes the neural network of the brain quite a few milliseconds to figure out what's going on in the world and to tip off our conscious minds. So even in what we think of as the present we have the advantage of hindsight. When tennis players return thunderous serves with flashy whipped forehands they are reacting faster than is humanly possible: in effect, they shut their eyes and obey the rules, the conventions they have absorbed in practice. About the only time they make a real mess of things is when they are given an absolute sitter: give them a chance to think, and all that well-grooved skill goes straight out of the window.

We think we are taking careful decisions, weighing up the pros and cons before deciding what to do, but actually we just obey (or resist) deep, well-trained reflexes. Perhaps this is what Carmen meant when she said that civilisation was a habit we were trying to kick.

There are plenty of proverbs to the effect that you can make up for lost time, but you need a following wind, and everything this morning was blowing into Luke's face. Life can be like that when you're skidding around on the thin ice above the deep waters of real time.

Come to think of it, there was something else that happened while Luke's father was talking. Luke was feeling around with his hand for a pen and wasn't really listening to the first part of the shopping list – but how can you display, on a printed page, simultaneous gestures? It's hard enough, in films, to tune into characters who insist on talking at the same time. In a book, you must be joking. Let's sneak a look into the future, and consider the first line of the next chapter: Luke took the stairs three at a time, and found a taxi almost at once. This sounds as though it makes sense, but if we're honest, how many things can you do in the same breath, in the same sentence?

Oh, at a pinch, if you wanted to make an issue of it, you could print pages with see-through flaps. Or you could print the whole book on transparent paper. The future would be at all times dimly visible, and the ghostly shapes of the past would quiver whenever you turned a page.

No, no, no. Even in literature, the future should be a closed book.

It isn't what you could call a failing that novels can't represent two people talking at once. In life, too, Luke often reckoned, you have to take things one step at a time. Those moments a while ago when the radio interrupted Luke's thought process – it's not as if the radio switched itself off each time he stopped hearing it. There were all sorts of other items we could have mentioned; there was even a traffic report, which Luke, perhaps surprisingly, could not be bothered to listen to.

We're not so different from radios in a way – we can only fasten on to one frequency at a time. But we have an advantage: no one else knows what station we are plugged in to. That's good news, because more than likely we're not paying attention at all; we're already busy working out what we are going to say next, or wondering whether this is a good moment to drop in that joke, the one about the mad professor and the lobster claw, but no, maybe later, don't want to spoil things . . .

Our own voice is the only one we can be sure of receiving loud and clear. All the others, well, there's invariably static in the air, a bit of crackling at the edge.

Luke's work with computers had taught him that simultaneity was an illusion, merely a matter of breakneck speed. He'd become quite excited about this in the months leading up to the bus escapade. But what if he was wrong? What if the rules that drove his software didn't make sense? Computers could only read, whereas everyone he knew could hear, see, smell, touch and all the rest of it. Sure, they had parallel processing these days, but it was only conjuring, not magic. They still lived in a universe of first things first. If we could only teach them an ounce of common sense . . . If they could have hunches, get the rough idea, give it a shot anyway, see what happens. We're not talking flights of fancy, or anything too ambitious in the creative line. But no — they wanted to know every scrap of data before taking the first elementary step, and if you didn't feed them information bit by bit they clammed up like, well, clams.

Luke had read about the latest experiments in which human nerve cells were grown into microchips. In the future, it seemed, it would be possible for a computer to have, quite literally, a nervous breakdown. Luke didn't like the sound of this: the idea of a marriage between organic life and electronics made him feel queasy. There were things, he didn't know . . .

Washing his hair gave Luke a refreshing sense of clean efficiency, whereas the telephone call made him feel like someone trapped by a red light. Amazing how an everyday occurence like that can change your view of the way things are going. We think we can keep track of time, but we are flung through the day like pinballs, in a series of hectic accelerations and momentary exhaustions. Maybe it's just as well: squinting up through the glass to see who's pushing the buttons is usually too depressing for words.

On balance, Luke didn't do too badly in those first forty minutes. He even had time to dream a little.

Nine o'clock

Luke took the stairs three at a time, and found a taxi almost at once. He had brought the rubbish with him, and was just shoving it into the dustbin when he caught sight of the orange light pulling out from the road opposite. He shouted and waved his arm, and the cab swung round and stopped in front of him.

Luke stared at the fold-down seats facing him, with their crude posters for pocket telephones. God: he could do with one of those.

Let's see . . . the latest he could afford to leave was, hmmm, assuming the train didn't take more than half an hour, ten o'clock would be fine. That would give him forty-five minutes at the airport. But with all the shopping – it was going to be close.

That settled it: he'd forget about the supermarket. He put a finger to his forehead to check on his frown.

The plane would probably be there by now. Early morning passengers from Italy would be taking cardigans from their luggage and looking out at the gloomy sky through the shimmer of hot petrol. Technicians would be fussing beneath the wings, pushing and pulling fuel hoses between the wheels. Tall girls with red fingernails and tied-back hair would be moving up and down the aisles checking for stray bags. Old women with stoops would be picking up newspapers and sweet wrappers. And a handful of nervous flyers bound for Rome might already be waiting by the check-in desk, glancing at their watches and wondering whether, with less than two hours to go until boarding, they had time to snatch some food in the Country Pantry or the Sky Grill.

Carmen's flat was only just off the main road, and Luke asked the driver to let him off by the shops. He couldn't turn up empty-handed. There was a chemist – would perfume do the trick? – and a jeweller. There was a florist called Blooming Lovely, a watchmaker's called Joseph Tarrant, and a bookshop, closed. There was a newsagent and an off-licence – that would have been good, champagne for breakfast – but it wasn't open. What else: a pizza place, a window full of lampshades under the sign, See the Light, a corridor with cheap antique stalls and a bicycle shop: Deals on Wheels. Ah, look: a delicatessen.

Luke bought two almond croissants and some fresh grapefruit juice. He knew there was a chocolate place further up, so he headed that way, but when he saw the music shop he smiled. Perfect. In less than a minute he had chosen a great aria compilation recorded in Rome and was back on the street. He paused in the newsagent, and when he reappeared the tapes were wrapped in black-and-gold paper, with a card. He walked round the corner about as fast as you can walk without actually running.

An old man with a long beard was tapping a white stick against the kerb. Luke hurried past him, sighed, and went back. Here, he said, taking the man's arm. It's clear, let me help you.

They crossed, Luke hurrying.

Thank you, the old man said. But a word of advice. Don't hang on to people's arms like that. It affects our balance. And he was off, striking his cane against the base of a lamp-post with a metallic clang.

Luke watched him go, then shook his head and turned away.

The all-night grocer was open and Luke managed to persuade the cashier to sell him a bottle of champagne. He watched as the boy put the bottle into a brown paper bag. It wasn't cold, but what the hell – it would make it seem like an occasion, give the morning a bit of fizz.

By the till there was a rack full of children's toys – small super-bouncy balls and dolls. Luke couldn't help noticing the cello-phane-wrapped model of a London bus. He slid it from its chrome peg and put it in the bag with the champagne.

Outside, having second thoughts, he tore away the paper and plastic and dropped the bus into his pocket. It was surprisingly heavy. If it hit someone it could probably do a fair amount of damage.

At the bottom of the stairs he stopped and wrote in the card. Not Carmen, he wrote, but you can't have everything. He smiled.

Oh, thank you, said Carmen, putting the package on the bookcase, and taking the bottle from Luke's hand. I'd almost given up hope. Where'd you get the jeans?

Yes, Luke bowed his head forward to inspect them. Sorry about these.

No, they look good. She leaned forward and kissed him. Ah, your hair's wet, I see.

Luke forced himself to shrug. Yes, well, I accidentally fell into the bath. Can't think how. Came out of nowhere.

Must have been awful.

He nodded at the bottle in her hand. You can open it if you like.

Oh, I couldn't possibly. Thanks, though.

Luke was tempted to grab the bottle and uncork it anyway. It wasn't as if he'd bought it for himself; he'd gone to a fair amount of trouble – broken the law – and for what? Thanks, though.

It served him right for trying to anticipate what other people wanted. You said what you thought they expected, and then what happened? You couldn't very well go round claiming you never meant a word you said.

I'm going to the supermarket anyway. For Christ's sake.

One of the great things about computers was that they were not capable of lying. Oh, they could throw what looked to casual passers-by like temper tantrums, but they never played fast and loose with the order in which things came. Yet people always said that they didn't count as intelligent, on the grounds that they never understood what they were doing, only mimicked what they'd been told. So far as Luke was concerned, this made them almost human. How else did children learn? Besides, what people said was mostly recycled bits of previous conversations. Luke wasn't always sure what he thought, or whether he thought anything at all. He would hear himself floating along with the general drift – and it was as if there was no one at the helm. Carmen had once said he was all washing, no line. It still hurt.

It wasn't that he wanted champagne himself. Coffee was fine by him.

Coffee? Carmen said. How long have you got?

Well, I ought to be gone by . . . well, certainly by quarter to. What's the time now?

About ten past, I think. The news finished a few minutes ago. What on earth have you been *doing*?

She was in the kitchen, so Luke couldn't see her look down at her hands. But he was vexed by this second reference to his lateness.

Thing was, he said, I had to go round the supermarket for my dad. He's stuck at home with a broken leg, and stupidly I volunteered to help. You wouldn't believe how many people go shopping first thing. Place was crammed.

Luke hesitated. The one good thing about having the shopping to do (even though he had no intention of doing it) was that it gave him a reason to keep things brief here. As always with a good fib, the sense of walking on dodgy ground made him feel defensive and irritated.

The real pain was that I was supposed to drop the bags off at Mrs Granville's. So I trekked over there and typical, she wasn't in. I had to lug the shopping back home. I'll have to try again later.

Carmen said nothing. Luke could hear the clink of spoons and cups.

So that's why I'm late, he said. I'm sorry. He put his hand in his pocket and let his fingers rest on the little bus. It was cold and hard. For some reason he felt nervous – he couldn't think why. Ready for action, Carmen had said. What was going to happen?

The news wasn't on any more. She must have turned the radio off while he was on his way up. He'd done it himself, of course, gone running to the record player to make sure the right piece of music was on – that gorgeous swirly bit that was so lovely she'd be bound to ask what it was, and he could say, What? Oh, that. He was not very proud of this eagerness to make a good impression, but it was nice to think of Carmen taking the same sort of trouble.

Oh well, Carmen called. Never mind. You made it eventually.

Luke sighed and walked over to the window. The morning was well into its stride. The rain had been swabbed off the pavements by people hurrying into offices, shops were beginning to run out of newspapers, sandwich bars were already building towers of buttered bread for the lunch crowd. He thought of Emma sitting at his desk, a Japanese–English dictionary on her knees. Outside, a queue of cars formed behind a van that had parked in the road, lights flashing. A couple of drivers hooted.

It had always been quite dark, this flat. It was surprising – you'd have thought that Carmen could have taken her pick. Or that she could have lived in any number of exotic houses while they were waiting to be sold. But she'd bought this place years ago, before the neighbourhood became popular and prices went through what they called the roof. As if roofs never fell in.

Terrible about those miners, Luke called.

The what? Oh, awful, yes. Though I can never bear to listen to news like that.

Luke sat down and looked at the painting over the mantelpiece. It was a close-up, quite a rapid sketch in oil, of a young elephant, a calf, brown-haired and with baby's eyes. Carmen had adopted it, and paid a monthly fee to keep it in bananas. She was thinking about a killer whale next.

He knew what she meant about the news: it was what he thought himself. But simply by asking the question he had somehow aligned himself with a contrary view. It was the same old story: he agreed with Carmen completely, but found himself trapped on the wrong side of the argument.

Who cared about the news, anyway? Apart from the mine disaster he could hardly remember today's headlines: police were still looking for that young boy, the pound was holding steady against the dollar, someone had been shot in Belfast, a genetic research laboratory had successfully bred a blue daffodil, the usual business. Once it had been read, it changed from being a summary of what was happening to the news, in inverted commas; and something really exceptional, like an earthquake, had to happen before they stopped repeating what they'd said last time. It made Luke's head spin to think of all the millions of things that happened in the world reduced to four or five choice items.

He picked up his parcel, wondering, not for the first time, why it was called a present. Why not a future? Why not a past?

You're really sure you don't want to open this? he said. He looked around for the bottle, but Carmen must have taken it into the kitchen. Luke had a sudden vision of a friend coming round and Carmen saying, Tell you what, I've got some champagne in the fridge, let's crack it open. And of course the other person would go, Ah, never could resist a woman with a well-stocked cellar, and they'd both giggle, and who knew where things would end up?

You can open it for me, if you want. Carmen was coming through, with mugs.

Well, no. It's for you.

Or you can tell me what it is. Here.

Thanks. It's elephant food.

Mmmm, my favourite. So, you're all ready.

Yup. Everything packed. I've just got to drop some stuff off . . . on the way.

Flat stuff?

He seems okay. Chap called Martin.

You should have let me handle it.

Well, I didn't want to . . . you know, it'd be a bore.

Commission's always welcome, though.

Well I could always change, if you really thought . . .

No, better leave it . . . Anyway. Cheers. Here's to Italy.

Right. Luke took a gulp but there was something wrong with his stomach: it felt empty and tense. He headed for Carmen's bathroom. Excuse me a minute.

It was warm and damp in there. Carmen must have had a shower. According to the magazines, most women were frightened to take showers when they were alone. Carmen obviously didn't read them.

Luke decided that he didn't really need to go after all, so he just splashed a bit of water over his face and looked in the mirror. He could see clusters of bottles all over the place. A wicker basket full of soap stood on top of the cistern, and two glass shelves covered with make-up ran along the wall above the bath. There was magic in the air. When Carmen said she was going to get changed, she really meant it: she would come into this chamber full of pleasant oils and smells, and emerge a few minutes later a completely different person.

On the wall above the radiator was a large frame filled with photographs: a collage of Carmen's life. There were shots of her as a young girl, lying on her belly in a bright blue paddling pool, shots of her kneeling in the snow, shots of her opening the door of her first car. Luke always glanced at the pictures when he was in here, in case a snap of himself had made it into her anthology. But so far, no luck.

He flushed the loo, for appearance's sake, and walked back towards the living room.

So what was it? he found himself saying. You said you had something, a surprise.

Well, it might be a surprise, I don't know.

Luke waited.

Did I ever tell you about my name? Carmen asked.

What about it?

Most people think it comes from the opera. You know.

Well, doesn't it?

What do you think?

I know. It comes from that opera. Luke's gaze flicked up to the black-and-gold parcel.

Exactly. It's odd you've never asked.

Should I have?

I suppose not . . . it's just that, people seem to imagine me as a sort of gipsy, just because of my name.

Luke didn't know what to say.

Actually, I'll tell you where it comes from. When I was born, my father owned a garage. I'd have been called Carson if I'd been a boy.

Luke tried to imagine Carmen as a boy, and shook his head. Look on the bright side, he said. You're lucky you're not called Tappet. Or Hub.

Carmen didn't seem to have heard. She was looking at a tall blaze of crimson roses, which she must have bought herself, unless they were a gift from a grateful client.

Is that it, Luke said. Is that what you wanted to tell me?

No. But it's always bothered me that I have this manly name. It's not manly. It's, well, it's sort of gipsy. Luke put on his best smile.

What I wanted to say was, I mean I know it's not the best time, with you about to leave and everything. But since you've raised the question of hubs, she looked up, I was thinking maybe we should, you know, get married.

There, Carmen said. I've said it. She put out a hand towards him and Luke, though he wasn't able to think of anything, made a mechanical movement with his own arm. Their hands didn't quite touch: they seemed to run out of gas at the crucial moment.

There was a space, then. The room seemed to get bigger. Luke tried to focus on one thing, but didn't succeed. Different words and pictures occurred to him. Some concerned his immediate surroundings: the white carpet with the orange highlights he had never noticed before, Carmen's pushed-back hair, the heat from his coffee cup; some had to do with his journey to the airport; some were obvious allusions to how he felt – a sense first of floating, then of sinking; and some had no bearing on anything at all.

He had read somewhere – there was a plaque at the office – that a single instant could decide a whole life. Usually he thought that any old instant would do, that life was like a tree trunk, that you could take a cross-section and see the same set of rings, the same indelible scars of experience, no matter what. But perhaps some moments carried a charge so powerful they could spark and glitter for ever. Was this one of those? It felt like one, but there might be others yet to come that would turn out to be far more important. Maybe, in a few years' time, he wouldn't even remember this moment.

He was looking at a pattern on the wall, which for some reason reminded him of the scratches on his tap. Don't forget the keys for Martin, he told himself. His hand hurt.

It dismayed him, so much so he felt his head move even though he was trying to keep still, when he realised that he was racking his brains like a student in search of the correct answer, or even one which would do for now.

There were only two possible responses: yes or no. But he didn't want to make a mistake; this wasn't like flipping a coin.

Was this truly one of those deep moments, a break from the everyday choice-crisis, something too big to see clearly?

In a flash, Luke was back on the edge of the road, his knee in a puddle of rainwater and soaked leaves, the traffic towering above, the breath of the engine warm and sickly against his face. He felt in his pocket again for the toy bus. It was minuscule – you could hide it in the palm of your hand. He searched his head, calling up new file after new file, desperate to come up with something in black and white. But it was all grey in there. And his brain felt like a broken disk drive: everything was jumbled.

This was what Luke had been saying to himself: how many of the words you said in your life did you actually mean? Did you rehearse them with your mind's mouth until you had them off pat? Hardly ever. Yet that's what Luke felt he had to do now, and he had less than a second or two – a slight pause would be forgiveable – to make himself word perfect.

He wasn't wearing a watch, but he could almost feel the second hand on his wrist sweeping round in a tight, vertiginous circle, hoisting him up like a bit of driftwood bobbing in a whirlpool, round and round in a fierce, endless spiral.

What could Carmen be thinking? Luke was aware of a rising giddiness and a strong sense of his heart beating. Imagine saying what she had just said and then having to wait. Look at her sitting there, lovely and decided . . . He felt faint and almost said yes right away. But simultaneously he felt dwarfed, as if to say yes would be somehow vacant, merely obliging. Was this what women felt when they were proposed to? It was one thing if they'd already made up their minds in secret – right, if he asks, I'll say yes. But what if it was a complete surprise? He'd always assumed that plucking up the nerve to ask was the hard part, but now he wasn't so sure.

And there was something else. He envied her. She'd said her piece. He was the one in the hot seat now.

Custard, he thought. Horseradish. Plums, if they're ripe.

He looked at her again, hoping he wouldn't meet her eyes. But she was looking at him in a determined way, her lips pushed out.

If only he was wearing better clothes. He felt untidy and taken-by-surprise.

Suddenly he remembered where his watch was. In his jacket pocket. What a relief: he wouldn't have to . . .

What had she said? I think maybe we should . . . She wasn't proposing, exactly, just suggesting. They could talk about it.

Wow, Carmen, he said.

Wow's okay. I don't mind wow. She grinned, as if she was letting something out. For a minute, I thought you were about to go and have a bath again.

Well then. Wow.

So long as it's not don't know.

Carmen, you're superb. The words astonished even Luke.

Thank you.

They both hesitated, as if there was nothing more to be said.

The thing is, Carmen said. You're going to say we haven't got time to talk about it.

I must admit . . . , the breath came out of Luke in a rush. I mean, this *is* one hell of a time.

Is it?

Oh Carmen, I don't know what to say.

It's not the saying. It's what you want to do.

What I want to do is say something. But I'm . . .

How about yes?

Erm . . .

How about no?

Not that either.

So it *is* don't know.

I . . . I don't know.

Well, that's a start.

It's just a surprise, that's all.

I did warn you.

Hardly. I mean, of course I'm . . .

Don't say flattered, Luke. Don't say it.

74

Why not? I am.

I know. Well, so you should be. But you're right: it's important to say the right thing, or to avoid saying the wrong thing. As soon as you say that, you have to say but, and as soon as you've said but you have to think of something to finish the sentence, even if that's not what you meant to say at all. So you'll say I'm flattered, but . . . and anything you said then would point you in the direction of no. I'll get those croissants.

You've thought about this, I can tell.

You bet I have, Carmen called. All night, practically. I wrote you a long letter. That's what made me think about my name.

I don't think I get that.

It was a way of saying that it was important to me, but you'd never thought about it. I'm not blaming you or anything. It's just funny, that's all. It just shows you.

But why now? I'm leaving in half an hour. Going abroad.

Exactly. If I didn't ask you now, when would I?

Anyway, Luke tried, you can say but and then have another but later on. An on the other hand.

Yes, but that'll take ages. We're both in a hurry.

This is . . . what can I say?

Luke really didn't know. What he wanted to talk about was how long it might take to get to the airport, whether it was all right to be there only half an hour before the flight, whether it was okay to ask Martin about getting the flat cleaned. He wouldn't even have minded talking about what Carmen would do in the coming months: was she going to stick things out at the agency or was she going – she'd mentioned it a few times – to have a crack on her own? Would she come out in the summer, or was she going to lie on a beach with the others?

He had to say something, though.

Carmen, this is big stuff, he began. I don't know if there's time.

How long do you want?

More than five minutes, that's for sure. This is our whole future we're talking about. He was pleased with that word, our.

Oh, the future. Who cares about the future?

That's what this is all about, surely.

75

Who says? This is about right now. The future, well, you could fall under a bus tomorrow . . .

That reminds me, Luke said, glad of an opportunity to change the subject. He groped in his pocket. Look, I brought you this.

A bus? Carmen looked surprised. Thank you. It's . . . sweet.

No, I didn't mean . . .

What was that about telling me something . . .

They spoke at the same time, and stopped at the same time. There was a moment when they were just staring at each other. Then Carmen smiled and gave a little bow and a wave.

It was just something that happened, Luke said. A few months ago. I don't think I ever mentioned it.

He paused, but Carmen wasn't saying anything.

I really did get hit by a bus. Luke couldn't think of a way of not making it sound melodramatic; perhaps that was how he wanted it to sound. I was leaving the office one night, and this bus hit me.

No, you didn't tell me.

It was a bit of a shock. Well, you can imagine: one minute I was about to cross the road, the next . . . wham. I had this massive bruise on my shoulder for a day or two. Amazing colours. Otherwise I was fine.

Well, that's all right then. Carmen put the bus down on the arm of a chair. It settled at a slight angle, as if taking a corner too fast.

Well, yes and no. I mean, I wasn't hurt or anything, but it wouldn't go away.

What, the bruise?

No, that was nothing. But the whole thing, it's hard to explain, it really shook me up. The fact I hadn't seen it as much as anything. I couldn't figure it out. I tried . . .

What's there to figure out? It sounds as if you were lucky.

Lucky? Well, yes, it could have been worse. I suppose it just gave me a bit of a fright, I don't know.

He reached for his coffee and held the cup in both hands. What I'm saying is, it's not that I nearly died or anything. But I couldn't figure out how come I didn't see the damn thing. It was right on top of me.

You just weren't paying attention. You were thinking of something else. It's a miracle it doesn't happen more often. And it's just what I was saying: you can't spend your whole life wondering what'll happen. It's too unpredictable.

You could say that again, Luke thought. But he was sensible enough not to say it out loud.

With me, he said, it had the opposite effect. Being knocked over made me think about everything: my work, my life, everything. And then when this job in Italy came up, I dunno. It all seemed linked.

What do you mean, everything?

Oh, you know . . . everything.

Me, for example. There was an extra lightness in Carmen's voice when she said this.

No, not you, no, course not. Luke spoke quickly. He didn't want to get into that – the whole point was to avoid getting into all that. Just me, mainly. What I was doing.

What were you doing?

Actually, it's to do with work. Here I am, spending all day trying to think of new ways to count cars, and, well, it just seemed ridiculous. I had this feeling I was missing something.

But you're going to be doing the same stuff in Italy, aren't you?

It's still a change. Faster drivers, you know . . .

Luke, I'm lost. I don't see what any of this has to do with . . .

You're right, I'm sorry. What I'm saying, in a roundabout way, is – all this work I've been doing, it kind of makes you focus on the way people make decisions.

Ah. I see.

Luke smiled a sheepish smile. You're right, of course. I can't make head or tail of it myself. And I don't want to bore you with all that.

Oh, you never know, Carmen said. I might understand it.

Luke winced.

Go ahead. Carmen was shaking her head, which seemed like the wrong gesture. Bore me.

This was getting out of hand. Luke took a deep breath. Okay, he said. To start with, you need at least a zillion meg of RAM,

77

and the software has to have trog files on both the inner and the outer loop, and if you're using Boolean algebra, say, then all the gate protocols have to be . . .

Very funny, Carmen said.

Course, if you have local bus mothercards with access to an Ethernet environment, plus FDDI or something, then it's easier.

Yeah, yeah, said Carmen. But eventually she smiled.

The thing about traffic lights, she said, concentrating again. They're pretty straightforward, seems to me. Stop, go. Could be there's a lesson there.

Exactly. Except you have amber too, don't forget. And all the lights are linked.

So you build a brain to keep things moving.

Yes, well, a bit more than a brain. But the thing is, you can't do any of this without wondering what intelligence is. If a bird finds the same tree each winter, we call it instinct, whereas if a child finds its way home after a party we think it's Einstein.

So?

So, what is intelligence? Is a thermostat intelligent? It notices when the temperature drops, and switches the boiler on.

Big deal. Give it a Nobel prize.

Okay. But if you imagine a giant network of thermostats, hundreds of on-off switches . . . That's pretty much what your brain does, keeps the blood racing to your fingertips.

But the brain does all that without thinking.

So can computers. At least, they can do it so fast they seem not to think. The great test is if you can't tell whether the thing behind the screen is human or mechanical.

Behind what screen?

It's an experiment they did. You had a conversation, using keyboards of course, and if you couldn't tell . . .

But why use keyboards?

Well, so you couldn't . . .

See that it's rigged? What happened if you asked the computer to speak up a bit: sorry, didn't quite catch that . . . ?

Look, it's all theoretical, okay.

So I see. But where does the bus come in? And what in God's name does it all have to do with . . . with what I just said?

Luke wasn't sure how they'd got on to this, still there was nothing for it but to carry on. The fact that I didn't see it, he said. I mean, my system can spot cars a mile off. It can work out their speed to three decimal places and calculate exactly – no estimates or anything – how long it would take to cross the road.

So?

So . . . well . . . Luke's face reddened a degree or two. He had tied himself in quite a few knots over this godforsaken bus, but Carmen didn't seem to be getting it at all.

Tell me if I'm not understanding, Luke. I've got things on my mind. But I don't see the connection. The bus missed you. You were lucky. You were dreaming about something and nearly got yourself well and truly run over, but you got away with it. Your work's a different matter. Who said computer intelligence was like human intelligence, anyway?

That's the point. It's different. Better in some ways, worse in others. Right now I'm a bit confused about which is which.

Oh, come on. Forgive me, but honestly . . . diddums.

I'm serious.

Well . . . so what? Sounds to me, Luke, as though you're bringing your work home in a big way.

It sounds stupid, I know . . . Look, it's two separate things. One, I crashed into a bus, and two, I was busy trying to see how far you could go with the idea of machines that think, and suddenly realised it was a waste of time. They once tried to get a computer to play with children's blocks, build a tower or something, and you know what it did? It placed the top block first. Over and over again. Pathetic. Maybe this has nothing to do with anything, I can't tell.

And I can't tell why we're talking about this at all. I'm sorry about the bus, really I am. I'm a little surprised you didn't mention it before, if it's so important. Maybe I'm not intelligent enough.

I didn't say that.

I know you didn't. Jesus. Can't I make a joke?

Carmen turned and walked into the kitchen. The radio came on. Music, quite loud.

79

Luke knew he had done something dreadful, but wasn't sure what, or when, or how. Part of him wanted to get out of here. He couldn't concentrate. But another part knew that it wasn't up to him. He was in Carmen's hands. What in God's name was he going to do?

He looked at the elephant and imagined, with a pang of jealousy, its small but forthright vocabulary. Animals had it easy. They could say, Hey look: food; they could say, Look out everyone, trouble; they could say, Why, hello, fancy a bit of . . . ; and they could articulate a kind of gaiety – as a bird, for instance, might sing out when it flew or splash-landed, after a long hot flight, in delicious cool water.

Part of the problem was that Luke had lost, over the years, the habit of talking to people face to face. Even to Carmen. He was more himself, somehow, on the screen, sending and receiving messages. He could say what he liked, and the other person wouldn't distract him with a smile or a sarcastic comment, or a weary motion with their hands.

Maybe everyone was like that, these days. Maybe what we all said was just the surface trace of a few deeper things. And when the time came for the grunt or whistle signalling yes or no, stop or go, it was impossible to get your mouth round it. He remembered some schoolbook reference to a historic vowel shift – surely, if the noises had changed, there'd been a great meaning shift, too. Maybe this phonetic lunge had steered everyone away from what they meant; if you were shocked, and your immediate response was to say Oh!, it would be most disconcerting if one day it came out as Oi!

But he had to pay attention: this was no time to let his mind flit about.

In the discussion so far there'd been very little body language. Carmen had been sitting on the arm of the sofa, her coffee cup in both hands. Every now and then she'd taken a gulp, but you couldn't read anything into that. Luke, meanwhile, had put his cup down after that first gulp, which had made his stomach fidget, and when he picked it up again he held it in both hands too, as if he was really appreciating it, though in fact he didn't take so much as a sip. He was sitting in the chair by the table, his left leg crossed over his right. He wanted to move because it made him lean back and he'd rather be leaning forward. But he felt for some reason that when Carmen returned, as she was bound to, he ought to be in exactly the same position. He didn't want her to think that things had moved on in her absence.

Perhaps this stillness on both sides meant something. Usually, they were loose. Luke wasn't at all the type of person who could sit still for very long, not with his long frame which ached if he didn't stretch it every now and then. And Carmen, well, she wasn't what you could call restless, but she would often lie back and across the arms of the chair, or plant her bare feet on the coffee table.

So maybe it would be more natural if he did move. He leaned forward. But this was a mistake, since it made him look tense. He looked out of the window to see whether it was still raining. Hard to say.

The radio went off again. Carmen was on her way back. He was approaching the time, he realised – though, in truth, only a few moments had passed – when he'd have to come up with a proper reply. He was hungry. It wouldn't take more than a few minutes to fry some eggs and toast some bread, or you could forget the eggs, just some marmalade or honey would be ideal; but he couldn't very well suggest that.

He hardly had time to complete the thought when he sniffed the bacon frying. Oh no! Carmen really *was* cooking something. How embarrassing.

Here we are, said Carmen. She put plates of bacon and eggs on the table. The croissants were in a bowl.

Mmmm, said Luke. Wonderful.

And here. I thought we might as well drink this, after all. Want to open it?

Luke tore off the foil and pulled away the wire clasp. For some reason a loud, festive pop seemed inappropriate, so he held on to the cork tightly and unwound it, lifting it away with an almost inaudible gasp. He filled two glasses. Champagne bubbles spilled up over the sides and fizzed down on to the table.

Cheers, he said.

Yeah, cheers.

81

But both of them just lifted their glasses and put them down again.

Luke glanced at the food, and then at Carmen. How could he just sit there and eat, as if nothing had happened, as if, oh . . . yummeee, the great British breakfast. Just what I feel like. I could eat a horse. Dig in.

He stole another look at Carmen. Was she thinking that she'd played her card and nothing could proceed until he'd played his? Or was she brooding on other things – the contracts she should have drawn up yesterday, the keys she had to collect.

Odds were, she was having a chat to herself every bit as elaborate as his own. Probably everyone did, most of the time. I mean, take what Carmen had just said about her name. She was right, Luke had never thought about it. Or if he had it had all been predictable – skirts, roses, dancing and all those skittish gipsy allusions which seemed to *suit* her, if anything. It was a lovely, bold, romantic name, the sort you never minded dropping. Carmen. It sounded good. He'd missed the garage connection, yet all her life she'd been plagued by it: in her own mind she had a name which smelt of oil and grease and metal and rubber and men's sweat. Amazing.

God, all that nonsense about thermostats . . . he'd made it sound as though he was comparing Carmen to a temperature gauge. Hardly surprising she wasn't impressed. But it was tricky enough keeping tabs on your own thoughts, let alone someone else's. I was thinking we should, you know, get married.

I mean, the idea . . . When people talked about it they implied a falling of curtains, a giving up of all kinds of innocent freedoms. But it didn't feel like that at all. In the moments following the mere mention of the word, the horizons of Luke's life seemed to tilt up before his eyes, giving him a view clear to the edge. There he was, worrying about where he'd put the shower hose, and before you could say Jack Robinson his whole life was the issue: how would it be from now on? Would he spend it with Carmen? His whole life? Luke was alarmed by the thought that he had rarely conceived of his life as having anything more than a beginning and a middle. And even the beginning he tried to put behind him whenever he could.

He let the palm of his hand curl round the toy. In a strange out-of-focus area behind his eyelids he could see Carmen at the wheel, hair swept back and eyes glinting as the great red vehicle bore down on him. He wanted to jump back, but couldn't move.

He tried to dream himself forward into old age, so he could imagine the future as if it was the past. Would he wish he'd put in more time at the office? Or would he regret the failure to break away, see the world? If he made the wrong move now, would he mourn the missed chance, look back and think: what a fool, I should have known I'd never meet anyone like her again?

The thought made Luke tremble. But one of the problems with marriage was that married people themselves gave it such a bad press. There were conventions involved: you had to join the club, make sad jokes about Her Indoors, wash the car on Sundays, groan about schools and hospitals, whine about the kids. Luke was not about to go along with that sort of talk. But give it a few years, a creepy voice inside him murmured, wait till you're buried under kids. Ask your mother, he'd be saying. I already did, they'd reply – she said ask you. Oh yes you did; oh no you didn't. Why, why, why?

Don't be stupid. Who said it had to be like that?

God, there was an ache in Luke's head. It was nothing to do with Carmen, he realised; it was the decision itself that was baffling him. He was suffering a slight paralysis in that area, and there wasn't a thing he could do about it. All he needed was to go away. A spell on his own would do him good, let things settle.

None of this made sense: he was the man who couldn't say no, wasn't he? But it was as if he could only make choices between things he could see. It was like being in a supermarket: did you want this luxury supersoft soap with the almond scent and the blue wrapper, or this one, the secret double-action formula for dry skin, with the free ten per cent extra. It wasn't hard to predict what they'd be like and the choice was simple – unless you were, as Luke was most of the time, keen to experiment with different fragrances. But how on earth could you make choices between unpredictable futures? There wasn't anything on the packet to tell you what you were getting, or how long it would keep.

Come on, said Carmen. It can't be that bad. Eat. It'll get cold.

She leaned forward and picked up a piece of bacon in her fingers. I'm starving, anyway.

Another thought made Luke tremble even more. Carmen didn't usually say one thing when she meant another, but was she trying to say that she was . . . ? Surely not.

I must say, Carmen said, standing up all of a sudden. Look, I'm not trying to put the pressure on. This isn't a race against time, I didn't deliberately wait till you only had ten minutes. In fact it would be awful if you said yes and then had to leave straightaway. I just thought and thought about it and wanted to get it out in the open before you went. Is that so peculiar? You don't have to decide now, if that helps.

Luke was astonished to find that they hadn't moved on. He tried to remember what he'd said so far, so he wouldn't repeat himself.

Do you want to know why I asked you now? Have a croissant. She took one herself, dipped it into her coffee, and gave it a munch. I mean not now this morning, but now in general. It's not for any of the obvious reasons – well it is, in fact, the most obvious of all. I'm not, you know, or anything, if that's what you're worried about. I'm not about to start painting cots and knitting little socks. I just thought, well, you must have wondered what I made of it, your going away and everything.

I thought you thought it was great.

Great for you. What did you expect me to say? Say I hated the idea and what would I do without you? Maybe that's what you wanted.

Carmen gave him a shrewd look after this. Then she continued.

But you're right. And I didn't mean to sound like that. I *did* think it was great. I mean, I was upset, of course I was. But you want the truth: I never thought you'd do it, and I was sort of impressed. Everyone's always talking about how they'll do this and how they'll do that – I do it myself, for God's sake – but you know that what they're really proud of is their company car or the chance of getting so and so's job when she leaves. It only really came home to me last night. If you just went off and, I don't know, maybe I'd come and visit or maybe I wouldn't, but even if I did there's no guarantee. And I had a vision of me receiving a few postcards and everything just dwindling, dwindling. New things would start happening to you, even if you didn't want them to. And that's when I realised I didn't want that, I wanted . . . and well, that's it. It was simple after that. I weighed up the chances of your asking me and they were nil – I don't mean anything, only that you wouldn't have time – so I decided to bring it up myself. I had two whiskies before you came.

She was looking down into her coffee while she said this, as if she was talking to herself, practising on her own.

You can say you're flattered again, if you like. Carmen attempted a grin.

Of course I'm flattered, Luke said. I'm so flattered I think you must have lost your wits. I can hardly believe it. Maybe that's the problem.

But Luke, there isn't a problem. You're the man who can't say no. Remember?

Oh yes, the man who can't say no. That's a laugh.

Well it's true. You can't. It's why everyone likes you.

Carmen, I don't know what's wrong . . . There's just a little bit of me that hasn't thought about it enough.

Your brain, you mean.

Well, yes. The other bits, well . . . they're all for it.

Ah, the other bits. How many of them are there, Luke?

I don't know. Loads.

Well, good for them. Carmen sounded tired.

No, seriously. There's an ill bit and a drunk bit and a sober bit and a lazy bit and . . . well, there's loads. You know, when you're ill it's as if you've never been anything but. Your memory seems to latch on to the last time you were feverish.

Carmen took a gulp of coffee and looked at him. She was doing something with her tongue around the front of her teeth.

I know, I know. Luke attempted to grin. You don't have to say it – it's ridiculous. But I feel like, I don't know, like a . . . like a nut, a cashew nut. Two halves held together by a film of oil.

And trapped in a shell.

Do you want to know something? It's not much fun being the

man who can't say no. I guess that's all I'm saying. It's one step away from being a complete idiot.

No, it's one step away from being a saint, Carmen said. You idiot.

But Luke wasn't laughing. There's no such thing as an individual, anyway, he said. His voice had become a glum monotone. If there are two bits you can always split them. You know what atom means? Indivisible.

Luke, Luke. Carmen was shaking her head.

But even Luke didn't know what he was on about any more. He looked up at her. It's not you I'm worried about, Carmen, he said. You're, well, you know what I think . . . It's just marriage in general.

There isn't such a thing as marriage in general.

I mean, church, speeches, to have and to hold. Godparents. All that.

Oh come on, you're just saying that. It's the people, not the thing.

You know what I mean. People can live together and everything without being married.

Well, the one thing we won't be doing is living together, right? You're going to Italy in about five minutes.

God, you're right. *Five minutes!*

And while we're talking about flattery, I might say, your enthusiasm is quite moving. Carmen took another bite out of her croissant. A gold-coloured flake clung to the corner of her lips, and Luke wanted to lean towards her and incline his face towards hers and . . . oh, forget it.

He couldn't touch his food at all. For a minute there he hoped that things were picking up, that they were breaking through into open space. But he'd ruined it. Where had it come from, this awful habit of conducting lengthy debates with himself? He couldn't have been like this all his life, because he was always being teased when he was young for having his foot in his mouth. He felt his stomach pushing against his belt. When had it happened: when had he become huge and silent?

Sitting over breakfast one time, there'd been this long silence, and Luke spent about five minutes wondering what he'd done wrong. But when he cleared his throat and started to ask, Carmen slapped her hand on the table and said, Great, I've been timing you. Seven minutes without saying a word. A personal best. Congratulations.

Well, it was true. At some point Luke must have resolved to chew his words before spitting them out, and now he couldn't stop. It occurred to him that he was at some level being deliberately maddening, trying to exasperate Carmen to the point at which she would throw him out, so that he could leave, relieved and indignant at the same time, as if he'd been cut off before he had a chance to say his piece. Was that what he was doing? He blinked.

You're right, he said. I'm being dumb, I know. But I'm in a state. I started out by losing an hour. And then people kept phoning, and . . . and I cut my hand on a . . . and there's this plane I'm meant to be catching. And now you come up with this. I'm stunned, that's all. I was on a different wavelength. I mean, God, it's fantastic, and part of me's jumping up and down. But I don't know where my head is today. I know you think I was being an idiot about the bus, but I swear to God, I was lying in the road with this damn great engine on top of me, and it just felt like my whole life had changed . . . You took me by surprise, and I've made a mess of it. I wish I had faster reflexes, but there it is. I'm sorry.

Carmen came and sat on the arm of the sofa. He could feel the warmth of her hip against his arm, and see the curve of her breasts against her shirt.

Thank God, she said. You've said something. Look, I can understand all that. I know it's a big decision. Christ, I've been up half the night worrying about it, wondering whether I've gone mad. She laughed.

There, told you so. Luke let himself smile, too.

Carmen picked up the bus and pushed it up and down Luke's arm. It left parallel white trails.

Great, Luke said. Run over by a Dinky toy.

I hit a bus once, too, Carmen said, giving her head a toss. In my driving test. I ever tell you?

Bet you passed, though.

Of course. The man was very nice about it. Said if I was planning to go round hitting passenger vehicles to make sure I gave them a proper clout.

Typical. I got failed for stopping at an amber light. I was only trying to show how safe and careful I was.

They failed you for that?

I took it very calmly. Went home and stuck my head in the microwave.

What went wrong?

What do you mean? My head came out like fried noodles.

Oh, you forgot to switch it on, then?

As if by magic, good humour seemed to have fallen on them. Luke put his arm round Carmen and hugged her towards him. She put a hand on his chest.

Look, she smiled. Why not ring Mrs Whatsername and say you're in too much of a rush. I can drop the stuff off later.

Luke stiffened. She'd never hear the phone, he said. She's deaf.

Well, I can thump on her door till she hears. No problem.

She was right, as usual, but this was dangerous. Damn. Why had he lied in the first place? It'd be great, he said, but don't worry. I'll nip round, it won't take a minute. Mrs Granville's meeting my mum at some flower show, and . . . oh, it's all too complicated . . .

Okay, then call your dad and say you're sorry, but you're right up against it and can't do this shopping. I can commandeer whatever you bought: what did you get, anything nice?

I don't know. Plums, a whole load of stuff.

I'll ring him for you if you like, say you've left. Then I'll ring work and take the morning off, and we can at least . . .

She leaned into him. Luke put his arm along her shoulders, and battled to control an impulse to scream. It would have been perfect, perfect. But he had blown it already by playing the supermarket card too early. What a bloody idiot. He wasn't a step away: he was the thing itself. It served him right.

God, he said. If only.

Oh, go on. It's a lie, I know, but only a small one. It won't hurt anybody – that shopping can't be urgent or he'd have asked someone nearer.

Luke put his head in his hands.

Carmen laughed and rubbed his arm. Come on, she said, what's the number? Tell you what, it'll work really well. I've got to show some people round a house near the airport. We can go down together. I'll stand in the garden waving a hanky when you fly over.

Luke groaned. He tried to blame his father, but deep down he knew it was all his own fault. In his mind's eye he could see his dad limping to the phone, resting his broken leg on an arm-chair. When he first learned of the accident they spoke on the phone and he said, so, plastered as usual? Very funny, I'm sure, his father said, but Luke could tell he wasn't even smiling.

It won't work, he said. It's a pain, but there's no way round it.

What do you mean? Carmen pulled away. Of course there's a way.

I can't explain it. There are things you just . . . have to do.

Oh, give me a break. It's up to you what you do. She stood up.

Was that true? It didn't feel true.

No, said Luke, still sitting down. I think, I don't know. We can't ring. I'm sorry, okay?

Luke. Carmen was facing him, standing on one leg, her knee on the chair beside him. She had both her shoes on. This is important, Luke.

I know. I know. But I can't . . . Luke kept his eyes down. He knew that this time he had really done it, but couldn't think of a way out.

Carmen pulled away from him. That's the dutiful bit, I pre-sume, she said. When she went over to the shelves and started making the books stand up straight, an air of finality blew over the proceedings, as if she was clearing up, as if it was over.

I'd have thought they had things delivered.

This was terrible. They do usually, he said.

They were facing away from each other.

I don't know, Luke said. It doesn't matter.

Doesn't matter? Carmen said it almost to herself. Then she turned round. But what do you feel, Luke? Forgive me for asking.

89

Feel?

Eff. Ee. Ee. Ell.

It's what I *think* that's important. Luke knew that desperation was leading him astray, but couldn't stop himself. This modern obsession with feelings, he went on. We're so keen to get in touch with our feelings that we're . . .

Losing touch with our minds. Yeah, yeah, I know that one, Luke. But we're not talking about – what did you call it? – a modern obsession. We're talking about me. And you, of course.

But the only . . .

And whatever you say, in the end it comes down to an impulse. You can analyse all you want, with your traffic lights and those thermostats you think are such hot stuff, but it doesn't change a thing. That's how it was with me.

I'm not sure it works like that. Luke wanted to yell. This was all wrong. Carmen had got it all wrong. But it wasn't easy to explain that they were having a row about whether or not he was going to do something he had no intention of doing, especially now.

You can be as not sure as you like. I felt it, last night, almost in spite of myself. I thought you'd be . . .

What, you mean you tried to ignore it?

No, I just didn't plan it. It just came to me. Someone reached in and placed this idea right in here.

She was confident, Luke could tell; confident that he would say yes. He couldn't think why, but it made him dig his heels in.

But how were you so sure? he said. About what you felt.

I wasn't sure, in the way of knowing, the way you know that two tens are twenty. It was more like choosing what colour to paint your flat. You chose – yellow, wasn't it? – and you didn't *know* what it'd be like. You just hoped for the best.

And once you've done everything yellow you convince yourself that it's the perfect colour.

That's life. Sometimes it's a disaster.

So you divorce yellow.

Don't be silly. I'm not proposing that we get divorced.

Well, you're right, in a way. I mean, so far as blithe notions like hoping for the best go, well . . . and I know this is going to sound cold and everything and I don't mean it to, but I believe that feelings are really thoughts. Thoughts you haven't bothered to think about.

So what?

Luke was a bit thrown by that. Carmen's comparison with the colour of his walls was unexpected. And he wasn't sure he had the heart to continue with this. He'd have to let things come out in the wash, start afresh another time.

I'm sorry, Carmen, he said. Some day I'll explain. I don't know why we're even having this conversation. But since you ask, yes, I always wonder if I'm really feeling something or whether I just think I am. Don't you? I mean, take a conventional emotion like . . .

A conventional emotion? What's that, like marriage in general? Generalisations are always wrong, Luke. You're just trying to kid yourself that your own little feelings are universal.

No, wait.

No, you wait. What's conventional?

Well . . .

All you mean is commonplace. Jesus. Last night I felt I wanted to marry you. Or maybe I thought it. What's the difference? It didn't feel conventional to me. It never happened before. What does it matter, anyway? I mean, oranges come from Spain or Israel or wherever, but when you eat one, it's an orange.

It's not as simple as that. You have to think, use your intelligence . . .

Intelligence? Oh, give me a break. Another break. Don't make it so complicated, Luke. I knew you'd make it all complicated.

She wasn't kidding, Luke thought. Complicated was right on the money.

But it is quite, he said.

Oh, it's so much easier to think that things are difficult.

Easier than what?

Carmen looked at him. Easier than thinking that they're simple. This is a straight choice, Luke, an easy one. A traffic light could do it – red, green, stop or go. And don't give me any of that crap about amber. Don't make it convoluted, please.

I can't help it. Orange lights do exist, you know.

Oh, let's not go into all that again.

Luke was getting lost. He spoke slowly, trying to feel the weight of each word on his tongue before it flew away. I believe there are feelings, okay, real feelings. But mostly there are just thoughts, that's what I think. Vague ideas masquerading as feelings. Most people . . .

By which you mean me.

No. Not you, Carmen. Far from it.

Ah, but I can see what you're doing.

I'm not *doing* anything.

Oh, maybe you just haven't thought about it enough. Once you've relegated my strong feeling, my *strong* feeling to the status of, what was it, a vague idea, a blithe notion? Well . . .

That's not what I meant and you know it.

Maybe I just feel it, Luke.

There's no need to get . . .

No need! Jesus. I ask you to come over and you spend hours doing God knows what. Don't even have the courtesy to ring. And then I find you'd rather deliver cornflakes for your father than have a cup of coffee with me. You won't make the slightest change in your schedule, and still go on about how conventional I am. God Almighty, Luke. And you expect me to be pleased!

No, I . . .

Just say no if you mean no.

I'm sorry about earlier. I tried to give you a ring.

Liar, Carmen said. I tried to give you one.

But you were engaged.

She slapped him then, hard and fast. It made a sharp cracking noise, the way slaps were supposed to. She was only a step away, and she just leaned forward and hit him across the face. It hurt like anything. Water sprang into his eyes, and he couldn't see for a minute.

He'd been slapped once before, years ago. Funny how the sensation came back: he could see the pine-clad kitchen in the new house by the ocean, could see the line of hills out of the window and smell the fresh mown grass drifting in the spring air, could see the startled look on his mother's face . . .

It was the salmon's fault. It was a special treat – a celebration meal! – but he couldn't eat. There was that horrid fishy smell: he couldn't bear it. His parents tried to urge him gently – just have a taste, you'll be surprised – but he refused to lift a morsel to his mouth. In the end his mother grew angry. It wasn't so much the fish she cared about as the atmosphere that had been spoiled. She declared that he would NOT be getting up from the table until he'd eaten it. Luke, who kept one eye on the time even then, and was anxious to watch something on the television instead of all this pointless eating, astonished even himself by tipping his plate upside down onto the table, folding his arms and glaring at his parents as if that was it, from now on he was going to tell them nothing more than his name, rank and serial number.

For a second no one moved. Then his father reached forward over the table and slapped Luke hard across the side of his face. Luke had never been hit by either of his parents before, so he wasn't expecting anything like that, and didn't duck or flinch at all. The palm of the hand caught him square on – his father seemed to be a bit of an expert.

Going to have to teach you some manners, his father said.

Manners, Jesus. At the time Luke thought they were the most boring thing ever. But now, when he looked back, he was ashamed.

Maybe that's what all this was about, too. Luke looked at the table, the uneaten plate of bacon and eggs which Carmen had bought and cooked as a special indulgence, knowing it was his favourite, the untouched bottle of champagne which he, after all, had allowed himself to get a bit worked up about. He heard Carmen's voice – don't even have the courtesy . . .

He picked up a knife and jabbed the top of the egg. A smear of cold yolk rolled on to the plate.

Manners, conventions, rules . . .

Carmen sat down, as if the air that had been buoying her up was bleeding away through some invisible puncture. For the first time Luke noticed the empty glass, with traces of whisky hanging in droplets down one side, on the mantelpiece.

I've got to go in a minute, she said, in a quiet voice. So have you. I didn't realise it would be like this. Look at us. You'd better go. You'll miss your flight.

Carmen, let's not . . .

I didn't expect you to say yes straightaway. I mean, I know it was unconventional . . . I hope that hasn't bothered you.

That word, again.

Of course not. Look, Carmen . . . The moment had come: he was free to leave. But the blood seemed to drain away to the side of his face which stung and felt red. If he left now . . .

Well, I'm not staying, anyway. Carmen began to move about the flat, taking a bag off the door handle and picking up a coat. She pulled it over her arms, giving her hair a flick to keep it clear of the collar. I'm sorry I've added an unpleasant twist to your busy morning, I can see you're anxious to get on. Feel free, have a peaceful breakfast. Polish off the champagne. Have a celebration. You can let yourself out.

Carmen. Don't be like . . . You can't . . .

What? She had the door open. Don't say it: can't walk out. Look who's talking.

He flinched, expecting the door to slam, but she pulled it shut with hardly any noise at all. He could hear her footsteps on the first few stairs, and then nothing until the door downstairs slammed with a crash which made the floorboards quiver. Luke turned around a couple of times. He wasn't thinking of anything at all. After a moment he took the whisky glass from the shelf above the fireplace, shook the drops into a sip and drank it. The alcohol made a warm spot on his tongue. He carried the glass through into the kitchen and turned on the tap in the sink. He was going to rinse it out, but in the end he just left it there.

The clock over the cooker said twenty-eight minutes past nine.

If you don't mind, we'll skip the next couple of minutes and say, for the sake of argument, that it's nine thirty. Those two minutes were hardly worth describing, as it happens. Luke stood in the kitchen lifting cups and plates, but otherwise he didn't move a muscle. He might have blinked, but that was it.

He was reflecting, naturally enough, on the trouble that a lie can cause. Carmen's brilliant idea of phoning his father — talk about killing two birds with one stone. But in producing the supermarket story ahead of its appointed place he had thrown a spanner into the workings of the clock. Who was it who said that if you never lied, you never had to remember anything? Lies and memory had one thing in common: they both played perilous games with the orderly progress of time.

In the middle of his rumination Luke realised why Carmen had wanted to avoid opening the champagne. It wasn't that she was ungrateful — simply that she knew there might well be a champagne moment on the way.

For an instant he wondered about destiny. We might think that since Luke is only a character in a book, he could afford to relax, knowing that his future has already been figured out. But he has no idea what lies ahead. He is in someone else's hands, and can't tell if they are safe ones.

All in all, Luke has been on the move for an hour and ten minutes, and the speed of his life, give or take the odd spurt here or there, should tally with the time it has taken to read this far. But you probably found that the last half-hour passed much more quickly than the first. Luke certainly did.

It's not surprising: there were innumerable pauses and hesitations in his conversation with Carmen; the commas and full stops were doing a lot of the work. They soaked up minute after minute, though they didn't occupy much space on the page.

Isn't that always the way? Where on earth do you draw the line? It would have been possible to fill that half-hour with entirely different experiences — there wasn't room to comment on the way Carmen nipped into the bathroom to brush her hair, and it would have been tedious to record all the occasions on which Luke fingered the double-decker bus in his pocket.

It wouldn't have been fair to mention that Luke spent an instant wondering where the word engaged came from — something to do with glove-in-glove, he shouldn't wonder — because he was surrounded by more urgent matters, such as what was he going to say next.

And of course it wasn't possible to include the steady fountain of thoughts which splashed through Carmen's head as she sat there, waiting for Luke to open his mouth. What, you think she was just sitting there? On the contrary, she was casting her own mind back to the time she met Luke. She couldn't remember that much about it — only that he was so shy and alone that she felt almost obliged to look in on him every now and then. It was part of her job, more or less: routine after-sales service. And his shirt that first day was a beautiful shade of green — her favourite colour.

By rights, a book that keeps up with the clock should be the last word in realism. But literature is like a bus timetable: it gives you the rough outline, but can't hope to include the thousands of tiny variations along the way. Even when you plan to be faithful you have to choose. Life is such a jumble of time-disrupting evasions, memories and desires that it is futile to count on things ever going like clockwork. Even clocks can't always manage that, and books struggle to navigate a sensible course through all the short cuts and cul-de-sacs, all those points where two lanes merge into one. And since books know the future, every literary marriage is an arranged marriage, or at least rearranged with the benefit of hindsight.

Besides, nobody can read and absorb, in real time, everything that happens in a single minute. Brilliant Achilles can bring a hundred doomed Trojans crashing to the dust; Lancelot can rescue Guinevere — for an epic hero, this sort of thing is the work of a moment. In

St Luke's Gospel, sixty seconds are ample for the performance of a miracle, or the salvation of mankind. Yet Luke and Carmen are capable of frittering a whole minute on a pause.

Have you ever seen those space-age photographic sequences they have in museums? The picture starts in outer space and is just a mass of confused colours. They magnify it by ten times to reveal a pattern of white dots on a dark background, and then magnify it again, zooming in, until step by step the earth emerges out of the gloom. We dive through the clouds and can make out a coastline, a city, a park, a lake, a group of picnickers on a rug, and finally a man's hand.

And that's where the fun starts. By rights we should stop at this point. But the picture keeps changing: we go inside the hand and see the ghoulish skeleton, bones fanned out in a ghostly close-up. A couple more clicks, and we can't see anything much, just a swirling chaos of neurons and quarks which resembles nothing so much as that very first shot from deep space.

Where does it all end? Here we are, focusing in on a few hours, eavesdropping on Luke's life in real time . . . yet we remain close to the surface. To reach the meaningful depths we would need a lot more time. (This, of course, is pretty much how Luke himself feels.)

These seventy minutes we've been watching – we could deal with them in a single sentence if we so desired: Luke was trying to figure out how he was going to fit everything in and still catch his plane when, out of the blue, his girlfriend Carmen said, Let's get married. On the other hand, why not twist the lens and come up with an hour-length paragraph; that would give us time to include the phone call from Luke's father and the shopping-list? And we can keep magnifying by ten until we hit real life.

But what if we keep going? The truth is, we could fill hundreds of pages about that one hour. If we wanted to record the exact rate at which Luke's hair follicles were declining, or the speed of his cell reproduction, we'd need thousands. And if we were keen to trace Luke's thoughts back to incidents in his childhood, or set them in a satisfying socio-economic context, we'd lose count altogether.

These things were happening, all right: heaven knows how many atoms fell to the bathroom floor when Carmen brushed her hair with that irritated flick of her right hand; or how many armies of bacteria began to feast on the edge of Luke's cooling breakfast. How many *molecules of water vapour rose from the coffee cups and made damp marks on the windows and light bulbs? And who can say, with any confidence, that there wasn't, even as they spoke about marriage and so on, the germ of a virus delicately forming in one or other of them, starting to gain confidence and throw its weight around? There were moments, to be sure, when Luke felt a headache coming on.*

We haven't even mentioned the saga surrounding Luke's car. That would make a story in itself.

Besides, nothing could be more arbitrary than to concentrate on Luke and Carmen. Other people were having a completely different time. Luke's mother was pushing through a thick crowd of people in a marquee brimming with scented lilies and daffodils, gorgeous camellias and orchids and rare anenomes. Carmen's colleagues were looking at her empty desk and taking telephone messages, wondering what could have become of her. Emma was doodling in a notepad full of Luke's bad handwriting, looking up as Brian hustled out of the office with a small suitcase in one hand and an expensive raincoat in the other. We could go on for ever.

In the wider world, well, it's hardly worth starting. Thousands of tons of sewage have been pumped into the world's oceans in the last hour and ten minutes. Millions of doors have closed, and millions of others have opened. Thousands of babies have been born; and some have died; hundreds of violent crimes have been committed, and an unguessable number of television-hours have been watched. Governments have trembled; some have fallen. The world has spun on its axis like the hour hand of a vast, universal clock.

But Luke can play games as long as he likes; nothing can alter the fact that he has less than two hours to go before the captain asks the cabin crew to secure doors for take-off.

Half past nine

There was a second or two when Luke thought that if he opened the window and called out, he'd be able to stop Carmen before she disappeared. But he didn't move, and by the time the clock had vibrated a couple of times it was too late. He tried to persuade himself that his body had gone to sleep for a moment and couldn't see the frantic signals he was sending, that word would get through and everything would be all right.

But he failed.

Oh well. If they had gone on talking much longer, he'd have been done for. As it was, he could sort everything out and still catch his plane, no problem.

And then what?

Oh well? What kind of a reaction was that?

Luke put his hands to his cheeks. Carmen had hit him. Unbelievable.

In a way it made him feel grand, even manly. Not everyone he knew had been slapped by a woman in a romantic fit. Only a certain kind of person could provoke feelings like that.

If only, if only, if only. But it was too late for that now. In making up that story about the supermarket he had broken all the rules; he'd taken out an advance without proper authorisation. He had only himself to blame if his cheques started bouncing.

He still couldn't believe she'd walked out.

Luke wasn't used to things you couldn't postpone, so he was astonished to find his hands shaking when he tried to open the window. The last time – indeed the first time – his fingers had twitched like this was when he was walking the wrong way down the road after the collision. Was this like that? Was this too big to see?

He was alone in Carmen's flat. It came to him that he needed to preserve an accurate picture of this moment.

But maybe it was just something to do with the noise doors made when they closed. Maybe they always gave you that hollow creamy feeling in your stomach.

He took the breakfast things into the kitchen, folding a piece of bacon into his mouth on the way. Delicious: he put the plates down and ate some more. Then he scraped the leftovers into the swing bin.

There was an empty whisky bottle in there, and what was this? A letter, addressed to him. Carmen's handwriting.

He shook the crumbs off and opened it. Darling Luke! he read. This might come as a surprise, and I'm sorry to be putting it like this, in a letter . . .

Luke leaned back and tapped one of his heels against the wall. It was the exclamation mark that killed him. And Carmen had never called him darling before. What had he done? For some reason he couldn't bear to read the letter right away; the thought of Carmen watching the moon curve across the night sky while she wrote out a marriage proposal was too much to take in at a time like this. And filching the letter from the bin felt stealthy; he needed to be far away from the scene of his crime to read it in peace. So he folded the paper, slipped it into his back pocket and started to leave.

That thing Carmen had said about his preferring to do his father's shopping than spend time with her . . . If only she knew.

There was no way to make amends, but he could wipe the slate clean, at least. He'd ring his father at once. The phone was on the top of a dresser in the sitting room, beside a large pile of brochures and details from the office. As Luke dialled, he glanced at a list of flats and houses in the area. Some of them had question marks pencilled against them, some had emphatic ticks.

Dad, he said.

Luke?

Yuh. Listen . . .

That was quick.

Dad, I'm not sure I have time. My flight . . .

Sorry?

I said I'm not sure I have time. It's too tight. I've got to be at the airport in . . . I'm about to leave.

I see.

Stupid of me. I should have realised.

I see.

There was a pause. Luke heard a sigh at the far end of the line and closed his eyes. Don't say another word, he urged himself. If he wasn't careful . . .

I really am sorry, Dad. You know how it is, when you're travelling and everything.

No, it's my fault. I shouldn't have asked. Your mother said not to worry you, but I thought you wouldn't mind.

I didn't mind.

We hate asking you to do anything. We know how busy you are.

Oh God, Luke thought. It's happening; I can feel it happening.

But if you haven't got time to help us out with a little bit of shopping . . . Not to worry. I'll do it myself, I suppose.

Look . . .

Don't worry. You go and catch your plane. I should have known: it's always better to do things yourself.

It's not that I wouldn't . . .

No need to explain. I know it's boring, having to go round the shops. You've got better things to do with your time.

Look, I'll do it, okay. I'll go now. Jesus. You can't be saying this, he said to himself. You cannot be saying this.

No, no, no. I'll think of something. Don't trouble yourself.

I'm going this minute. I'll drop the stuff off at Mrs Granville's, okay. No more discussion. I'm on my way.

Well, if you insist. Oh, something I forgot? Stewing steak, couple of pounds.

Bye, Dad.

Luke put the phone down and looked up at the ceiling. Damn, damn, damn. It was a good job he was going abroad. A long way from here, that's where he needed to be. At this rate he wasn't going anywhere, but what could he do? He couldn't say no, could he?

Wouldn't it be great if you could buy time? People spent their whole working lives selling it, mostly on the cheap. So there ought to be a place – a market, a clock exchange – where you could help yourself.

How would it work? You couldn't just walk in, say that's okay, thanks, I'm browsing, find what you wanted and write a cheque on your way out. It wasn't like groceries: there was no superstore where you could wander down the aisles filling your wire basket with minutes and hours – taking care to look at the sell-by dates – and waiting in line at the tills, perhaps deciding to use your credit card so you didn't have to pay for it there and then.

Or maybe that's what a supermarket was: a place to buy time.

Dream on. Time was like property; you took a lease for 99 years, or 87 years – or 999 years, if you were an optimist – but in the end, no matter how much you paid, all the rights reverted. And time was a tough landlord: it would hit you with an eviction order as soon as say good morning.

Luke used to think that if you wanted an extra hour, all you had to do was get up earlier and it was yours for nothing. But even then it was only a loan: you'd sneak in an extra chunk of sleep as soon as you could and be back to square one, and sometimes you were charged interest and there was nothing for it but to have a hot bath and an early night.

Only when he shut the door of Carmen's flat did it occur to him that he might never open it again. He touched the letter in his pocket.

He was trying, he knew, to avoid thinking about what had just happened, but it was there, on some obscure alternate screen or hidden file inside his system. Every time his mind drifted in that direction he felt weak all over, as if his heart could no longer pump enough blood to his hands and feet.

On the stairs, for instance, the light, which was on a timer, went out, and even though there were glimmers lower down it was quite dark, and Luke had to fumble along the wall to find the button. And he felt a burst of Carmen's scent in his face and had to reach for the bannister.

Or outside, when he emerged into the rain, and it was colder than he expected: some heavy drops tipped from a gutter, and Luke felt cold watery needles pinning him to a grey pavement he might never, thanks to what he had just said and not said, see again.

The houses opposite, the parked cars, and the advertising hoardings on the corner were streaked with dirt. The air round here might look clean, but everyone knew it was loaded with household dust and grime from fires, invisible drifts of ash from all those cigarettes, and mud washed from the wheels of the cars and trucks that stopped at the lights. It licked the painted windowsills and billboards, and no one noticed until they were filthy.

In fact, now that he looked, he could see a few trees breaking into leaf. Even in the city, nature wouldn't take no for an answer.

He might have to take care of this headache. Pills: that was something else. Might as well get a supply while he was about it.

What time was it? It was absurd: for the price of a hamburger he could buy a new one and know how long he had, instead of this constant guessing and hoping. Of all the days to forget his watch . . .

Tell you what, though. (He was grabbing all the shelter he could as he hurried out into the main road.) Why didn't he buy something and take it to Carmen's office? Some token that would keep things open – a plant, or a book, or . . . He could visualise the look on her face when, eyes still a little red, she found the package on her desk, the way her head would tilt forward, hair tumbling over her eyes . . . He could write her a note: I thought I'd give you a ring anyway, ha-ha-ha. Maybe her hand would go up over her face when she saw what it was, and she'd look at the clock on the wall to see whether there was time to grab a cab to the airport to say, I'm not engaged, darling, the line was busy, that's all . . . But no, forget it. You couldn't shell out for a ring just like that. Who was to say there wouldn't be a much better one down the road? You had to do these things with a certain solemnity: you wouldn't expect to find a jewel worth buying until you'd seen hundreds. You had to be sure it was right. It was for ever, after all.

But say he got lucky. Say he went into the jewellers and the man said, Ah yes, how much was sir wanting to spend?, and Luke would say he didn't have a fixed sum in mind (giving a relaxed smile), he was just looking for now – and there, right there on a piece of blue satin, would be this fantastic ring. Simple, of course, Carmen wouldn't want anything big or multicoloured. Luke would try it on his little finger, forcing it over the knuckle with a grimace, and then hold his hand up and watch light spill out of the stone. And the price wouldn't be too bad, and Luke would nip to the bank and get them to clear the cheque right there so he could take the ring away with him . . .

He was so excited that he did stop to look into the window of the jeweller by the chemist. But in the rows and rows of almost weightless pendants, chains and earrings he could see nothing that chimed with his hopes, and anyway he caught sight of a man inside peering over the top of some old-fashioned glasses. So he ducked away and hurried on.

What was it he needed? Christ, he didn't even have the list.

It was enough to make him burst into tears. He wasn't sure whether all this confusion flowed from one source – whether he had triggered all this himself – or whether he was being assaulted from all sides at once. Carmen, he said to himself, come back, you don't understand, it was all a misunderstanding.

There was nothing for it: he'd have to see what he could remember. Breakfast stuff. Mustard, sugar, tins of sweetcorn and tomatoes. What else? A bottle of cider? Oh yes, coffee, beef, chops. It would be all right once he got in there. He could walk up and down and know what he needed when he saw it.

That ring idea: where had it come from? Most of Luke's best daydreams were deliberate set-ups, but that one seemed to come from nowhere. It was as if someone reached in and . . . no, don't be silly. Was it possible, he thought, taking a wire basket from the clump by the door and then changing his mind and going for a trolley, that Carmen was right, that these things weren't ideas as such but the outward sign of deeper feelings? Or was the thought itself so cheering, so full of drama and excitement, that it warmed back into an emotion? Which way did these things run? He remembered Carmen saying, So what? and the whole picture was right there in front of his closed eyes – Carmen running out of the office, him waiting to board the plane, Carmen jumping from a taxi and pushing through the glass doors, passengers shouting in alarm as she shoved them aside – then cut to him filing down the ramp towards the aircraft. But he didn't have the energy to hold it in his mind for very long, or rather, he'd seen these scenes in films and God, were they unconvincing. Besides (this was the part the films always left out) the thought of what it would actually take – the haggling with the bank, the incredible haste – made him open his eyes again.

Probably he would have blinked in any case, because after the flat light outside it was pretty bright in here. The supermarket was, as all of them were nowadays, laid out in a way designed to make you buy more than you wanted to. Luke knew some of the tricks – they were well known: the way they always had flowers and fruit by the entrance, to entice you in if you were hesitating; the way they made sure to bake a bit of bread or brew some coffee at the back so there was a fresh food smell to tickle your hunger – why else would you buy a tin of treacle sponge? The way they kept the few things you were bound to want – bread, milk, meat, vegetables – as far apart as possible so that you'd have to walk along aisle upon aisle of soup packets and biscuits and fancy new cereals you wouldn't have looked at otherwise. Christ, look at all these new pasta shapes: Batman, Bugs Bunny, the Flintstones. You could eat your favourite cartoons now, along with some alphabetti or, a new one on Luke, numberelli. The amazing thing was that even though you knew this you still went, as it were, off-list every now and then, and even felt grateful. Well, not today, thank you very much. Luke would help himself to what he'd come for, and that would be it.

The supermarket had an empty, early-morning feeling. Even the trolleys made no sound. There was heel-noise, but that was it. Out in the city's offices, people would be at their desks by now, empty coffee cups by their elbows; half-finished crosswords would be tucked in briefcases ready for the journey home; cafés and restaurants would be spreading cutlery and napkins over the tables. This place would probably fill up at lunchtime: there was a decent sandwich section. But now it was perfect.

Okay: he'd leave the fruit till last – didn't want it to get squashed at the bottom. Tins first, the cheese was up ahead. He pulled cans from the shelves and dropped them in the trolley. He could probably have crammed everything into a basket, but it wasn't worth the risk. And since he had the shop to himself, the trolley was just as convenient.

Convenience . . . hang on a minute. It was another bit of sleight-of-hand with the clock, an attempt to bring deep time, that absolute next-next-next number cruncher, to heel. Luke was standing in front of the tinned vegetables, looking at baby carrots in brine, when he had this tiny interior outburst. His arms were full of tomatoes and sweetcorn and he was tipping them into the trolley. His hand had started to bleed again, and possibly it was this which was bothering him, rather than the inadequacy of the wire baskets, which he wasn't even using. But that word, convenience . . . it had never occurred to him before, but surely it meant . . . marriage. It must be from the Latin for coming together, it was to do with convening and conventions, to do with manners and rules.

He didn't know what to do with this insight, but he had a fleeting sense that he was close to making some solid connections. Getting married was – what – conventional? . . . convenient? He couldn't quite put his finger on it, but was there some odd sense in which marriage was a time saver?

So what?

In theory, he ought to be at the airport by now. He could check in, have a beaker of refreshing tropical fruit crush at the health bar and stroll through customs as if he had all day, the very picture of patience, indifferent to the chaotic fugitives sprinting from queue to queue looking for the shortest one . . .

Hey, but seriously.

He located eggs and frozen peas. Horseradish, of course. Otherwise, his mind was blank. There were a few so-called necessities he could do with himself: razors, shampoo, aspirin, toothpaste – ah, one of those for Dad as well. Where were we? He kept thinking about bottles of cider, but couldn't think why.

He reached behind him to check the letter. Still there.

High ridges of food passed in front of him. Each time he

reached the end of an aisle he had to swing the trolley round just right, the way you had to if you were moving fast through an airport with your luggage piled up. He was starting to sweat.

What had Carmen been thinking at the end? That it was all over? Surely not. They had hardly got going. So far as he was concerned, there was lots more talking to be done. Or was it . . . Luke's cheek burned. Things had changed, he realised. This might not be up to him any more. Carmen could have made a decision of her own by now, could have changed her mind.

Oh, put yourself in her shoes, for heaven's sake. Once you'd raised a subject like that there was only one unambiguous answer: yes. Yes, yes, yes. Anything else meant – there was no escaping it – no.

He of all people ought to have registered that there were only two sides to this. But what could he do? He scanned his internal directory to see if there was an option he hadn't thought of.

Here he was: bacon. Bung a packet of sausages in as well. Plus some of this horrible-looking breakfast slice. He knew his father hated black pudding, so he picked out a couple of juicy ones and threw them in.

In other circumstances, if he wasn't going away for example, there would have been more to discuss. Like, if the answer was no, was that a no, not ever or a no, not just now? It made a difference.

Was she angry, or just upset? He tried to remember something he had read in a women's magazine. What men don't know about women's moods.

Excuse me.

He moved out of the way. A voice cut into the music for a second. Someone was wanted at till two.

Upset was all right: it would leave her room to say, oh, she was wrong, no, really, it's okay. But she had a right to be angry. Standing at the end of two aisles, one containing biscuits and pet food, the other bathroom equipment, Luke felt that he might have given her a good look at the kind of person he was, and when it struck him that this was exactly what he had been seeking to avoid, well . . .

What if he had? There was always . . .

Emma? Luke.

Luke! My God! Where *are* you? In mid-air?

No, about nought feet. In the sky lounge.

Well it's *lovely* to hear you. I posted those letters.

Emma, it was just to say . . . I haven't got long. About coming out . . .

Yes, I'm excited. I had a word with Brian. He said all right.

Great.

You're sure it's okay?

Yes, perfect. We'll do Rome. I'll be Audrey Hepburn.

But the voices in Luke's head faded. He knew he was trying to lift his spirits, and it wasn't working. Carmen's face kept drifting into the picture, wavy hair touching the corners of her mouth.

What was he doing? Surely he wasn't about to start comparing Emma and Carmen as if they were different sorts of pizza on the supermarket shelf, one of them deep pan, the other with an exciting new topping.

Luke almost left the trolley where it was and walked out. He stared around him at the tins and packets and felt giddy. All this mad labour . . . fruit from the Philippines and Indonesia and South America hacked by hungry men and women and loaded into trucks bound for the coast . . . coffee beans and tea from exotic hillsides mashed into frozen tubs on mile-long ships . . . noisy bottling plants and canneries in the suburbs . . . huge food-refining factories around the airport . . . all that shattering industrial effort just so he could walk around snatching hygienic food into his chromium-plated trolley.

Look at all this: Golden Turkey Pizzaburgers. Bacostix in Crispy Crumb. Chicken Donut Hoops in Malaysian Satay.

A tiny girl wheeled past. Help me, someone, she cried. Help me, someone. Everybody seemed to be ignoring her, so Luke did the same.

It was enough to make anyone's head spin. Luke had been told by a friend that, in a hostage situation, the standard training was to ask the kidnappers if they wanted something to eat. When they said yes, you said, What, chicken or fish? If there was a pause, you had them. Experienced nappers would shout that they wanted food and they wanted it now or the kid would get it.

Novices would go, Er, chicken, no, wait a minute, make that three chicken, one fish. (This at least was how things would go according to the manual: real life might not be so neat.) And then you'd go, How do you want it cooked – fried, roast, cold? And they'd have to decide again. And you'd say, Want anything with that: fries, a baked potato, how about ketchup? And something to drink? Maybe some fruit – we've got some ripe plums. Or what about chocolate? Plain, milk, ripple? You could keep it up for ever, and unless the people inside realised what was going on, they'd lose control. Having to decide put you at a disadvantage. Sandwich bars worked on the same principle.

Luke knew this feeling. Didn't everyone? You only had to watch television to see people going on about the supermarket as the symbolic or mythical incarnation of the, er, consumerist hegemony in a decadent, er, post-capitalist society. And it had happened to him before, in shops or canteens, this kind of customer panic. It was as though you were perched on a thin crust which could cave in at any minute (like the roof of a mine, Luke thought with a guilty start). You wanted to tear away the screens which came between you and the food, junk all the paper and tin, and rip off those enthusiastic recipes telling you how to make a mouth-watering tuna and bean bake by adding the contents of this sachet to (fancy that) some tuna and beans.

Perhaps it was only vanity, a natural distaste for the idea that he was in the slightest degree predictable. He always hated it when he read, for example, that the big food chains conducted elaborate weather forecasts, so that on sunny days they could fill the sandwiches with prawns and save the beef for when it was cold. Was it so easy to anticipate what people would want for lunch – people who'd be scanning the shelves thinking, hmmm, what do I *really* fancy today? If it looked like snow they'd leave the lettuces in the fridge and order more juggernauts full of chops and potatoes and soup. Luke resented the idea of being easy to read, an obedient consumer, so much that quite often, on those August days when the tarmac in the roads melted and glistened, he'd fill his basket with stew and cocoa and red wine, waiting until there was ice on the windows before he would let himself buy spring onions and radishes. You would have thought that buying things nobody else wanted would be cheaper, but for some reason the reverse was the case. Luke had never forgotten the New Year's Eve dinner he'd prepared: the strawberries had cost a fortune, and even the ice cream wasn't reduced.

He gazed at the racks of seasonings. Creamy onion and herb sauce mix. Check these out: Green Cuisine tomato and broccoli quarter-pounders. And while we were here, why was the healthy eating option always lasagne?

There was a condition, Luke remembered hearing about it, called dyspraxia, or something like that; it made people suffer a choice-crisis. In most areas of life they were fine, but ask them if they wanted tea or coffee and they'd collapse. Toddlers would rage and weep, and parents would grow furious: Dad would tell Mum not to spoil the kids; Mum would tell Dad not to be so hard on them and anyway, a little attention from *him* once in a while might not be such a bad idea.

Sometimes Luke thought it was a question of scale. The geography of food production – the ceaseless milling and churning and loading across the great oceans, the truckloads of vegetables burrowing into tunnels and hovering over the waiting holds of cargo ships – it was all, all of it, too big to see.

At other times it seemed to be more a matter of detail, the feeling that you had been targeted by cost imperatives and considerations of distribution and marketing that had nothing to do with you. The irate motorists stuck at the lights never suspected that there was a traffic god up there, with green lips and big red eyes, and that his name was Luke. Nor did the people buying all these new and improved goods, all these individual tropical milkshakes.

Luke felt as though the surface of the earth, no thicker than the skin of one of these apples, was splitting; his feet were sinking into a hot sponge core that went down and down for ever. The more he struggled, the deeper he sank.

He wished he hadn't said blithe notion. Or conventional emotion. Or modern obsession. Carmen was right: he was ridiculous. Look at him trudging up and down the polished tile alleys like a trained mouse, taking pleasure – pride! – in the way he handled his trolley, keeping the wheels well aligned so no one would think for a moment he wasn't a dab hand at this.

What sort of dog food? Tender chunks of lamb and beef, with a rabbit, vegetable and spinach pasta? Mr Happy Nouvelle vegetarian mix with the refillable trial pack? Luke looked up, half expecting to see a shelf of dog wine.

There was a favourite line which the exact-science types at work were always repeating. It was some famous writer saying that whoever could make two ears of corn grow where only one grew before would deserve better of mankind than the whole race of politicians combined. Well, various people *had* spent long years of trial and error and come up with astonishing high-yield crops, and where were they now?

Luke picked up a bottle of cider. It must have been a great day when someone cracked the problem of how to seal fizzy drinks. Bottles of ginger beer all over the table, sheets and sheets of drawings, a small mound of bright shavings where the metalwork was done. And then, snap, simple.

Luke took a deep breath. You wanted to be depressed by the mass market? Fine. Stunned? No problem. It was only yet another choice you had to make. If you picked the former and bored people with insights into how things really worked, all you were doing was asking them to see you as a perceptive free-thinker who wasn't willing to take shit from the big boys. And if you went for the latter, weren't you just inviting people to think of you as eager and bright, interested in everything, not closed to the wonders of life? Everything you said was an advertisement for whatever aspect of yourself you were promoting at the time. Sometimes you felt like seeming weighed down, and sometimes you wanted people to think of you as a bon viveur. Take your pick.

Luke was interrupted by his father's voice. Cream, sugar, custard powder . . . If he could stay on this frequency he wouldn't forget anything. But custard powder: what on earth would that be with?

And what time was it? Excuse me, Luke asked someone, a girl. Have you . . . ?

I don't know. Quarter to ten-ish.

Thanks.

Tick, the world went. Tock.

He still didn't know how he had ended up in here, though he had a vague feeling that it was where he deserved to be, that he'd brought it all on himself. But it wasn't fair: you told one small fib, and one thing led to another, and soon you were sunk. The plane was leaving in an hour and a half. And his flat was still . . .

He was glad Carmen hadn't opened his present. It was nice to think of her opening it when she got back, seeing her name on the front and having no one to thank. Unless she didn't open it: what if she took one look and dropped it in the plastic bin beneath the sink, along with the milk cartons, the eggshells, the empty whisky bottle, and the letter.

Luke was walking past glistening polythene bags of minced beef and slabs of liver and steak. His heart felt heavy, as if it needed more room. If only he could sit down and think for a bit; it ought to be straightforward: did he want to get married, or not? He leaned over the meat counter to let someone past, and felt feverish in the refrigerated fumes of conditioned air.

He ought to get something for Martin. A bottle of whisky? Very funny.

It struck Luke just then that there was a reason why he hadn't said yes to Carmen. It was a good reason, even if he hadn't been aware of it at the time. He leaned on his trolley and almost smiled. He was getting somewhere at last. Because the thing was, surely, it was quite out of the question to say yes, let's get married, and then look at your watch and say, Right, nice idea, sure thing, I'll be off then. If you said yes you had to stay – what else could you do? You had to drink champagne or something, loosen your tie a little, if you know what I mean. Carmen would have put her toe behind her heel and leaned back into the cushions, saying there was lots of time, no need to rush. Yes, that was it: this whole business was Carmen's fault – really it was. She'd put him in an impossible situation. Luke was sure that she'd be the first to admit it.

Carmen, he imagined saying to her. I found your letter. I've been such a fool.

No, it's me, she would say. My timing was terrible. But look,

I've bought a ticket on your flight. We can have a great weekend in Rome, forget all about it.

He could get himself a bag of sweets for take-off, to stop his ears clogging – butterscotch would be good. Assuming he was on the plane, that is.

Why didn't he cancel his flight?

The thought landed without warning. Luke couldn't say where it came from. Someone reached in, he said to himself.

Yes, why not book another one for tomorrow or the day after. What was he talking about: two hundred pounds? It'd be great. They'd have time for a proper talk; he could relax.

Dear oh dear. Luke navigated a route to the counter where green and yellow lights flared down on the lemons and pears. He picked some apples with an absent mind and wandered over to the tills. Standing up an aeroplane seemed wrong, not like missing a train or a bus or even a person. It wasn't only the money. And you could convince yourself that it was glamorous: Yeah, a few things came up so I skipped it, trashed the ticket, what the hell. But a flight was a solid commitment. You knew weeks ago when it would leave, and couldn't start pretending that it was not convenient. You had to live as if something was fixed.

Anyway, what was he planning to achieve by staying? The one thing keeping him going was the thought of leaving. Things might look different from Italy.

He switched off for a second and scanned the other shoppers, who were nosing around, leaning in occasionally for a closer look like people in an art gallery. But the whole point of galleries was that visitors were as receptive as possible, whereas these faces were hard and fixed. Art, travelling, shopping . . . sometimes he thought the world was composed of only two things: queuing and choosing. And trivial things were always barging their way to the front. Wake up, wake up. Luke shook his head. There was a shorter line over by the sign saying EXIT, but the woman in front had a trolley filled to the brim. This one would be okay unless people started writing cheques, and then the girl on the checkout would have to ring her bell.

It was a relief to be standing still for a second. It was like an interval, a chance to stretch your legs before you got locked into the second half.

Why did he want to analyse all this, anyway? Wasn't this what Carmen had been trying to say: that every now and then you had to take the plunge. It was as easy as riding a bike. If you fell off the first few times, big deal.

But this wasn't like cycling, except for the feeling of going round in circles.

Luke caught sight of himself in one of those round, convex mirrors these places used to keep an eye on the customers. His face was swollen, and the rest tapered away almost to nothing. All around him were piles of primary colours and bright patches where cellophane caught the electric glare.

Luke could not ignore a nagging feeling that all this reflection wasn't going to help. This wasn't one of those lateral puzzles to which you knew there was an answer. This might be a trickier thing, a problem where the harder you thought about it the more you got lost.

The music switched to something classical. What the hell was it? Luke started to hum along under his breath.

These people in the queue ahead of him. The woman at the front was quite young, with pale arms. Then there was an old man holding a single frozen pie and a carton of apple juice. Then another woman, older, her head wrapped in a scarf, purse ready. Were they all married? How had it happened?

Did he have everything? Damn – pastry. And plums.

There was already someone behind him, and he couldn't face giving up his place. Hang on: he wedged his trolley against the rim of the food slide, said, One second! to the woman at the till – who was busy tapping prices in and probably wouldn't know what he was talking about – and trotted back to the freezer chests. There were about a million different sorts of ice cream, all kinds of packed-up curries and shrimp platters and low cal five-course meals. Hundreds of pies, too: chicken, ocean, shepherd's, captain's . . . vol-au-vent cases, quiche starter-packs. No pastry, though.

Ah. He grabbed two.

On a malicious whim, he leaned over the cold tubs. His father had a thing about prepared food: it infuriated him. Luke picked out the most prepared thing in sight – Norfolk Ham Cobbler: tender gammon chunks in a rich country-style pineapple batter sauce – and grinned.

By the time he got back to his trolley the woman had gone in front of him: she only had a packet of peppercorns, and Luke didn't have the heart to say anything. He could imagine how cross she must have been. Probably having smoked salmon or mackerel or something for lunch, or someone important coming round. It was very distinguished, using this fabulous global labour-saving machine to buy a few pellets of spice and nothing else.

It would give him another minute of peace, at any rate. He could listen to the music. Sounded like opera. On guitars.

The thing about queues was their abject surrender to the authority of time. There was no way to tinker with priority. It should have been possible to gauge how urgent were the needs of the customers – in which case Luke would have gone straight to the front – but no, it was first come, first served all the way.

I was thinking, Carmen said inside his head, I was thinking, maybe . . .

The words seemed unremarkable. But then it was never the words themselves that carried the charge.

Darling Luke! This might come as a surprise . . .

He stared at some bottles of Calvados, which had full-size apples hanging in the liquor. It wasn't even worth wondering how they got them there.

He could remember a time, years ago, when he'd been sitting in someone's garden trying to think up ideas for films. One of his friends was a director – at least, he wanted to direct – and had told Luke how it worked, how you had to submit treatments, short summaries of the story, and then, if they liked that, develop a full screenplay.

It sounded easy to Luke and, one weekend, when everyone else went for a long walk in the surrounding hills, he found a biro and sat down at a slatted table in the sun.

By the end of the afternoon he had written out several stories. One was a comedy about a man – or it could have been a woman, it didn't really matter – who agreed as a bet to try to live by the ten commandments for a whole week. The story pushed him through all the usual scenes and showed how hard it was to live like that, but twisted when it dawned on the hero that there was something immoral about trying to live a moral life on a temporary basis, to win a bet.

Another described someone up for a prize, some prestigious award. He didn't know if he would win, but agreed with his wife, in an emotional scene the night before, that if he did he'd announce that all the money would go to charity. Well, the next day he did win, and when he walked up to make his speech he was full of good intentions. But as soon as he began to speak he filled up with doubts. If you were giving to charity you should do it privately, not boast about it. And then, which charity? There were so many. And wouldn't it be insulting to the others to make such a grandiose gesture? So he didn't say anything. He tried to explain all this to his wife, but she wouldn't accept any excuse, and not long afterwards went off with a fund-raiser. In the last scene the hero, all alone, would receive a postcard from Nairobi.

There was another one – it wasn't hard to dream them up – which involved someone watching the television and seeing some awful scene in a far away place – a flood or a famine. The hero would decide to get a lorry and help out. So he gets everything together and drives off, but while he's gone he gets fired from his job, and what's more one of his daughters gets pregnant and maybe commits suicide. It was going to be a real tear-jerker, this one. Underneath it would be full of ironies about what happens if you watch too much TV, if you start thinking that electronic pictures beamed in from outer space are more real than your own life. That sort of thing.

Luke's favourite was about a fisherman. There wasn't nearly enough fishing in films, he thought. This one would describe the adventure of a man who loved fishing so much that he could never eat fish. Most mornings he'd be on the river at dawn, but whenever he caught anything (salmon and trout were what he went for) he'd just kiss the head and return the fish to the stream. His family would poke fun at him all the time: they had a bottomless supply of bad-fisherman stories to embarrass him with. But one day he cast into a deep pool and hooked a real beauty. He played it for a long, memorable afternoon, going up-river all the time. Twice he nearly lost it when his line wrapped itself round a rock or tangled in a low branch, so he waded out into the current and worked with water up to his chest. By the time he landed the fish he could see that it was exhausted to the point of death. So he took it home, and the family greeted him with lots of merriment. The old man and the salmon, they said. His wife made a big thing about cooking it, and even laid on some candles. But one of the children suddenly claimed to hate fish and refused to eat it. There was a big argument. All the children ended up in tears – over a stupid fish, what did it matter? The man, left at the table on his own, reached out a reluctant fork, lifted a frag-ment to his lips, and found it so delicious that he ate as much as he could. After that he never fished again, though he ate salmon whenever he could, almost all the time, in fact.

There were other stories, too (not one saw the light of day), but what Luke remembered about that afternoon was that he had made a note, during a spell when he couldn't think, of the things that were running through his mind. He couldn't say now what they all were, but the list went something like this:

So, what would be a good story for a film? Oh, the sun's gone in. Listen . . . I know that tune . . . the warmth on forearms when the sun's out, the way the hairs stand up when the wind blows . . . Shall I have another cigarette now or wait? . . . Maybe make some tea in a minute, then have one . . . A spider crawling across the white page . . . I could kill it, but I won't . . . Would I write different things if I had different coloured ink? . . . Maybe a story about a woman who lives alone and dies, and the local people wonder where her money is . . . Even here you can't escape industry: aeroplanes above, radios in the distance, traffic some-where over there . . . The scent in the garden: why can't perfume makers get closer to these superb plant fragrances? . . . The grass looks greener through sunglasses . . . What birds are those? . . . What's that crackling in the woods up there, a squirrel? . . . There's tennis on the television, I could be watching . . . I wonder when the others will get back . . . I could find something to read . . . Say the film's made, can I wander around on location, chatting to actresses? . . . What kind of a speech would I make if it won an Oscar or something? . . . There's an idea: a man prepares a speech about giving the money away, then doesn't do it . . . Who could play the man? . . . I really should ring my mum, haven't spoken to her for a while . . . Could you live like this all the time, just sitting around making things up? . . . What are my favourite films: what do I like about them? . . . Gosh, it's warm now . . . there might be some sun oil in the bathroom I could borrow . . . I think maybe I will have a cigarette . . .

And so on. But Luke soon saw that he'd been concentrating too hard: quite a few times he'd paused to think of new things to write, and part of his purpose had been to introduce a jerky, random element to the list. Even in life you had to have some system for deciding which things were more important than the rest. You couldn't just take everything as it came. Posterity would look after it all in the long run, but who could afford to wait that long?

There was a clock over the sliding doors. Luke was astonished to see that it was only 9.54. Not bad. Not bad at all.

Plums. Damn.

He hurried back to the fruit. Were these ripe? They were almost the same colour as that bruise on his shoulder: dark purple and red in the centre, with traces of yellow and green radiating outwards in a confused traffic-light effect. Luke squeezed one, and thought of Emma.

But were they ripe?

Luke was fed up with presuming, with supposing, with guessing, with wondering whether this or that was the case. What he wanted was a less provisional life. Speculation was fine, but there were risks.

I mean, it was quite something to decide that you wanted ham, when you could have had beef or lamb or pork or chicken or turkey or mince (by the time you'd got that far you'd already have rejected the idea of fish) – not to mention the far-out meats: poussin and pheasant, veal and pigeon, rabbit and quail, hare and reindeer. Perhaps you wanted to show off, do something really special – like that time Carmen came round on his birthday, and Luke prepared a cheese soufflé, forgetting that timing was everything and that she might well be on the late side. Well, if that was the case, you probably would have put a cross against ham quite a while ago.

But even if you successfully negotiated this cat's cradle of influences and settled on ham, you had to choose between American, Suffolk, Canadian, Norfolk and probably Somerset and Wiltshire too; you could have it baked, smoked, honey-glazed or spicy; thinly sliced, carved in lazy wedges or chopped. Want the fat trimmed off? There was almost no end to it. Easier, and quicker, to pick up a tin of long life Old Oake Gammon (from Argentina).

Would these people please hurry up. The man with the apple juice was writing a cheque. Unbelievable!

Maybe the reason he was refusing to entertain the idea of missing his flight was because it was the one concrete appointment he had. He'd made the decision ages ago, weighing up the pros and cons – was Friday a good day to travel, was an early flight better, if you booked long enough in advance did you get the cut-price fare. It was too late to start over again. It was done with.

Would Mr Apple Juice never move?

He was trying to keep his mind away from Carmen, but it was clear even to him that his musings had in some sense been shunted, swung around from left to right as they crossed the points and diverted towards a different line of thought.

But did this disqualify them?

Luke had often wondered whether, if he was somewhere else, he would have different ideas. If, for instance, instead of coming into the supermarket he'd stepped into a taxi and let the gentle rocking and lurching carry him along . . . what then? Would he have been preoccupied with images relevant to the way the cab rode the bumps in the street and weaved through the traffic. Would he have had thoughts related to ideas about U-turns and short cuts, or congestion and pollution? Probably.

And would he have reached a different conclusion? Hard to say. He hadn't actually reached one, had he?

His turn! The girl waved a hand at a sign and muttered something.

Sorry?

Five items or less.

You're not serious.

The girl shrugged, then started processing his purchases. Luke's shoulders sagged in relief. If she'd wanted to stand on ceremony he'd have been done for. He loaded the goods into plastic bags and paid with a credit card. They had one of those new tills where you slide the card along a groove and everything happens automatically. The machine hesitated and Luke grappled with a sharp fear of rejection, but in the end it clicked away. On the receipt, printed in pale grey computer script, the machine recorded the total: 1962. The year he was born. Time really was money.

The hours and minutes were written on there, too. It was six minutes to ten. If he wasn't on the way to the airport by quarter past he might as well cash in his chips.

By now they would have automatically debited his account and flashed details of the transaction half-way across the country. Expensive software would have whisked the numbers into the innards of the big processors in head office, and poured a little more sand into the hourglass of his monthly debt. Oh yes, they had the technology all right. In real time, too.

But from now on he had to concentrate one hundred per cent. Letting his mind wander up and down stray footpaths was out. Otherwise, before he knew it . . . Or maybe that was the way to miss a flight: to deceive yourself into believing that there was still time until, whoops, too late. Perhaps, though he couldn't admit this to himself, he had no intention of catching the plane, but wanted to keep up appearances. This way you wouldn't have to make your mind up at all, you could just keep putting off the moment when you finally realised that you had to go no matter how much more there was to do. And usually you'd find that all those things that seemed so pressing could just as easily be done later.

For instance: what was to stop him posting the papers to Martin and phoning him from Italy?

Stop it, he told himself. Stick to the plan.

The doors slapped back with a beep, triggered by some invisible radar, and a blast of hot, electronic air from above cascaded between Luke and the rain.

Now: a taxi.

But you couldn't just stick to a plan no matter what. It might be a good idea one minute, but times changed and you had to go with the flow, use your mind like a rudder, flick it this way and that in a series of minute responses to the shift in the current. And hope for the best that you didn't nudge yourself out into the white water, where you couldn't do anything to help yourself.

Luke took a deep breath. He didn't seem to be able to think of a single thing where the opposite wasn't also true. Now he was wondering whether to wait for a cab or whether he might as well start walking. It wouldn't take long, whereas if he opted for a taxi and had no luck – you couldn't rely on anything – his goose would be cooked.

One or the other – it didn't really matter. But if he decided to wait for a cab he would need the courage of his convictions. He couldn't hang around for five minutes and then decide to walk. That would be a feeble waste of time. Or would it be a shrewd cutting of his losses? He shook his head.

This was madness, madness. Luke could see he was approaching dangerous waters. A flash of disgust ran through him when he realised that he was actually able to make himself so agitated. Christ, you've seen the pictures: those creatures with huge, old man's heads and legs like coat-hangers. You only had to consider what went on in the world, Jesus. Surely you weren't going to have the cheek to start bitching about how many choices you had, about how tough it was to waver between Belgian lettuce and Dutch endive.

He'd said something to Carmen once about how they lived in difficult times, but she was having none of it. We're about the luckiest generation that ever lived, she snapped. For one thing, we've got away without a major war, though the way things are going we might not be out of the woods yet.

Luke never found it easy to talk in these terms. Right now, for instance, he couldn't concentrate on anything, not with these plastic handles digging ugly white creases into the palms of his hands.

Probably it was best to wait here for a taxi: it was a busy enough road.

He put the bags down and imagined briefly saying, Yes, Carmen, yes, yes, the way people did in books. Just thinking of it made him feel better. Some of the stiffness slid out of his shoulders and even his headache seemed to evaporate. A miracle! Apart from banishing – as if by hitting a delete button – this whole tortuous thought process, making the big choice would put all the smaller ones into the shade. If he said yes – well, what would it matter, in the scheme of things, that the plums were sour?

A marriage of convenience. What was wrong with that? There were plenty of places in the world where brides and grooms were lined up by their families. It was a lot less trouble, you had to admit.

Mind you: saying no would have the same effect.

Too late, he saw the taxi, windscreen wipers going hard. He shouted, and for an instant the driver seemed to slow down; but then he picked up speed again and accelerated through the green light up by the tube station. Luke swore. Try finding a red light when you needed one.

But hold on – you couldn't start talking about marriage as if it was a handy way to save time, a labour-saving device (for a start, it didn't come with a malfunction guarantee). Some decisions were more important than others and required more thought, that was all there was to it.

Luke was used to the idea – this was computers teaching him a lesson again – that every piece of data had equivalent weight, that the number of blips the brain needed to buy a house was the same as the number required for a bar of chocolate. But this notion was being consigned to the scrapheap here and now. It was all right for computers, they weren't sentimental. It wouldn't worry them that a house was meant to last, according to the particulars, 999 years; whereas the chocolate might well be gone in five minutes.

Across the road, Luke noticed as he stood in the rain, the doors of the church opened, and a man came out onto the steps. From behind him came the sound of organ pipes. The man pushed up an umbrella and then waited, rain spattering beside his polished shoes, looking up and down the road, as if he was expecting guests. He inspected his watch a couple of times.

Luke felt like going in. It looked dark and quiet. He hadn't been in a church for years, but it was like riding a bike: you didn't forget.

It occurred to him that the man standing there like a shop-keeper in search of business might be just that – a shepherd without a flock. It rang true: this had never seemed, to anyone except estate agents, an area ripe for conversion. And you didn't see too many adverts, among the thousands for detergents and cars and banks and breakfast cereals, for matins and evensong. The world was nervous about promoting things we needed, as opposed to those we merely wanted.

Luke felt a surge of sadness. It must be awful standing there in the wet, watching people file into the supermarket, passing by the counters, helping themselves to pieces of lamb and whatever else had been sacrificed to make their lives easier, receiving a brief blessing at the till before passing, glad in heart and replenished, back into the street.

And it looked so small, wedged in there between two tall office blocks made of tinted glass. The whole point of churches, Luke thought, was that they steepled or spired above the rest of the world, a reminder that there were things in life too big to see. But that was the trouble with cities. In villages, the church was the Church. Here, there were hundreds. And they looked like toys.

It was . . .

But heavens above! He couldn't afford to hang about like this. Rain or no rain, he was going to have to walk.

Sod it. He'd forgotten the stewing steak.

For a moment there, Luke might have been on to something. Time went on for ever: convenience was a way of snipping bits off for your own private use. If you could put the two together, if you could bring about the marriage of time and convenience, you could put your feet up.

Luke had visited a psychiatrist many years before (even Carmen didn't know this). It was not long after he first came to the city. He was struggling to come to terms with the particular conditions of urban life, and was put in touch with a man who specialised in such cases. Luke was shown a sheet full of blotchy pictures, and had to say what he thought they represented. One of them was a circle with a crude slash across the middle. Luke said he thought it was the world, or one of those planets with rings; then he identified it as a practice golf ball. The man looked at him with a tolerant smile.

Eventually, desperate for an interesting answer, Luke said: a cashew nut.

It was only a joke, but the man sat forward. Now we're talking, he said. Say a bit more about that.

He seemed to want Luke's life story. But how could you cram a whole life into a few one-hour episodes? Was it important to start at the beginning and work through from there, as if there was a coherent sequence of causes and effects? Or should you take a cross-section, like a tree, and hope that the rings showed accurate deposits of past experience? Luke, who often endured nervous flutters about the reliability of his memory, was shocked to see how much had slithered away, like sand in an hourglass.

But he did his best, and the psychiatrist seemed happy, especially when Luke told him about a dream he'd had several times. It was about a man who wanted to live a life of perfect seclusion. He built a remote garden and planted explosives all over the grounds to keep the world at a safe distance, but after a while he started to forget where the dangers were. Luke couldn't remember how it ended – he always woke up before things came to a head.

The psychiatrist said that if it happened again, he should take notes. He wanted all the details.

Afterwards, Luke concluded that life was like a book: you revised as you advanced, so the past kept changing. When people told him that books were artificial, that they couldn't represent life as it really was, he replied that life was artificial too: a few hours of everyday existence contained years of random memories and buried hopes.

What's more, life didn't only have length – it had breadth and depth too. The cross-section was what counted.

It was shortly after this that Luke sat on the lawn and tried to study his mental traffic flow.

On reflection, the cashew nut analogy wasn't bad – two halves which seemed to fit together but could be separated by the smallest tap of a fingernail, the slightest knock on the shoulder or slap on the face. It was certainly an improvement on Luke's previous notion: that he was a snowflake, swollen by the weight of experience as he fell through life. Even this made a kind of sense: he was sure that events of any sort – emotions, thoughts, whatever – had mass. And he was convinced that new ones could displace old ones, the way you could tape over music you'd outgrown, or call up a new file while the old one was still running. The catch was, it did involve a certain abdication: it assumed that you fell through life without even trying to steer a course. What was it Carmen had said, that he was all rudder, no helm?

It took a while for Luke to see that snowflakes lacked the individuality he was after. They tended to drift around with other snowflakes, vulnerable to any old puff of wind or minute shift in the temperature. They were part of the snowflake community. And in the end they melted.

This nut idea wasn't going to fly either. As Carmen had pointed out, nuts had shells. And they weren't like birds, scratching away with their nibs when they felt ready to face the world outside. They were trapped in there until some higher power – a squirrel, a thrush, a chimpanzee, a multinational nut franchise — decided to crack them apart and gobble them up.

For Luke, the dilemma this morning was simple: he had an awful lot on his mind, but didn't have time to think about it because of everything he had to do first. If he was looking for a way to marry these two halves of himself, to find the gear that would engage life on the surface with life in the depths . . . well, it was staring him in the face. He had only to reach out his hands.

What he wanted was to discover imaginary time. Many names have been devised for it: eternity, posterity, history. It is the engine of all sorts of fringe psychic phenomena — dreams that come true, sensations of déjà vu; but it is also the driving force behind any literature that attempts to persuade the reader that a whole life, or several generations of lives, can be embraced by something that only takes a few hours to read. As soon as you read the words Once upon a time . . . you've stepped into this imaginary world, where whole years pass by in a flash and someone seems to have arranged it so the past and the future are walking up the aisle, hand in hand, smartly dressed and with bands of gold in their pockets.

For centuries, it was a philosophical question. Did time exist, or were we just imagining it? Then science got in on the act, bending its mind to the task of measuring infinity and making it seem as if time had solid characteristics which could be nailed down and defined. It was no easy job, even for the experts: sometimes they racked their brains and felt as if it would go on for ever. But various enthusiastic mystics have come along recently and declared that all you have to do is shut your eyes, wrench your knees together and chant for a while, and you'll dip your feet into the profound well of cool, refreshing imaginary time.

It's a bit of a come-down. In ancient times sun-worshippers lined up the solstice with huge stones, and paid attention when their bright god signalled it was time to thatch the hut. Today's sun-worshippers worry about harmful effects, and ration their devotions. The modern sun sports a health warning.

Did time exist? Or had we just invented a way of making timetables work? Was a broken watch still a watch? Was a river that didn't flow still a river?

There were people in the world for whom the idea that this was the end of the twentieth century was a joke, the last gasp of an imperial presumption. All the millennial gushing, which seemed to spring from some infinite reservoir, was of purely local interest.

The only sensible course, it seemed, was to absent yourself, to find some secluded garden with high barricades, and bask there in exquisite solitude.

These were the thoughts that made Luke frown as he stood there in the rain outside the supermarket. In fact, he watched them fall into his mind in the space between two raindrops.

He only snapped out of it because it occurred to him to wonder what time it was.

The clock is the enemy of imaginary time. It wants us to forget that behind us lie fossils, and ahead lies God knows what. It has been besieging real, deep time for centuries, drawing the noose ever tighter, dragging it into the shadows of our lives and into the shadows cast by shadows. But how on earth was Luke supposed to know that, with all that he had on his mind?

Ten o'clock

Luke had only walked about a hundred yards, and was just getting used to the idea that he was going to get soaked, when he saw a taxi nodding over the hill towards him. He tried to raise his arm to attract the driver, but all he managed was to shake the plastic bags. He felt one of the handles rip, but it held. As the taxi braked and pulled in beside him, its front wheel thumped a puddle and sprayed Luke's shins with cold water.

The sensation was familiar, for some reason.

He had to put the bags down to get the door open.

He gave the directions and slouched back.

Can I turn this on? He touched the heater with his hand. The bags had made his cut start bleeding again. Terrific.

Go ahead.

It's pretty wet out there.

Tell me about it.

Luke pushed the switch and warm air came streaming out. He rubbed his damp hands.

Sorry it's not far.

Job's a job.

Listen. I've just got to drop this stuff off and pick up my things. Don't suppose you fancy going on? I'm heading for the airport, but need to stop on the way.

Nah. Wouldn't catch me on that motorway at any price.

Oh God, jammed, is it?

Some sort of slow-moving vehicle. Two lanes wide. Hang on. He spoke into his microphone.

The radio was full of voices which Luke couldn't unscramble.

Solid as a rock, they're saying. Course, we don't mind, it's all money. Hope you're not in a hurry.

Not specially. What time is it?

Time? Just turned ten.

You know those lights after the cinema. If you turn left there and go up the hill, I'll get off at the top.

Luke leaned into the corner. He needed a rest from all this backwards and forwards thinking; he wanted to be more like a second hand – trembling with each passing instant, never flagging or looking back. Or like a microchip, taking each game as it comes, giving every little scrap of data and every signal from on high its complete attention. This was a state of mind well worth imitating.

Driving was a help. Luke would often sidle into a daydream at the wheel, especially on familiar roads. He could change gear, indicate, turn corners and accelerate almost without thinking, leaving him free to rehearse what he was going to say when he arrived, or go over what he wished he had said to the people he'd just left, and would come up with next time he got the chance.

But there were no short cuts, and, what's more, every time you were distracted – the lights went red, or a bus pulled out bang in front – you were startled and had to go back to square one. Or else something would come into your head, even though you were trying to swim away from the shallow end, that would bring you back into the world of appointments and schedules, the world where you were supposed to be.

Where you off to, then?

Sorry?

The airport, you said. Where you off to?

Oh, Italy.

What, holidays is it?

Work, I'm afraid.

Watch out for the brothers is my advice.

The what?

Brothers. You know, Italian girls? Had a mate once . . .

Oh. Right.

Luke fingered the letter in his pocket. He'd read it when he got home.

Going with the flow, swimming with the current: all these familiar sayings sounded like ways of moving at the right speed – keeping up to the minute, keeping abreast . . . But if you were going at the same rate as the water, it was impossible to tell how fast you were going: everything drifted along in the same way. Only if you hit a rock could you tell what sort of a river you were in. And each attempt to swim a bit faster or turn uphill created a turbulence that knocked the rhythm out of your stroke and left you gasping for air.

What about marriage: was that going with the flow or against it?

Up the hill, wasn't it?

What?

Left here?

Oh, sure. Yes.

Where was he? What time was it? He'd better pay attention.

The taxi stopped in the middle of the road and the driver reached backwards out of his window to open the door. At some point in the last couple of minutes it had stopped raining.

Thanks for the traffic update, Luke said. Better get the train, I guess.

Cigarettes. He'd forgotten the cigarettes for the gardener. He smiled. All that fresh air, poor man probably needed a good smoke. Ah, and boxes, too, don't forget.

His legs were still wet at the back where he had been splashed. And he was wearing his good shoes, the ones he was travelling in, which were much too delicate to take urban rain in their stride.

This morning would have been a lot less complicated if he hadn't accepted this damn stupid job in the first place, if he'd carried on the way he was. Carmen wouldn't have . . . Yes, he'd brought all this on himself.

He could imagine what Emma was thinking: Lucky bastard! Here we are in the office at the crack of dawn, while he just gets up and catches a plane to sunsville. All right for some. She should see him now.

It didn't occur to Luke that maybe they weren't thinking about him at all. Perhaps they had forgotten he was going, wouldn't remember until they saw his empty desk or found a new recruit sitting at his screen. Oh hello, they'd say. You must be . . . Chap before you couldn't take it, pissed off abroad. But it's not as bad as all that, don't worry. Have you figured out the coffee yet? Some of us are going to the pub at lunchtime, if you want to come.

The newsagent shook his head. No boxes. Not yet. In the afternoon, maybe.

Luke bought a paper and the cigarettes. There was a clock behind the till, above the lighters and matches. Five past ten.

How about plastic bags? he said.

These?

They looked fine, a decent size anyway. The orange-yellow motif didn't matter.

I'll have five, Luke said. No, better make it ten.

He offered the man a pound.

No, no. That's okay.

Well . . . thanks. Tell you what, though. I'll have another packet of these, please.

For himself. What the hell: the way today was going . . .

Outside the shop a tall man in a coat mumbled something, and Luke hesitated before he understood what he wanted.

Here, he said, putting down his bags and fishing out a coin.

Sir. The man's hand took his arm with a surprising softness. Sir, thank you, sir, but it's like this . . .

It's all I've got, Luke said, bending over his bags.

It's like this, sir. God bless you, sir.

The man didn't have a bad face. He might even have shaved. On another day Luke would have been happy to chat for a while, take him for a sandwich somewhere warm. But this morning . . .

Who was he kidding? Even Luke couldn't pretend that he would have treated the man to lunch if he had all the time in the world.

Oh well. Beggars couldn't be choosers.

Luke watched the numbers go by – 89, green door; 87, yellow; 85 with the cherry tree; 83 without a number you could see . . . Mrs Granville lived at number 41.

The doors, the trees, the number of pints listed on those little clock faces people put out for the milkman – were these essential differences, or was this no more than the pebble-dashed community, pushed and pulled by the same forces, surging out in the mornings and ebbing at night, like stones raked up and down a shingle beach?

Roman columns around the front door at 61; 59 with the broken window above the porch; 57's satellite dish fastened high up between the bedroom windows, where the curtains never seemed to be open.

Luke knew this road too well. When he first arrived he used to enjoy wondering what went on behind these doors. They all bought the same batches of food and newsprint and petfood and the same carpets and household utensils from the same Home-Care store on the main road. Yet they managed to lead lives that seemed unique, as if they had a choice. It didn't often dawn on Luke that their lives might amount to more than the sum of their purchases.

His hand was sore and he was leaving; and he was glad. He breathed in and imagined the odours of Rome – exhaust fumes, hot car bonnets, oily food and warm wine. This road didn't smell of anything but rain.

He was now level with number 45, 43. Thank God, the lights were on. That would have been the last straw. Luke pushed the button and listened to the tubular chime. He wondered whether they could change the tune, or whether they were stuck with this one.

He prodded the button a couple more times. Inside, he could hear voices raised in anger. God, it sounded as though they were having a fight.

That you, Frank?

Frank?

Oh, it's Luke. Come on in.

The door opened, and a middle-aged woman stepped out. She leaned her face forward, and so did Luke, but they both turned their cheeks to the same side and ended up with kissing foreheads.

The voices carried on shouting.

I'm worried about Mandy. She's been so down since Red killed himself.

And you think that's why she lost the baby . . . ?

It must be the television, one of those soap operas. Talk about loud, though.

I can't stay, Luke said. I've brought these. It's kind of you to help.

Yes, your father rang. Cup of tea?

No, I really must . . . I'm in a bit of a hurry.

No, I wasn't worried, Mrs Granville said, and smiled.

She'd got worse, Luke thought.

I'll just drop these off, then, he said. Or shall I put them in the car?

The car?

To take to the flower show, for lunch. Oh dear: he'd have to shout. For my mum. He pointed at the bags.

Yes, your father phoned, Mrs Granville said.

Oh, did I tell you? I ran into Chip at the yacht club this morning. No, how was he?

I reckon he's still coming to terms with his mum's heart attack and that awful car smash. Don says his knee's so bad he might never surf again.

Luke tried not to listen, though it was impossible not to hear. Will you apologise for me, he said. I forgot the stewing steak. He made chopping movements with his hands. Stewing steak. For stew.

Yesterday?

Stew Wing steak! Luke glanced over his shoulder to see if anyone was listening. Oh, never mind. It'll take too long to explain.

Yes, it's filthy, Mrs Granville said, peering out at the sky. But the television says it's going to clear after lunch.

This was impossible. He'd better just dump the bags and leave.

I'm sorry I can't stay. Luke tapped his wrist, and grinned.

So you're off to Italy. Good for you.

If I ever get there.

Wait a minute. Mrs Granville turned about and set off up the stairs, holding on to the rail all the way. Do shut the door, she said without turning round. There's a draught.

Luke stepped inside and pushed the door to, but made sure it didn't close. It was like a greenhouse in here. Looking in, he could see the back of a black leather sofa with a newspaper over the armrest. The crossword was nearly finished. How anyone could concentrate with that programme blaring . . .

I really must run, he called.

Here it is.

Mrs Granville took the stairs even more slowly on the way down, leading with the right leg always, then letting the left catch up before attempting another step. Luke had wanted to help her, but didn't see what he could do. He felt hot and feverish, and Christ, she was slow.

In a flash he imagined seizing her foot and pulling her down. He had a vision of her head crashing against the bannister and then nothing else moving . . . Then he could get out of here.

He was shocked by this thought, which he hadn't remotely intended to have. What was happening to him? His right knee twitched and ached.

You might as well have it, said Mrs Granville, holding out her hand. I don't suppose we'll be doing so much travelling, what with this hip.

Luke wasn't sure what it was at first: a looped chrome tube attached to a cord. Then he realised.

Oh. I see. For coffee. Or tea.

You just plug it in and put it in the mug. We had an adaptor for the car somewhere, but I can't find it. It's jolly convenient.

It's . . . that's lovely . . . Thank you.

We used to drive to Italy a lot, Frank and me. In our younger days, of course, before Edward. Nearly forty years ago, can you believe that?

Luke understood that she was giving him something precious: a piece of her past, a piece of her marriage. But if he didn't watch it he might be in for the whole story.

Thank you, he said again.

Well, you never know. Mrs Granville kept a hand on the shelf above the radiator to keep her steady. The effort of standing up seemed to trouble her.

I must let you get on, Luke said, opening the door.

That's a Floriatum, Mrs Granville said. That's what it sounded like, at least.

A what?

That tree, she said, pointing. Floriatum.

Oh.

It's terribly old. It's our pride and joy.

What's a Floriatum? Luke asked, being polite.

It's a tree! Mrs Granville gave her head a shake to show what she thought of today's young people. It's terribly old. Goes back to Henry Moore's time.

Henry Moore?

You know who Henry Moore is, surely?

The sculptor?

No! Mrs Granville looked exasperated. No, no, no! The king!

Luke stared at the tree for a minute. Then he said: Well, it's lovely. But I must go. Give my regards to, erm, Frank.

He'll be sorry he missed you. He was in Italy, you know. In the war.

I expect it's changed a bit. Anyway . . .

Oh, those bags. They'd better come in here, where it's cool.

She led the way into the kitchen. Luke wound the plastic handles over his hands and lifted. The kitchen was, if anything, warmer than the hall.

Henry the Eighth, she must have meant. God almighty.

In here. Mrs Granville headed for a room at the back of the house. There were boxes of apples everywhere and large glass bottles full of red liquid. That's Frank's wine. I'd give you some, except you wouldn't want to carry it.

No, that's fine. Be a bit coals to Newcastle.

Luke put the bags down and turned to go. His thumb was bleeding again, so he put it in his pocket. The cigarettes.

Oh, I nearly forgot. He pushed the packets into the nearest bag, on top of the plums.

Cigarettes?

For the new gardener, he said. Lance, I think his name is.

Oh, look at your hand. It's bleeding.

Luke made a fist to hide the cut. Oh, I must have caught it. Never mind.

Here. Mrs Granville was rummaging in a drawer. I've got some plasters. Or some TCP. Here.

Luke tipped a little of the fluid into the cut and resisted the temptation to yell.

I'll let it dry first, he said, holding on to the plasters. Thanks for these, though.

Well. Have a good trip. What time are you off?

Pretty soon, I suppose. Luke forced himself to smile. You need to allow plenty of time.

Very sensible. Very sensible. I'm the same, but Frank? Always leaves everything till the last minute.

Bye-bye. Hope your hip, you know, gets better.

Bye-bye, Luke.

Luke waited to let a car go by – he was pretty careful about road-crossing these days – and then jogged across the road. When he reached the pavement he increased his speed and jogged round the corner. He was only a couple of streets away.

He jumped up all four steps to his own front door. It felt good to get a bit of exercise. He wouldn't mind running round the block a few times.

Before he opened the door he leaned out to the right and lobbed the porta-kettle towards the dustbin. Usually he missed, but this time it went straight in: there was a sharp crack of breaking glass.

Inside his flat, he rested against the front door to catch his breath in the stale, damp-carpet air of the hallway. The newspaper and the plastic bags he dropped onto the small table, and bent to examine the post.

His thumb didn't enjoy tearing open the envelopes, but Luke ignored it. What did we have here: a mail-order catalogue – adjustamatic beds, agriframes, sun loungers; and a bright yellow competition form – £75,000 could be yours! Three phone cards from minicab firms, an individually-wrapped biscuit sample, and a leaflet from a pizza company: you could have a Caribbean Scorcher delivered to your door, no extra cost. And look here, a pamphlet from an exclusive singles club. Dear unattached friend, it began.

What was he doing reading these, when he had Carmen's letter burning a hole in his pocket?

Darling Luke! he read. This might come as a surprise, and I'm sorry to be putting it like this, in a letter, but I've been wondering what it means, your going away like this, and I think I understand what you're trying to say, and only want to let you know that I agree we've been drifting along a bit lately, and think I understand what you're doing.

Luke smiled. These long, looping sentences of hers. In life she was clipped, but on paper she could go on for ever. There was something about the tone, though . . . He read on:

I wish, of course, that you'd come right out and say what you mean, but some of that might be my fault, as I know I take advantage of you sometimes, and you always let me get away with far too much. But I think it will be better for both of us if we regard this as a good clean break . . .

A good clean break? What the hell was she talking about? Luke put a hand on the table, though whether to steady himself or whether to touch wood it was hard to tell.

I'll miss you a lot, Luke, and I fondly hope that you'll miss me a bit, too. If things had been different we might have found a better way to work things out, but it's obvious we're heading in different directions and the last thing I want to do is hold you back. I think you're doing the right thing going to Italy, by the way, though of course it's not that flattering to me, and I know . . .

There was more, another page at least, but something had gone wrong with Luke's vision. He turned the paper over and glanced at the end:

All love, C. xxxx
PS I finally started using that computer program you made, and guess what, it's brilliant. You're a genius!

He needed to think. It didn't make sense. When she said she'd been up all night writing, surely she didn't mean . . . this.

Luke felt his face grow hot. It hadn't occurred to him that Carmen too might be vacillating and uncertain. She wasn't simply waiting, on the shelf, for him to decide. Was there another letter somewhere, in her handbag or under her pillow, which contradicted everything she'd said in this one? Or had she changed her mind on the spur of the moment?

There had to be a way of seeing her again. She was probably at the office by now: he could catch her on the phone.

Or better still, he could surprise her.

He thought for a moment.

She was right, he was a genius! She'd said something about a house she had to visit near the airport: he could go and find her there. The office would know where it was.

He ran to the phone and began to dial.

But then he wondered: what if she answered the phone herself? He couldn't just say he'd found her letter and thanks for those kind words about his software, and by the way, thanks for breakfast, too.

Did she want to marry him, or wasn't she fussed either way? He was about to wish that she'd make her mind up when he blushed. That was rich, coming from him. You imagined you were free to think anything you pleased, but some thoughts had to be earned.

He put the letter down on the corner table, behind a lamp shaped like a lobster claw, with a pink shade. A present from his old friends Jonathan and Kate, an unwanted wedding gift: they made no bones about that. They were going to give it away anyhow, so he needn't thank them . . . Luke said he could use all the illumination that was going.

He remembered their wedding – they went soaring off in a hot-air balloon, and the guests jumped into their cars and chased them across Warwickshire. It was a miracle no one crashed, hurtling down those narrow lanes looking straight up into the sky. Kate had saved her bouquet and when they came in to land in the field by the aerodrome she threw it, from what everyone agreed was a fair old height, towards the waiting cars. It bounced on the bonnet of Luke's sporty car. Maybe the lamp was a peace-offering; but the fact remained: Luke was glad to have that scratch.

The thing that got him was that Jonathan and Kate had only known each other for such a short while when they decided to get married. They met on a boat somewhere, had a rapturous few days, and that was that. It had always baffled Luke. How could they have been so sure? Jonathan hadn't spent any time looking around, comparing prices, seeing if it was cheaper in *Exchange & Mart*. He'd just plumped for the whole deal in one go.

Come on. No time for this. He had to move fast. Luke was aware that Carmen's letter ought to have distressed him no end. She was saying they should call it a day, after all. But the truth was, he felt invigorated. He hadn't decided to say yes, but he was determined to decline the resignation implied by her letter. He was not going to take no for an answer.

Right, here was the plan. Iron a shirt. Bung the remaining junk in the plastic bags and shove them in the loft. Pick out a few books.

First he'd find his watch and make sure it was right. There it was, in his jacket pocket.

He knelt by the phone, which was still on the floor, and rang the speaking clock. The Time, sponsored by so-and-so, is ten, eleven, and fifteen seconds, precisely. The words were a jumble of pre-recorded tones, plucked out in sequence like pop records in a pub music system. They'd even detached the voice from the time, now. Luke wondered whether the people at the exchange had their favourite times, the way the voices came together. Go on, play ten past three again, I love that one. It was like the new phones: you could almost play tunes on them: 445345 – on the office phone at least – was pretty close to the National Anthem. Maybe it was the number of a castle or a palace.

But he still had a few minutes, that was the main thing. Once he'd found out where Carmen was heading he could get a taxi in no time.

All these cabs. He was ashamed to be having such a thought at such a time, but honestly: this morning was costing him a packet.

He wasn't going to make the same mistake twice, though. He'd put on some new clothes.

The ironing board was in a built-in cupboard by the window in the kitchen. A mad place for a cupboard, and whoever put it there needed their head examining: it blocked out half the light and made it awkward to lean out over the gardens, which you wanted to do quite often in the summer. But Luke had never got around to taking it down, and besides, where would you put everything?

Hello – what was this? Luke reached to the back and pulled out the mirror he had made, the one that reflected things the way they actually were.

He rubbed the dust off and tried a smile or two. He looked different, and the smile looked anything but convincing. He carried the frame through into the bathroom; he had half a mind to mount it on the wall and give the new tenants a surprise. But there was no time for pranks, so he just left it on the floor.

Back in the kitchen, he leaned over the ironing board, trying to find the lever which allowed the legs to come together and lift the board. He took care to keep his fingers out of the way. It was bad enough having one hand out of action. And the iron . . . oh, don't say he'd packed . . . no, there it was, underneath those dishcloths.

He put it on the charger-pyramid and switched it on. A woman in the shop had persuaded him that this was what they were all going for these days; the cordless iron. And she was right: the wire was a nuisance – the part of the shirt you weren't ironing always snagged on the cable and creased. But she hadn't been quite honest about the number of times you had to put the iron back on to its dynamic plinth. It stayed hot for about thirty seconds. After that you had to give it more juice.

There was still a bit of coffee in the mug. It was cold and tasted of honey. What was it Carmen had said? The flowers need the bees, and the bees need the pollen. She always made things sound so simple.

At the back of his mind her face seemed to be watching him with a serious expression.

The shirt was in okay condition. A few grand sweeping motions would probably be enough, and he didn't have to worry about the back too much. He'd be wearing a jacket.

He was anxious about the time all this would take, but pressed clothes were essential if you wanted to feel like a new person. When you said you were going to change, you had to mean it.

While it was warming up, Luke noticed a sealed envelope and tore it open. Huh, as he thought. A gas bill. It was red, a final demand, and it had a lot of strict warnings about the penalties for not paying in time. But the box said £27.43 CR. He was in credit. Did that mean that if they didn't come up with the money, he could cut their gas off?

On the back of the envelope he wrote: *Shirt, washing up, tidy, hoover, keys to Martin, ring Dad, check drawers, books, phone for taxi, phone C. . . .*

No, forget that. Go back to previous version. Scrub it. I mean, okay, I will ring Carmen. But I don't have to write it down here, as if it was the equivalent of checking the drawers. Jesus.

Now that he had started he realised that he had a long way to go. *Letter to Martin; bills, cleaning, etc. Bank, B'card ch of address. Lira airport. Tapes, etc.*

Crikey. He wasn't sure what that final etc. meant, but there was bound to be more he hadn't thought of.

But if he didn't think of it, he wouldn't do it, so it had no place on the list. Neat, or what?

Or maybe the etc. was more general, an optimistic aside in the hope that there were, somewhere, more interesting things to do than the ones that had made it onto the list. Well, of course there were. But wasn't it typical that all the most profound parts of a life were relegated, because of more immediate concerns, to a pigeonhole marked with an old Latin tag?

Oh Christ, the phone again.

He could always let it ring. He often wondered whether to have one that would not accept incoming calls. He was as happy as anyone to talk along a fibre-optic cable with someone miles away; yet he always jumped when the phone rang. You had to stop what you were doing and open yourself up to something new. And they deliberately made it sound urgent, like a fire alarm. They wanted you to pick it up. For them, time was money all right.

Hello?

Oh, you're still there.

Dad?

I was thinking you might have left.

I got your stuff, you don't have to worry.

That's what I was going to say. The man rang to say he'd look at the boat another time. So I'm free to go myself . . . Luke?

Yes, I'm here.

Luke was staring at a branch of the tree outside his window. It swayed into view and then away again at regular intervals. It must be breezy out there. He hadn't noticed. Maybe it would blow the bad weather away.

But you did it already. Well, I'm glad I caught you. I was just about to set off.

Mrs Granville's got it now. I might not have remembered everything. It was a bit of a . . .

Luke could see the look on Carmen's face. You'd rather buy cornflakes for your father than spend half an hour with me. He closed his eyes. His right hand seemed to move of its own accord to the cradle of the telephone. It hovered over the black circuit-breakers for a second, then pressed down with surprising delicacy.

Everything went quiet.

He looked down at the marks on the back of the envelope. A list of things he was supposed to do. Was he going mad? It was rubbish, all of it. An honest list would go:

> *Do I really not want to marry Carmen?*
>
> *When I imagined being with Emma in Rome, was I serious?*
>
> *Why am I going to Italy of all places?*
>
> *When I'm seventy, say, will today be memorable?*
>
> *If I died tomorrow, what would I wish I'd done?*

He stopped there, though in fact he wasn't writing this down. One reason you avoided questions like these was because you didn't know the answers. Or was it that you didn't want to know? Or you knew, but were trying to carry on as if you didn't?

Help. Luke felt the room melt.

That question about Emma, for instance. He didn't mean it — he included it out of a sense of mischief, a desire to impress himself as unpredictable. Whereas Carmen, that was the big one, the heart stopper. The others were just thrown in to make it seem less significant, one item among many.

He put his hand to his face. The slap had quite faded from his skin, though it was still etched hot and sharp in his mind.

Why had he put it, almost without thinking, that way round? Did he really not want to marry Carmen?

It wouldn't take long to devise a marital advice program, load in all the factors about, er, marriage in general, Carmen's particular character, his own priorities, and so on. He could run it like a spreadsheet, feeding in what-if scenarios and letting the results print out in their own sweet time.

His own priorities. That was a laugh.

He wanted Carmen, no doubt about it. Did he want to marry her, that was the question.

Luke was sitting on the floor, he discovered. He didn't seem to be in control of what he was doing.

Oh, in theory he could have whatever he wanted. But the rules had changed. As of today, if he wanted Carmen he had to marry her.

You needed two consecutive green lights. If the first one was red, well, you might as well switch your engine off.

He wanted to get up, but when he tried to pull his leg back underneath him, nothing happened.

It was natural to want to keep his head down and let big questions like these fly harmlessly overhead. He had to be careful not to get out of his depth. Yet wasn't that exactly where he was trying to go? Out to where the water was deep, out beyond the reef, beyond the banks and shoals, out to where if you stopped swimming and let your feet drop a fathom towards the sea floor you could feel how cold it was down there. If he wasn't careful, he'd wake up one day, an old man, and find he'd spent his whole life in the shallows. Mind the pennies, they'd say, and the pounds will look after themselves. So if you minded the minutes, the years should take care of themselves?

You might end up wondering where the hell they'd gone. There had to be such a thing as second wise, hour foolish.

Those digital clocks – yes, them again: Luke was starting to think they were to blame for everything. They had this way of making the hours sound like years, and stopped you seeing how small they were. Take the time of his flight: 11.15. Wasn't that the year of the Magna Carta? Or was it a century after, an hour later? Anyway, there were probably major crusades going on, and several important cathedrals would have been under construction or, if not that, then at least a twinkle in some bishop's eye.

Which came first: the ticking or the . . .

It couldn't be right that petty matters like what time of day it was should be allowed to elbow aside great historical events like those. In early times they understood this, and used the real words. The twenty-four hour clock: the very name had something imperious and boastful about it, as if it never slept, or the sun never set on it or something, as if it thought it might smuggle in another twelve hours without anyone noticing. It was a typical modern vanity: great dates (1815, 1914, 1945) were just smothered, made to sound no different from train times.

Talking of clocks, what the hell was he thinking of? Luke felt bloodless, damp, faint and a little sick. His head was buzzing, too. He seemed to be drowning in these foolish thought-eddies which had nothing to do with anything. He didn't have much more to get done; if he kept going he could be out of here in ten minutes and track down Carmen. But his mind had slipped its moorings. His hand was full of pins and needles, and too heavy for his arm. He could no longer drag it back into service. What was happening?

Had he remembered the horseradish? And the pastry cases, had he got the right sort? He blinked.

If he hadn't tipped the taxi driver he could have given that old man outside the newsagents more money. He was probably still there, working through the morning to raise enough for a bottle of cider. And here he was driving himself to the edge of something because he didn't know which way to turn. Beggars couldn't be choosers. Lucky them.

He put his head in his hands. The effort of raising his arms made him clench his teeth and scowl.

Hang on, though. In the next century, things would get even worse. Thanks to a single work of science fiction, we were almost bound to call the year 2001 two thousand and one, not twenty oh one. It was possible that we might revert, in 2010, to twenty ten,

144

but by then the damage might have been done: we might already be married to two thousand. For ten centuries – maybe for twenty, maybe for more – we had counted in hundreds; now we were going to decimalise time, or decimate it, by another notch.

And the result: the digital clock would triumph: it would be the sole owner of all the deeds in hundreds. People would one day pick up history books to find that the battle of Waterloo had been fought in one point eight one five, that Columbus had sailed the ocean blue in one point four nine two.

Luke, who was only point zero two seven, wouldn't even be able to murmur, as his elderly relatives were fond of doing, that he wouldn't be there to see it, thank God. Barring accidents, he'd be there all right, telling people how he'd said it would come to this, but would anyone listen, oh no.

It was the kind of thing that he ought to write to the papers about. He could start a correspondence. Probably someone at Greenwich had it all worked out already, and would write in with some shiver-me-timber anecdotes about marine life . . .

Stop it! Stop it! Luke clutched his hands over his ears. All this dreaming, it wasn't him any more, it was someone else inside his head. Please, he thought, go away. Leave me alone.

He stood up and paced the room. A minute ago he had been cold; now he was warm, as he had been in the supermarket, with bright partitions of food stacked around him. With his eyes shut it was almost as if he were back in there, almost as if the tins and packets and bottles and plastic bags had invisible hands that reached out towards him, tapping him on the shoulder, fingering him by the pocket and dragging him along the aisle with a ghastly cackle.

Are these plums ripe?

Sorry?

I was wondering if these plums were ripe?

How should I know? Ha, ha, ha, ha, ha.

He put his hands to his ears and went into the bathroom. The first thing he saw was his novelty mirror. He didn't hesitate. He put in one short step, like a horse adjusting before a fence, and jumped into it. Both feet landed in the centre with a smash that was softer than he expected.

Just before the impact, he turned his head to one side and caught a glimpse of himself down there, flicking his chin the other way.

Then . . . well, he wasn't quite sure what happened next.

Luke blinked again and wondered what the time was. He felt as if he had been asleep for ages but no, his watch said twenty one minutes past ten. He must have been out for an instant, if that.

Jesus Christ. These little bits of glass everywhere. He'd have to . . .

What was happening? He'd lost his mind for a moment. More than anything he wanted to lie down. He was aware of a hundred different things, but all he dreamed about was Carmen coming in through the door and switching him off, telling him not to worry. His system was about to crash, he could tell. Please log off now.

Had he fallen asleep? Please God, not twice in one morning. Or was it something worse? He couldn't help thinking of the time, years ago . . . but no, stay away from that . . .

He walked through into the sitting room, turned the television on, and channel-hopped with the remote. There was a quiz show, something educational about levers, a black-and-white film set on some sort of ocean-going liner, and a studio discussion. Luke would have been happy to watch the people talk . . .

But the phone was ringing. Perhaps that was what had brought him round. He switched the telly off and went to pick up the call, but was too slow.

His father, bound to be. He'd have to pretend they'd been cut off.

Now what? He tried the radio. They were talking about a plane crash in Canada. The jet had hit some geese high up, that's what they thought, and the pilot hadn't been able to wrestle the plane to an airport. So he landed on a frozen lake instead.

So he *what*?

The ironing, when he finally got down to it, took no time at all. He was even able to use his cut hand without too much discomfort. He laid the shirt over the arm of the sofa and was about to make a pile of books when he had an idea.

His finger hurt a bit when he dialled. The number six was quite stiff; you had to give it a wrench. It was annoying if six was one of the last numbers, and got stuck half-way – you had to begin all over again. But it goes without saying that Luke preferred it to the ones with buttons. He was fond of all dials and circles.

And today he got it just so.

Is Jonathan there, please?

He heard someone call: Jay, it's for you. Take it over there.

Hello?

Jonathan, it's Luke.

Luke! Where are you?

At home. Just leaving.

I thought you would have gone by now. I kept trying over the weekend. We wanted you to come over.

Oh, I was out, I guess. Shopping, you know.

So you're all set?

Give me a break.

Yeah, I know what it's like.

So anyway, I was just phoning to say goodbye, you know.

Luke, are you okay?

Me? Fine. Why?

I don't know. You sound sort of . . .

Tired, I guess. I was up half the night packing. A minute ago I was just sitting down doing something and I kind of fell asleep. Just for a second, you know, like in a theatre.

Well, you can sleep on the plane. When's the flight?

Eleven fifteen.

Christ, Luke. You should be there by now. Is anything wrong?

Oh, it'll be okay. I've been later.

I know what it is. Cold feet, right?

No, I don't know.

Hey, no backing out, okay? Kitty and I are planning our trip.

How is Kate? Kitty.

Oh . . . she's well. We thought June. What do you think?

147

I was just going through everything. Found some pictures of your balloon.

Oh, right.

You know, the one on your . . .

Yeah, a whole year ago. Amazing.

I was wondering . . .

Still got that dent in your car?

Nope. Someone else has got it now. Did I tell you about the final indignity? You know someone kept bashing in my window.

Yeah. That dangerous area you live in.

Well I got so pissed off I wrote a note. No radio, no cassettes, no money, no valuables, so don't bother. Stuck it in the window. Guess what happened.

They stole the whole car.

No. But they did the window again. I went down, oh, day before yesterday, glass everywhere.

Bit optimistic expecting they could read, I suppose.

On my note there was a scribble. Just checking. That's all it said: Just checking. Unbelievable.

Lovely.

So I had to take it to the garage with the window out. He knocked off a hundred pounds.

Plus how much for the dent?

Ah, the dent. Don't suppose they'll look after it the way I did, eh?

Well it's not every day you get hit by a bouquet from a hundred feet. A direct hit.

What, you were aiming?

Well, not at you in particular. But at the cars in general.

The cars in general?

Luke, it's great to hear from you, but you've got to go.

Yeah, got to.

What, you don't want to?

I don't know, Jay. It's been a bit of a weird morning.

What happened?

Oh, nothing. Everything. It's a long story.

Well, save it, Luke. Whatever it is. Ring me when you get there, if you like. Anything you need doing?

No, I'm all set.

How's the Italian?

Oh, she's fine.

Yeah, yeah.

I've been taking lessons. Speak it like a native.

Liar.

Of West London.

Hey, whatever happened to that girl you were seeing? The one you were telling me about.

Who? Oh, Carmen?

O'Carmen? You make her sound Irish.

Yeah, yeah.

Great name, though, Carmen. You were pretty serious about her, I thought. How come we never got to meet?

Oh, you know, it wasn't that sort of . . . We're not, we were never a couple, like you and . . .

God, don't you hate that word. Couple – you make us sound like rolling stock. I know we got hitched, but . . .

I only meant, together.

Anyway, Kitty's gone to Glasgow this week, business. So I'm off the leash. Pity you're leaving.

Er, yeah. I'd better be off. Tell me, though. When you proposed to Kate, Kitty, what did you say?

What?

You know, how did you put it?

I went down on one knee, pledged my undying allegiance, said I'd forswear all dainty pleasures and begged her to make my happiness complete.

Really?

Damn, Luke, what's the matter with you? Of course I didn't. I just asked her. Might even have made some joke about riding into the sunset, embarrassing as it may sound. Why do you want to know?

And Kitty, what did she say?

She said I was a typical Aries. Luke, what's this all about? Thinking of naming the day?

Oh, nothing. Some research I'm doing on timing. How'd it happen so fast?

Chemistry, sheer chemistry. Hey, Luke.

Yes?

I'm wanted on another line. Ciao, okay?

Sure. Bye.

Luke put the phone down with a feeling of tremendous and unanticipated sadness. He felt as if life had taken a wrong turn. He could see the other cars still tearing up and down the motorway, but he was on this little private road, and there was no way back.

There was nothing for it but to carry on. It would be worse if he missed his plane on top of everything else. Jonathan was right. This was crazy. He had to live in the present, and had to wrap things up fast.

Those drawers . . . He moved mechanically, not hurrying but working step by step. He emptied the contents into the bags without bothering to see what he was dumping. He scooped up the stuff on the floor and pushed that into the bags as well. There were some fitted cupboards with smoked mirrors on sliding doors; he went through these as well and found a few old shoes, a squash racquet, some blankets, a lampshade and a power drill without a plug. Everything could go straight into the loft. Thank God he lived on the top floor – up around the water tank there was plenty of room.

The hoovering didn't take a minute, either. The plastic trunk which sucked dust back into the stomach of the vacuum was covered with drying strips of sellotape, but it still worked, even if you did sometimes have to fetch a fork and skewer balls of rubbish out of the nozzle where they gummed up the flow. He held the hose in one hand and pushed the suction-pad across the floor. He usually enjoyed the little noises it made, the sharp rustle when he managed to persuade a bit of paper into the chamber, the tinkle if a drawing pin or coin was inhaled by accident. But today he didn't notice, not even when he zizzed it around the bathroom and all the bits of glass and mirror rattled up.

He stowed the machine at the back of the kitchen cupboard and checked the time on the clock set into the cooker. Nearly twenty-five past. He registered it like a tug on a lead, with a sort of blind careless obedience. Perhaps dogs felt grateful for that sharp strangling feeling on their neck, perhaps it made them feel they had their feet on the ground.

Darling Luke! he thought, when he found the letter. He put it in his jacket pocket along with the bus and the watch. It was getting crowded in there.

Wait. Carmen, please wait. I'm on my way.

A quick note to Martin.

Dear Martin, Here are the keys. The big one does the downstairs, the two smaller ones do the door to the flat. I do suggest you have the place cleaned, but will leave that to you. I think you know how everything works. One thing I haven't mentioned is that the water pressure varies and you get an air-lock in the pipes to the bathroom. There's a hose under the sink and if you attach one end to the mains and the other to the tap you can squirt the air bubble up to the tank. Also, in high winds the boiler . . .

That wasn't such a hot idea. He didn't want to put people off. If the boiler went out, well, they weren't stupid; they'd be able to figure out that you had to light it again. He crossed it out and added: *I'll let you know my address as soon as I have one. If there's an emergency, contact . . .* He put his parents' address.

I hope you manage to find someone, he added. *If you don't have any luck, let me know and I'll stay out of the country for good!*

He folded the paper, squashing the sides to squeeze it into the envelope, and wrote Martin's name on the cover. Then he put the letter in his briefcase.

You would have thought – Luke would have, anyway – that he could have found someone, a friend of a friend of a friend, to rent a place like this. Then he could have shaken hands and avoided all this bureaucracy.

But he had come up empty. He had this idea that the local newsagent had a window crammed with cards saying URGENT: ACCOMMODATION NEEDED, MONEY NO OBJECT; but right now, not a sniff. He asked around, and everyone said, Sure, they knew lots of people – but it turned out they didn't. It was as if they thought it would be rude to say, Actually, no, can't think of a soul. Oh well.

Books: what should he take? The Darwin, of course. He needed to find out how the fittest survived.

Talking of which . . . He was feeling better, thank God. He didn't know what had happened back there, some kind of imaginary fit or seizure. But it seemed to have gone away. He found his packet of cigarettes and lit one, using the flame from the cooker, bending down low and burning a few hairs on his eyebrow. He had forgotten about the illicit shadow that crossed your mind every time you lit up, and quite enjoyed seeing it pass over once again. He wondered what he'd say to Carmen: that he was feeling better? That he had just thought, for a millisecond, about dying?

He wasn't fooling anybody with this, not even himself. The chances of finding out where she was and intercepting her were slim, but he had to try. She'd said he preferred to buy cornflakes for his dad – well, he was willing to gamble his plane ticket on the chance of proving her wrong. Would that do?

He still hadn't chosen his books.

But by now he'd spent almost too much time thinking about it, and the clock was ticking away. Plus he was feeling light-headed from the cigarette. The guidebook was safely packed, so he was okay for maps and so on. He settled for a mixture of thrillers and classics, a book on modern philosophers, two teach-yourself-Italian books, and also a novel Carmen had given him last Christmas and which he'd never had a go at. It was inscribed: To Luke – No Hands! love C. Well, now was the time: it was big, with daunting bits of Latin – but she said it was brilliant, and he was bound to agree.

At first she was surprised he was so fond of books. I thought you computer guys didn't like anything without sockets, she said.

I'm not a computer guy, Luke said.

He went on to say that reading and writing were in for a big comeback. That's what screens are for, he said. Soon everyone'll send each other written messages instead of phoning. Much more fun. And now you can get great little hand-held faxes, so instead of sending a postcard you can . . .

Come on, concentrate.

In among the books he found a notebook with unruled pages, a black cover and a red spine. He couldn't recall having bought it, but perhaps he could keep a journal. He could start by telling the story of this one day, though to be realistic he would have to start now, while he was in the middle of things. The whole point of going was to take a long, cool-handed look at himself. Writing things down would encourage him to keep his eyes peeled. It was like photography (only harder work).

Or maybe the opposite. Luke didn't own a camera, but he liked the idea of single moments frozen out of context. It was good to rip special instants out of everyday life and mount them on a wall. But he was unnerved by what photographs left out: the main thing was that someone was taking a picture, but this you rarely saw. It affected Luke's reading, too. On every page Luke's mind would turn to what was left out. If a woman went to bed one moment and was out riding horses the next, he would try to reconstruct what had occurred in between. Probably the maid prepared her riding clothes – it was hard to imagine the woman herself fishing them out of the laundry. The same went for the horse – surely she hadn't got up early for some grooming and feeding. One of Luke's staple questions was: didn't the phone go in all that time? Didn't she read something or overhear a few words on the radio? There were a thousand things that could have happened, and he found it hard to take on trust that the details he was offered were the essential ones.

So how would it go? He picked up a pen and began to write: *Friday. Half past ten. Darling Carmen, What I should have said was* . . .

He put the biro between his teeth.

Oh, to hell with it. He was too tired to think straight.

He stuffed the books into the big suitcase and hauled on the zips.

It was unbelievable how many things were still lying around. There was still stuff in the sink, for God's sake. Luke began in the sitting room, sweeping a few relics from previous foreign jaunts – a small plaster owl, a miniature Leaning Tower of Pisa, a bottle of black ink in a glass cockerel, a bullfighter's sword and a stuffed matador – from the shelves. The mantelpiece was fine, except for one invitation – the invitation to Jonathan and Kate's wedding – which Luke, after a brief hesitation, threw away. The plant on the windowsill could stay where it was, along with the cigarette lighter in the shape of a duelling pistol, and the hotel ashtray.

In the kitchen it was just a question of putting away a few glasses and cups. As he moved along, opening and closing the slatted wooden doors – if they were wood, that is; they were probably some nasty composite – he turned on the taps and squirted some washing-up liquid into the sink. Hot water plunged down, raising a mound of suds up and almost over the sides.

There were already a few plates from several days ago in there. He drained the cup of cold coffee and let it sink, then groped round for the things underneath.

A mistake: the water was steaming. Luke pulled his hands out quickly and thought he'd been fast enough, but then the stinging began. The heat (of course) got into the cut again and made the blood pulse. A few drops of blood dripped onto the snowy clouds of suds. Maybe that's what happened when geese hit planes. Maybe blood stained the top of the sky for a while until it seeped through and mingled with the rain.

It was a real drag, this hand. It wasn't the pain or inconvenience so much as the idea that he was leaking. He let water from the cold tap fall on to his fingers, moving his hands around to let it soothe the worst, the most scalded parts. It wasn't serious: his hands weren't burned, just surprised.

The water was a better temperature now, and Luke stacked the plates and cups in the cunning, false-bottomed draining cupboard above. He used to have one of those brushes, but it wasn't anywhere in sight, so he used his fingers, feeling the snags where the breakfast cereal had stuck.

Getting the plug out was always a bore: these days you had to coax a knife down one side and pop the thing out like the top of a bottle. But then – this, he had to confess, was one of the wonders of the flat – the way the sink drained was quite something, a virtuoso piece of plumbing, a flash of domestic theatre. It made one loud gurgle and then just seemed to swallow the entire tank in one gulp. It was pretty dramatic. Here, Luke would say to people. Watch this. They'd all stand around while the water swirled once and vanished – it was wonderful. It didn't even seem to matter if there were things in the way – teaspoons or bits of potato or leeks. They were the worst, though it always pleased Luke that you could plug the flow with a leek. But nothing could slake the thirst of this sink. Luke hoped, as he watched the water buckle and disappear, that whoever inherited this place would appreciate it as much as he did.

Time to go. He pulled on his coat, made sure he had his keys, and picked up the luggage. He took his watch out of his pocket, had a quick look, and put it back. On his wrist it would have felt like a manacle.

He'd been awake – he calculated – for only two hours. In a way it was remarkable he had done so much, but he still felt behind. Life was like that. You tried to bob along on the stream, hurrying, waiting, keeping up with the clock. And it was always as if you were swimming *against* the flow: time came up ahead and vanished behind you, and it was uphill work trying to make any ground towards the head of the river, towards the source, before you grew tired and time gathered you in its arms and carried you down to the open sea.

But it was not clear whether the source was up in the mountains, or out in the deep part of the ocean.

What Luke really wanted was to run like a trout into one of those deep pools and have a breather from all this swimming; to be able to drop below the surface towards the heart of things and relax, knowing that the thrust wasn't so strong down there, that it didn't take so much energy to keep yourself pointed in the right direction, that you could drift along at an even tempo, not having to worry about rocks or rapids or anything else.

He wanted, in other words, to escape from shallow time. But it was easier said than done. For a fresh half-hour he'd swap . . . but you couldn't make deals like that, couldn't haggle about the price. It was fixed.

That thought occupied Luke for as long as it took to turn both keys in the lock. Inside the flat, too late, the phone was ringing.

He was gentle with the door on to the street, closing it with his fingertips. But it still sounded like a door closing. He had a keen sense that he had forgotten something, but didn't want to dwell on it. He was on his way, at last. The Mediterranean summer stretched out ahead of him, blue and warm as far as the eye could see.

It's hard to know how to describe shallow time, because our modern senses are maladjusted. At first a worthy attempt to impose order on agricultural and ceremonial life — when the sun went down over the lake, it was time to sow the seed — our view of time grew into the beginnings of mathematics: early students of the stars marked each sunset with a cowrie shell in a buffalo horn, or jammed rods in the ground to measure shadows, and time began.

Or even earlier than that. In China they would light gunpowder trails, secure in the knowledge that a ten-yard line was worth about five minutes. In Greece they would ensure equal speaking time for their orators by letting sand fall through a funnel. And then there were water drips, hourglasses, rolling-ball machines and other elaborate devices for calibrating leaks into hours. It wasn't until much later that time gained a human form, received a face and hands which would meet, every hour or so, kiss and part again, for all the world like two strangers saying hello and for a moment becoming one. In its search for a more reliable dating-agency than the circuits of the stars, the world soon set great store by its chronometers, its clever cogs and ratchets, its faultless quartz and microwave pulses; gradually it fell to thinking that time must have existed before all these toys. The sands of time, these days, suggest infinite depth.

Back then, they probably had the sense to regard the new machinery with the good-natured, practical disdain it deserved. But ever since, and with accelerating fervour, we've tinkered with and grooved and tailored our clock until we can no longer think of it as just a useful technique for remembering the Pharaoh's birthday. These days, the way we measure time seems like time itself.

The irony is that through the vigorous exploration of new technologies in engineering and science we had succeeded in achieving a representation of time that made explicit, unlike all those funnels and filters, the shape of the universe. We should have stopped there, happy in the knowledge that we had hit on a realistic method. But now, as Luke had noticed, we were busy abandoning all this in favour of extra accuracy – a shallow thing beside the grand symbolic circling of hands, which was being allowed to slink away over the horizon out of sight and out of mind.

Because the truth is, we can't keep in step however hard we try. We have our own pulse. A couple of drinks, or a brisk walk, and our hearts beat a little faster. A lie-down, a mid-afternoon snooze, or any sedentary occupation, and the beat slows to a crawl. In the next half-hour, Luke will see an entire year flash before his eyes in the time it takes to complete a simple taxi ride. Yet we go on insisting that five minutes is five minutes, and that these deviations are just products of a fevered imagination.

We all know what they say about a watched kettle. But time is not even the same in cities as it is in the depths of the countryside. The demands of an urban timetable have very little in common with the shepherd's calendar. Everyday life in a traffic jam sharpens your pulse and warms the watch on your wrist no end. Sometimes you walk out of the cinema and discover that while you have been travelling huge distances and encountering remarkable new people, the world has been standing still – no time has passed: the same newspapers line the kiosks, the same pigeons peck at crumbs, the same litter fills the bins. But other times you emerge to find that it's dark, and it's as if the world has moved on while you sat suspended before the screen, doing nothing at all.

Yet deep down we still believe it's all the same to Father Time. All the classical scientists presumed that time was an absolute. They liked pointing out that if the age of the world was represented by the Eiffel Tower, then human habitation would occupy only the skin of paint on the top. Deep time, they called it. It's meant to be a depressing idea; it seeks to show us that life is a shallow business, a brief ignition in a universe of death, a sudden green light in a gridlocked traffic system. We live, they seem to say, in an hourglass, and are hardly ever aware of the faint slippage beneath our feet as the sand runs away in a steady, unceasing stream.

But now we know that it's not quite true, this sense of time as a stately structure with solid, changeless proportions. It's as unstable as the sand that trembles through the neck of the glass. And the higher you go, the faster time flies. Climb into a collapsed star, and time hardly moves a muscle.

In theory, what we should have – no doubt they'll devise it some day – is a watch that takes some of this into account. A few electrodes in the brain to measure the work-rate of the major synapses, a couple of inconspicuous probes into the cardiovascular system to keep track of the pulse rate, and we could have a time-scale which expanded and contracted at variable speeds. It would resemble a taxi meter, which has the basic gear built in but allows for some fine tuning on top, in the all-important area of shallow time where most of us live.

There would be some inconvenience. You'd have to know whether you were fast or slow if you wanted to catch the news, or were meeting a train. And you'd have to be willing to wait a bit if you were joining someone for lunch, in case they'd had a slow morning. But you would know, at any given time, how old you were, in years far more interesting and relevant than the ones we now swear by. A young man like Mozart would under the new system have been about 186 when he died, instead of the notional age which history recognises. Some old people, on the other hand, might be dismayed to find that, in their declining years and with their eyesight fading faster than they'd care to admit, they were barely out of their teens.

Best of all, a fluid clock would shatter the illusion that moments are repeatable. Luke might harbour fantasies to do with living exclusively in the present tense, but it was misleading to imagine that any one time – ten to eight, say – would soon come round again. As Carmen often said, you had to recognise that each moment might be your last.

Easier said than done. We are stuck with shallow time, and live like hounds on the scent of an imaginary fox. We used to believe that God or someone was out there running up streams the wrong way, covering His tracks; but recently we've grown used to the idea that there's nothing out there at all, we're just doing this for the exercise. And something stops us from lifting our gaze towards that line of hills *in the distance until we reach them, and then we can't see them any more. Besides, we've been trained. If our noses come away from the ground for an instant, someone cracks us with a whip.*

Half past ten

As Luke walked down the hill towards the station, he realised that it might have been Carmen phoning.

God! That's what he had forgotten! The address of the house! A genius, huh?

All right: he'd call her at the office when he got to the airport. It was the least he could do. He kept walking.

But not for long. He couldn't go without seeing her, he knew that for certain. He wasn't saying what he meant by it, but he was not, repeat not, getting on any aeroplanes until he had found her.

And look, there was a God, after all. Here was a phone box, with no one in it. Luke left his cases outside and checked his pocket for change. He had lots.

He dropped a coin in and dialled Carmen's office number.

Hello? Carmen? It's me.

Jenny here. Can I help?

Yes! It's about this house she's supposed to be showing. I said I'd meet her there, but I don't have the address.

Hang on.

Someone must have it. I'm late as it is . . .

But Luke could hear a hand over the phone. Through the fingers, he could hear voices.

What if she was there!

It gave him a buzz to think of Carmen sitting at her big triangular desk, doodling the shape of a large letter L. But what if she came to the phone? He battled to stop himself flinging the phone down.

Who is it calling?

Luke. Listen, I only wanted . . .

He stood on one foot. He was bursting. Another thing he'd forgotten to do before he left.

Hold on, I'll try to connect you with someone who can help.

Luke clamped his knees together. This was one of those new vandal-proof kiosks with the top and bottom sawn off. If a car went by you couldn't hear a thing. A bus changed gears three or four yards from where Luke was standing. He hoped no one was speaking.

Hello? Luke?

Yes. I'm here.

Hi, it's Finola.

Luke couldn't remember which one she was.

Hi.

This house, it's on King's Parade. Number a hundred and one.

Whereabouts is that?

Don't know for sure. But it says on the details it's two minutes from the station.

Thanks, Philippa, that's a real help.

Finola. No problem.

He pushed open the door and squinted in the sudden blast of wind. Then he picked up his luggage and carried on down the hill. He really did need to relieve himself. He sucked in and tried to ignore it.

There was an awful lot he hadn't done. All the things with the bank and so on he hadn't touched. But it didn't matter. There weren't any stern officials around to tap him on the shoulder and stop him from travelling.

This bag was getting heavy. All those books.

He hadn't been paying much attention to what was going on outside, but he had to stop now because there was a little cluster of people on the pavement. Three large black cars were drawn up in a convoy, double-parked. One of them – the big estate – was full of flowers. Everyone was wearing dark clothes, suits and coats.

He started to cross the road to keep out of their way, but stopped again when he saw four men carrying a coffin out of the house and pushing it into the boot of the car. A man tottered behind them with small, drunk steps, wheeling towards the hedge. A younger woman came up behind him fast and put an arm on his, to steady him. She had a small black hat on her head, with a veil over her eyes and blonde hair flowing out the back.

Luke had never been to a funeral, and never wanted to. One of his friends (a contemporary from school), had died years ago, a few months before he came up to the city and a long time before he met Carmen. They all watched her decline into that dim, panic-stations phase before the drugs took over. And then, one day, she wasn't there any more.

Luke had done a bit of phoning around after that. One of the numbers he tried belonged to the dead girl. It was her flatmate he was after, but the answering machine cut in and there she was: Hi, it's Amanda, now don't go away and DO leave a message. I'll get right back to you.

I mean . . . awful. Luke remembered slamming the phone down and staring at it, staring at this machine that was supposed to rope people together in a huge lattice of articulate threads . . .

He wasn't able to shake the sound of her voice from his mind for months. In fact, he tried the number again a few days later, to see if anyone had thought to change it.

That was the time when Luke had been, to say the least, a solitary person, living an interior life so beguiling that he lost interest in other people's. Luke had an image of himself perched on that big armchair in the therapist's consulting rooms, poring over illegible pictures . . .

One or two of the people over there were sniffing hard and looking about as if they couldn't believe this could be happening on such a grey, unmemorable day. They stood there, gentle and patient, touching each other now and then or leaning close to murmur something. One of them wore an old-fashioned pocket watch.

As Luke drew nearer, he could see they were standing outside number 17. God, it must be old Mr Sutherland, the man who used to sit on a deckchair on the pavement and say hello to passers-by. He was a keen mower, and could often be seen hoovering the tiny lawns of his neighbours. Even in the winter he was out there cleaning up, keeping down the weeds.

And now he'd been mown down himself. Luke shuddered.

As he walked past he couldn't resist pausing beside the great black car and asking one of the undertakers.

Mr Sutherland, was it?

I couldn't say, the man said. Better get a move on, whoever he is.

The engine of the car was ticking over. Luke blinked. Mr Sutherland was dead, but he was still running late.

The drivers held the doors open and people climbed in, taking care, helping each other. No one pushed ahead or tried to steal the best seats. Luke watched as the drivers closed the doors, saw the same young woman run back and lock the house, waited until she'd climbed in next to – what, her father, was it? And he didn't move as the black cars nosed out into the road and rolled down the hill, as quiet as worms.

Orange light glared off the polished roof of the car nearest to him. One of the streetlights still burned, even though it was the middle of the morning.

When Luke carried on walking it was with the sensation that life had swung close and brushed him with a light touch against his neck, like a wasp coming close, like a breath of something mortal and significant.

What was it? He walked on, not noticing the weight of the luggage or the ache in his hand.

That streetlight . . . yikes. Luke's professional reflexes twitched. You couldn't afford to let traffic lights switch themselves on when they felt like it. But this seemed typical of our urge to drive the darkness out. In the city the rows of lamps blocked out night, which made the roads safer, but slashed away the rope that bound us to the stars or, if you preferred, drew neon blinds down on the night sky. Every afternoon, long before the sun sank away towards America, we switched on. We were light addicts.

Listen, this was no joke. He had to go right now. He looked around – there, a gravel alley between houses. Probably it led to a garage round the back, but it had high walls. Luke did a quick left-right to check that no one was watching, and then slid his zip down.

Ah, that was more like it. He felt warmth returning to his limbs as he relaxed and let go. He kept his coat fanned out so that if anyone did catch sight of him it wouldn't be too obvious what he was up to. He swayed a bit so as not to create too vulgar a puddle. A few more seconds . . .

If Carmen could see him now . . .

Did it have anything to do with her that he avoided imagining himself in the back of one of those cars, or was that pushing it? Oh, from time to time he pictured himself knocked out of the reckoning – usually he was going to someone's rescue when it happened – but this was only ever theoretical, a way of indulging the presumption that people would be shocked to hear the news.

I mean, what would Carmen say if he stepped in front . . .

Well, go on, what would she? Luke felt stunned. While he was going about his morning, Carmen's life was proceeding, at exactly the same speed. Who knew what she might have thought and done by now? She'd already changed her mind once.

He was having a breathing problem. He took a couple of big gulps, which only made his heart beat even faster. All that thinking . . . and he still hadn't registered that it wasn't up to him. He'd given Carmen time to do some thinking of her own, and . . . God, what had he done?

He had to stop worrying about water that was already under the bridge. He had to face forward.

Anyway, Carmen had the same attitude: it hadn't seemed to strike her that he might say no. Not that he had, of course.

He reached the main road and paused. It was odd, but he couldn't face the idea of rushing any more. He didn't feel like taking another step. He didn't want to go anywhere at all, let alone Italy. But he did want to be lifted out of this hole he was in. I need to get away, he told himself. I need to be on that plane. In some way it is my last chance. Yet he could no longer make himself hurry. Whatever happened would happen, whatever he did.

A taxi pulled over and Luke bowed his head and stepped in. He gave the driver the address and then, obeying an unusual impulse, sat down in one of the fold-down seats. He didn't want to feel too comfortable, and it would be nice to travel with his back, as it were, to the future. He began to rehearse his speech to Carmen, but his mind was empty. He checked his watch – twenty-five to eleven – put his elbows on his knees, dropped his head down into his fists and tried to think of nothing at all.

Luke was no more nostalgic than the next man, but he was prey, like anyone, to the occasional wondering glance over his shoulder. He didn't have any clear idea how things could have been other than the way they were; the dark magic of circumstances usually left him perplexed. Had there been a moment when the rest of his life became inevitable, or had he stumbled through the maze with his eyes closed? He didn't know.

He had lived in London for years, though he was a suburban boy. He grew up in one of those dapper, soldierly towns in the commuter belt, where the dense suburbs begin to invade the open countryside. Not that there was anything open about the country round there. Ugly brick towns lay in a ruddy crescent along the curve of a river which no one ever saw. Some of the local councils had made game attempts to promote the pleasures of the river, posting jolly cartoons at the railways stations show-ing families walking along wooded banks or single men sitting hunched over fishing lines.

He didn't have many memories of life back then. Carmen seemed to have much sharper recollections from the year she'd spent there when her father was stationed at the military college. Luke was alone a good deal: his dad was at the office and his mum worked too, as a swimming instructor at the public baths; and he didn't have any brothers or sisters to tease or be teased by. So he grew up tall, serious and on the gloomy side.

It was hard to imagine his mother young and in a swimsuit, hammering a loud-hailer with her whistle and shouting at the children to kick . . . kick . . . kick.

What Luke did with himself he couldn't say: they had a big garden, and he would build hideaways in the woods at the bottom, and pretend there were people worth hiding from.

He did remember the curtains in his bedroom. They were as blue as the Pacific, and had ships printed on them, with the names and crests in ribbons underneath. At night, when the breeze swayed in through the open window, it was as if the great ships had put to sea. Luke would reel off the names – Ajax, Achilles, Hood, Victory – and imagine they were breasting those airy folds with a crash of salty spray. He could almost hear the harsh woop-woop-woop of the sirens calling them to arms. They never actually fired their guns – the enemy was invisible, out of the window, over the horizon – but they were always casting off from their dark moorings and setting out to meet their fate. Sometimes, on windy nights, Luke would open the window as if he could control the sea lanes, and he would watch the ships slip anchor and surge into the swells and troughs of the deeper ocean. For a long time all he wanted, when he grew up, was to be a harbour master.

Nor had he forgotten the annual pilgrimage to the military chapel at Christmas. They would try to be early, but more often than not ended up at the back, behind a white pillar with the names of the fallen engraved in gold. Luke would listen to the carols and look for patterns in the dead gilt. Outside, if the weather was right, he would watch the other children making snowballs and wish that he had a brother, someone to throw things at.

He recalled, too, hearing his father swear once while he mowed the lawn; and this was the first time he sensed that unhappiness might exist at home, that his parents might be people whose lives had taken a wrong turn.

And he never would be able to erase from his memory the fierce, feathery sensation of wasps on a young child's skin. He had kicked a nest, not knowing what it was, and the swarm was upon him before he could move. Someone smeared him with butter and vinegar, and to this day he could not taste mayonnaise without feeling the poisonous tickle of a wasp's legs.

But otherwise he couldn't remember much.

According to his father, things changed fast. Progress rushed down a new motorway and tore away the old crooked buildings and the open spaces. What had been a town of hedges became a town of fences and walls. What had been a high street, a military training college and a train station became a civic dream of office blocks, shopping centres, Do-It-Yourself Superstores, drive-in hamburger stations and endless, endless brick and birch estates.

No local myths stood in the way of development. There were no stately homes or ancient burial mounds that anyone knew of. There was one old lady, if you wanted to stretch matters: a tiny grey woman in a big coat who pushed a barrow loaded with stray dogs along the roads surrounding the golf course. But she was just a curiosity, and since she was the only thing the town was famous for, everyone was a little ashamed of her. And the land owned by the army up on the ridges remained a place where children could ride their bikes up and down the steep sandy slopes. The army, in fact, provided the neighbourhood with its only solid tradition: the local paper had pictures, every year, of the annual passing-out parade, cadets marching and saluting, one of them holding high the sword of honour. This ceremony survived unscathed, while everything else felt the keen edge of novelty.

Carmen must have been in the audience once or twice. Luke tried to visualise a slim, corn-haired girl with white socks and an eager expression, pointing at the young officers as they marched by.

Luke straightened when the taxi turned left. There was a paper on the floor, and he spread it on his knees to scan the headlines. Someone dead in Northern Ireland. An election in Germany. A row over missiles. Extraordinary . . . oh, it was last week's.

He gave up and tried to close his eyes. And as the car ferried him towards an uncertain future, in his mind he was travelling in the other direction.

When his parents moved to the guesthouse on the coast they said it was a way out of the rat race: plenty of bracing walks along the cliffs and real log fires. Fine for them: for Luke it was an eternity of washing up and serving coffee to elderly couples in the morning. It wasn't until he came up here and ran into Carmen . . .

As he sat there, with his suitcases nudging his knees, his life suspended between two places, Luke shivered. It was so like the time he first came to the city, a bag in either hand. What a disaster that had been. He had found it impossible to cope with the hectic, crowded life up here. He took a job stacking shelves in a stereo shop and spent most of his spare time playing computer games in big, anonymous arcades. He would sit on those stools for hours, his knee twitching in time with his accelerator button.

He had arrived on a spring day much like this one: grey, blustery and unsure what season it was. By the summer he had become quiet, by the autumn lonely, and by winter he was in trouble. The following spring, after the world had completed a revolution, he started to visit the psychiatrist. All he had to do was make up a few stories about isolated gardens, salmon, wasps and ships in the night, and the man seemed satisfied. The odd thing was, it made Luke feel better too.

All this thinking back – it was like the old days.

To begin with, Luke saw city life as a challenge and tried to meet it head on. As the years passed he became a sort of city-artist. He tried to appreciate the freedom that went with solitude, the easy-going way people ignored each other. There was nothing in particular that Luke wanted to do with this liberty, but he liked the feeling that he was available, should anything turn up.

He'd have to be on guard to make sure that Italy wasn't the same thing all over again. Like a snake shedding a dry skin, Luke felt layers of experience peel away and leave him back where he started, a young man on his own.

Was it cold, or was it him?

There were moments, in that first year, when Luke enjoyed being alone. The city emphasised, rather than diminished, his sense of self-importance. All those people, all those lives, all those purchases and sales – the whole vast metropolitan shudder never resolved itself into anything like a community, so there were no constraints. Not everyone liked this, but Luke learned how to exploit the machinery of urban life: where to stand on under-ground platforms to be near the exit at the other end, how to fix things and what to buy, where to linger and where not to go. There was a tongue – you couldn't call it a language – and Luke soon became fluent. He knew that not everyone could decode the barks and groans, the hoots and rumbles, the smells and patches of rubbish growing like fungus along the edge of roads – and was proud to be an initiate.

He thought – in one of his enthusiastic reveries – of the city as a dictionary, a place for flicking through, for treating yourself. It was full of hidden passages, alleys, roots. There was no sense trying to read it straight through, trying to comprehend it as a whole. You had to use the index (the A-Z) to plot tricky courses through webs of derivations and transformations. In an idle moment Luke had once calculated how many different words could be made, in theory, out of the 26-letter alphabet. The figure came out at 64 followed by 35 noughts. Written down, it went:

6,400,000,000,000,000,000,000,000,000,000,000,000.

Even this was arbitrary: it assumed that no word could be more than 26 letters long. And since it contained a great number of words that were obviously ridiculous – words containing nothing but the letter 'p' 26 times, for instance – he was happy to knock off a nought or two. Even if you restricted yourself to five-letter words, there were 1.8 million different combinations. None of the dictionaries mentioned more than a couple of hundred thousand words in all, so the language was running on a very low throttle indeed: it was using only a fraction of a percentage of the words that were in the tank.

My God. It was hard to believe he had ever really been like that. These days he thought there were too many words, not too few. If it was up to him, he'd write a book that ended with words screaming and melting as they went to the torch, or into the darkness.

It was nice to see that he was no longer his old self. Starting work with that computer outfit had made a difference, of course, but it was Carmen who had flung the rope and pulled him out of the grim isolation that threatened to turn him inside out. Surely he wasn't about to turn his back on all that?

Well, no. But neither was he prepared to let his own past blackmail him into any hasty decisions now.

What had she said? Look in the mirror, Luke.

He could understand, now he had a moment to reflect, why she hadn't wanted the champagne. It wasn't merely that she wanted to wait for a more festive moment, as he'd first thought.

She was already zonked on whisky. He should have been quicker on the uptake. It had taken him a while to get over the sting of her rejecting the bottle. Now he could see it didn't mean anything.

Did that mean that her proposal wasn't serious, just the drink talking?

He had not, he realised, lost the habit of stubborn, morose reflection. Back in his flat, before he left, the interminable talker inside him had run wild and out of control. It was obvious that the seeds of a lonely speculative nature were still buried in there. He had to be careful . . .

And that's what he'd been trying to say, too.

The number said it all. Even if you multiplied it to take account of the other languages which used the same alphabet, the answer showed that the world had not yet done more than shave the top off the opportunities on offer. Language was as thin as the coat of paint on top of the Eiffel Tower, as shallow as life itself.

Take a word like the. (This is how Luke would introduce the subject.) Someone had calculated that it accounted for one in twelve of the words in regular daily use. Yet by the law of averages, he had worked out, it stood only a one in 64 billion billion billion billion billion chance. It all proved, he would go on to say, how little explored the alphabet was. We're sending people to Venus, he would smile, but the big mysteries are all right here.

Luke hadn't ever minded the baffled looks this sort of remark drew from people who didn't know him: they had a right to be confused.

People would sometimes argue that the reason the alphabet was so underemployed was that there weren't enough things that needed names, but Luke would have none of this. He had more faith in the idea that billions of non-existent words were lying in wait, just biding their time, waiting for the bugle to blow. Otherwise – he would say, letting a little note of triumph creep into his voice – what's the point of having so many letters in the first place? We could make do with half the number.

For a while Luke had a theory that all words were really one word: he imagined that you could link them together by following each root back to its source – but he soon gave this up as hopeless: the dictionary defied him all the time. It was the same with the city-gazetteer: how could anyone hope to stamp an identity on a place so scattered and confused, with so many trails petering out right, left and centre?

It was odd how easy it was to remember all this stuff. It must be lying closer to the surface than he thought. Unless some trick of circumstance had turned over the topsoil and exposed the white roots lower down.

It goes without saying that Luke was not, in that difficult year, a great talker. (He'd improved out of all recognition, though as Carmen could testify he was still prone to word-caution.) He could never hear nouns and verbs and adjectives rolling off his tongue without wondering why he was using these particular ones, and not any of the thousands of others which were at his disposal. Even short conversations made him feel tired; long ones were almost too exhausting to contemplate.

Reading could be like that, too, especially where the lavatory or the bath was concerned. Luke went for thrillers at these times, often ones he'd already read. Sometimes he would spend as long going through the shelves looking for something suitable as he would having the actual bath. This was true particularly if you'd had a busy or stressful day and this was an important bath coming up. If you'd been out in the wind and the rain, or sweating round bright department stores with nothing to think of but a hot tub, then it was vital to make a wise choice, and the extra minutes weren't wasted.

It was rare for Luke to drop a book in the bath, though it had happened. Usually it was when he got one of his hands wet and had to turn the pages one-handed. He'd lay his little finger on the outside page and tweak the other one with a thumbnail, hoping to prise it loose. Then he'd shift his grip on the spine, cradling it in his palm for a risky split-second while he rolled the book to the left, clearing the fingers out of the way as fast as possible. Sometimes he completed the manoeuvre only to discover that he had forgotten what had just been happening. The sheer concentration demanded by the one-handed page turn was enough to dislodge all but the most gripping stories. This was another reason why you needed something action-packed; you wanted to be able to carry on without feeling you might be missing a decisive twist.

Sod it, the taxi driver said, braking hard.

Luke twisted round to see what was going on.

Red bleeding light, the man said. Always the same along here.

If you keep an even speed you should get green all the way, Luke said. Long as the road's clear.

That'll be the day.

Luke pulled the window down a little to let in some air. If he lost his grip on the daydream, he'd start wondering whether Carmen would still be at the house, whether his plane would wait for him, whether this, whether that. For now it was better to keep things at arm's length.

Lavatory books were different. You weren't there for so long, so you needed something chopped up into small chunks: an anthology, for example. Most people tended to associate the lavatory with humour, and left stacks of strip cartoons, treasuries of amusing anecdotes, and funniest-thing-that-ever-happened-to-me books by celebrities. Luke couldn't go along with this. The last thing you wanted just then was to burst out laughing. No, he found it an ideal time for a brief but intense concentration on lofty, abstract matters. All that releasing implied a certain slipping of earthly bonds: Luke often browsed though rarefied discussions of philosophy in there. Encyclopaediae were good. There'd be enough time to look up Aristotle or Aquinas or Zeno – and you could learn something.

The thing was, you didn't want to have to turn the page too often. Something about the process demanded a certain stillness from your upper body, so a large-format book (weight was no problem – you were well positioned for heavy volumes) was perfect. And the other thing about the encyclopaedia was that there was always the lucky-dip aspect. You'd look for one thing, and end up with another. This suited Luke, who liked to think he cast his net wide.

It also tallied with his anxiety about the gap between what people wanted to say and what they actually came out with. He hadn't, if he was honest, invested much of himself in that conversation with the taxi driver. Nor had the driver – that was obvious. He was too busy looking out for traffic; or perhaps he was wondering whether it would be quicker to turn left here and cut out the roundabout, checking his watch to make sure he still had time to pick up his wife from the supermarket.

Or maybe he had bigger problems: a child lying in hospital, a frightening letter from the tax man crushed in his wallet.

Neither of them was about to confide his real preoccupations. What could Luke have said? You haven't by any chance got any thoughts on whether I should get married or not, have you? Only someone just asked me. Left at the top, please.

You couldn't express most of what you felt: most of it was locked up in the vast, latent vocabulary of outer language.

This contradicted, Luke realised, what he had told Carmen about feelings being thoughts. So perhaps feelings were like time – the word we gave to things we could not quite put our finger on.

Or take those conversations with Emma and Jonathan. They weren't saying much, just signalling a desire to keep the line open – though that in itself was no small thing. Better than the old days, when he would watch television until his eyes hurt, persuading himself that it was a way of keeping in touch with the world, a window – when really it was exactly what it said it was: a screen, purpose-built to keep the world at bay.

He found his packet of cigarettes, thought about lighting one, and frowned when he saw the sign. Thank you for not smoking. Extraordinary: you gave up for months and then had just one, and the next thing you knew you felt deprived if you couldn't have another.

Why didn't he instruct the driver to forget it, go straight to the airport? But it would have been like a ship not stopping to rescue survivors. And if Carmen wasn't there he'd . . . he'd think of some other way. What would he tell her: that he wanted to keep the line open?

Don't think about it. Don't. He forced himself to close down that file and open another.

Planes, buses – no, delete them, Luke had never been able to read on coaches of any sort – cafés, restaurants, beaches, bed . . . you couldn't read one book in all those different places. For the beach, naturally, you needed a cliff-hanger, something to take your mind off the sand between your toes and the sun on your shoulders and the glowing tanned girl-ankles that went softly before your eyes every time you squinted sideways. And don't forget armchairs: there was always a chance that one day you might decide to read for once, and would fetch a cup of tea or, since this was a special occasion, a beer or a glass of wine, and you'd sit down and read, the way people used to before life changed. That's where the Darwin came in.

Besides, it would be interesting to trace a path back to the origin of things.

On the whole, though, Luke wasn't sure that it made much difference what you read. At the height of his introspective stage, he had an extremely hazy approach to books. The key thing was that you were reading, rather than eating or watching television or playing games. Just as, in the city, if you troubled too much about where you were at any one time, if you let the map come into your head for a moment, the capricious size of the thing could knock you sideways, so it was with books. If you tried to make sense of everything, to see where it all fitted in, you could go mad. Luke possessed no unusual knowledge about the history of books, but he knew that for every one you read there were thousands you would never come across. It was enough to make you give in right there. Any decision was bound to be arbitrary, so what was the use? He read, as it were, with his eyes shut.

He was also a natural devotee – back in what he now jokingly called his bachelor days – of small advertisements. Every week he read the lonely hearts columns and the sad lists of items for sale: even the innocuous ones – exercise bikes, labrador puppies, fridges – made Luke feel invited to speculate on the heartaches which led to their being advertised. It was quite common to see fur coats or record players tagged as unwanted presents, and once Luke saw this: Diamond wedding ring, incl. single sapphire, hardly worn. He tore it out and carried it in his pocket for a few days, and very nearly rang up just to see what sort of woman – or perhaps man – could have been brought to this. He would gaze about him in the streets or in the underground, wondering whether maybe this man was selling his double bed, as new; or whether that woman was looking for companionship, likes music, walking, food, photo appreciated.

With preoccupations like these, it was not surprising that Luke had lost touch with his friends. He tried to rationalise it by telling himself it was hard to justify knowing some people when there were so many millions of others. You could only scratch the surface, so why bother? But he couldn't hide his loneliness from himself. Even Jonathan, who came up to London at about this time, couldn't tempt him out of his seclusion.

I mean, look at them. The window was streaked with rain, but the cab was on an elevated bit of dual carriageway, so there was a view. A few church steeples poked above the melancholy rooftops, and nearby there were old craters that had been turned into car parks or rubbish dumps; but mainly it was like driving through an orchard, lines of houses whipping by, row after row after row. Here and there patches of grass refused to give up the ghost altogether. Otherwise, empty washing lines flapped, and a few children's bicycles lay stuck in the mud. The grey sky bristled with aerials and satellite dishes, which gave people a clear view of the far side of the world, but blotted out the street they lived in.

Carmen hadn't even seemed to notice how odd he was. Once or twice she remarked that he was kind of shy, but that she liked that. This was fine by Luke, who could hardly admit how much he liked the fact she wasn't shy at all.

One summer they went swimming in the river. It was a hot day, and they'd been to the races. (Carmen's idea: she just stopped by in her car with the roof down and said, jump in. It turned out she knew someone who had a horse running – it didn't win.) On the way back the traffic was bad all the way along the motorway and suddenly Carmen went, I give up, and headed for the exit ramp. It was hot, she said. She knew a place where they could swim, cool off.

She went through the town and down what looked like a dead end. On either side big houses grew like trees out of miserly lawns full of laburnum, hibiscus and forsythia. They all looked locked-up, uninhabited. Where the road turned left at the bottom there was a lane going straight on through some trees. Carmen went as far as she could, almost to the edge of the river, then stopped.

They got out. It was the beginning of dusk. Birds were chirruping all over the place and the air was full of bees. The water looked slack, and over on the far side, beyond the line of boats that lazed against the bank, a herd of cows bent their heads to the grass and flicked their tails. The last thing Luke felt like doing was jumping in, but Carmen was already stripping off.

People will see, he said.

So what? she said. It was one of her sayings. They'll only be jealous.

She had all her clothes off now. Except for her tanned face and arms, she looked pale. She stood there looking at him for a moment, her head tilted. Luke was still fully dressed. Then she smiled to herself, turned and waded in, keeping her brown arms high until the water was up to her waist.

Luke followed, running into the water, crouching in case anyone was on one of the boats.

We don't have towels or anything, he thought, but didn't say a word.

He was a strong swimmer, so it didn't take him long to catch up. Carmen was treading water. She tilted her head back and hair spread about her face like a fan. Luke took a handful and lifted it in his fingers, watching the river water glisten in the evening sun. He hadn't known you could do things like this.

See? Carmen moved a little closer to him and brushed against him. Luke could feel her legs kicking, and then she reached down and tickled him, so lightly he thought he might have imagined it. See? she said again.

The water was cold, but Luke wanted to push his feet down as far as possible, until they froze. The surface hovered with warm flies.

In the distance, if you listened, you could hear the cars on the motorway, inching forward in a haze of fumes and radios. One or two cars would have pulled in, too hot and thirsty to continue. And here they were, holding each other now, moving closer together and holding tight, keeping themselves afloat with small, thrilling movements of their legs as the river rolled them gently,

gently downhill at an even pace which felt, for the few moments that followed, like the pace of life itself.

See what I mean? God, had he made an awful mistake? Was it too late? As he sped towards her, the gap between them seemed to grow with every minute. He felt like a man with his hands on the boat and his feet on the jetty. He had to decide whether to jump before it was too late.

It was odd, after the swim, how different the houses seemed. The sun splashed warm colours over the brick and all the windows were open. A squirrel sat up on a sunny patch of pine needles and quivered its nostrils at them. A couple of swans swayed to the water's edge, fluttered their tails as they settled, and floated off downstream.

Luke felt like shouting hellos to everyone he could see.

The cab jerked as it pulled away from the lights.

Oh, he was tired. Tired of himself, tired of his life, tired of this morning. Please wait, he urged the plane. Don't go without me. I need to be taken away from all this.

From all what, though? Even he couldn't argue that he was suffering from anything that wasn't self-inflicted.

He opened the newspaper – at random, of course – and found himself staring at the entertainment section.

The old Luke, the previous version, always took an academic interest in the latest shows, concerts, lectures, sporting events and films. If anyone asked him what time a particular play started, or where the nearest late-night chemist was, he knew the answer. No one ever did, but who cared?

He also memorised timetables, just one small aspect of his attempt to comprehend the goings-on in the capital. Sometimes he would stop – it could be anywhere – and knowledgeably reflect on the movement of buses and trains into and out of London. In his mind the city would suddenly resemble one of those microscopic images of cell life, or one of those speeded-up time-lapse films; it would merge in his mind with an image of all those miniature highways built on electronic circuit boards – an early harbinger of the comparison he would later draw between data flow and traffic. He was especially fascinated by any natural phenomenon in which the substance would come and go while leaving the form intact: he could watch candles burning or rain falling for twenty minutes or so without thinking of anything else. In the summer, he would visit the parks and watch the water sprinklers whacking the grass, round and round. Sometimes, as he watched the endless flow, he would detect minute rhythms in the way the nozzle threw its cold jets onto the warm earth, and he would feel himself to be on the brink of an unusual perception; but it was always just then that a small child would run into the spray to cool off, and the moment would be lost.

In the end, what Luke could not adjust to was the chatter of signs and words that rained on the city every day. Inevitably, he limited himself to foxy dashes between familiar haunts, as if he didn't live in a city at all. When he saw the mad scurrying from place to place – so much purposeful movement everywhere, up and down escalators and across dangerous bus routes! – it was hard not to feel lost and in peril. But once he had withdrawn a little he found he could enjoy the tidal race of the population as something driven by the moon, as something solemn and inspiring, like the slow unfurling of a wave on a wide, empty beach.

Eventually, some time between Christmas and the New Year, he decided that to read the city's lips required a renunciation, a perception that the city's inexhaustible lattice of unconnected threads would support him only if he stopped struggling. The city belonged to no one, and claimed no allegiance from any of its inhabitants. Nor did it have what you could call a face – it had a million faces. It was much too big to see: even from an aeroplane it seemed to go on for ever, and seen from within, it blocked out the horizons. That was why travelling underground was so peculiar and appropriate: it gave the impression that you were submerged, nosing around in the shallows, running along the walls of steep underwater cliffs, coasting towards familiar pools. Luke often walked across the parks – which many people he talked to insisted were the best thing about the place – but the pleasure he took in them was of an uneasy and unusual kind. Out in the open he felt nervous, as though he had broken cover.

Living the true city life was demanding: keeping his footing took up most of Luke's energy. Oh, he forced himself to be as sociable as the next man: rubbing along with the people you bumped into was an important urban talent. But until Carmen, well, there was that Canadian girl who came in to the hi-fi shop one day looking for a camera, but it never really got off the ground, and he hadn't minded when, after a few weeks, she decided to go home. The only thing that made him sad about it was that she didn't mind either.

Was this the life that was awaiting him in Rome? He was shocked to realise how little he knew about the place. It had seven hills, didn't it, so there should be some good views. And it was antique, so it wouldn't be full of high-rise buildings. That was a relief. Luke had been to New York once and wandered around, like everyone else, with his head tilted back and his mouth open. But then it struck him that American cities weren't built vertically because the people liked it that way. It was simply that they'd been built after elevators had been invented. And then the commercial imperatives of property speculation stepped in, and there was nothing anybody could do.

Ironic, really. All that space, and they insisted on living on top of one another.

Luke rubbed his eyes and pulled the guidebook from his luggage. But he didn't get further than the front cover, a picture of two lovers kissing by a fountain, the sun sparkling off blue water and white marble and glinting in the spray behind their heads. Everyone agreed that Rome was romantic – but it had never struck Luke before that to be romantic was to be in some sense Roman. He was going to the right place, he said to himself.

But he couldn't bear to read about all these ancient sites and splendid masterpieces. The thought of people living and dying and being romantic two thousand years ago frightened him. So he carried on brooding.

In the summer, when everyone else was out and about, Luke mostly stayed at home and concentrated on imagining the city from there. But in the depths of winter he put on a coat and walked all over the place, from tree to tree, street to street, laying his finger – as he saw it – along the metropolitan pulse.

What he heard on his walks was not so much the demented soundtrack of the city's daily life but the more general, less audible noise of building and collapse. Wherever he went he could hear the whine and thump of drills, the iron ring of scaffolding and the scream of smashing glass. On clear days he could sometimes catch a dragging sound, like the surge of waves, as rubbish poured into bins and flooded out of the city. He could hear the steady rumble of cranes as they swung round overhead. He was even aware of the city's wheezy lungs, as a million cars and vacuum cleaners and air-conditioning units and people breathed in the oxygen which gusted in from the oceans, and breathed out smog.

Sometimes, even now, the city could swallow Luke up just like anyone else. Back then, as spring approached, even he became aware that his was an unusual life. At odd moments, when he was walking through the zoo or queuing for a ticket somewhere, a kind of vertigo could overcome him. He could get quite confused when the people in the kiosks asked him what kind of ticket he was after, or where he wanted to sit. There were so many seats, and it was annoying having to be confined to just one angle of vision. Sometimes he would be so flustered he would have to leave, though he was not above rejoining the back of the queue when he had calmed down. Impatience was not one of his vices.

This sense that he lived in a world of vast numbers, a queasy feeling that his grip on it all was feeble, and that he might fall through at any minute, was always lying in wait for him. Despite his determined efforts to keep it caged by pondering every eventuality, it could still spring out and surprise him. When this happened — and thank God it was quite rare — he could almost see himself vanishing, in front of his very eyes, taking his place in the numberless horde around him, shuffling this way and that as though pushed from behind — or led from in front, you could never tell. At times like this, he would imagine, for a moment, that he had been afforded a glimpse into a higher order; as though, if only he could get it into focus, he would take a step forward.

By this stage he had a well-developed enthusiasm for computers, and he was an early fan of the various high-tech magazines that sprang into life around then. It was here that Luke nurtured his fondness for binary distinctions. They seemed, at the time, to offer a way out of all this.

There was only one place where he never read anything at all, and that was on the underground. He never sat down either, even if there was no one else in the carriage. It seemed wrong to him to try to pretend that you could sit down, as if in an armchair, while you were rumbling along beneath the city through the dark tunnels like a mole, not knowing which direction you were going in. He preferred to stand in an aisle and hold on to one of the small sprung truncheons that hung from the curved, grubby ceiling. He even enjoyed staring through the windows at the black tunnel walls. You could see the cables rushing by – and Luke would attempt to guess what colour they had originally been – and every now and then, when the train crashed out of the darkness, there would be an exciting view of the fat grey London sky. There was another game he liked to play down there: he would attempt to guess, every now and then, exactly what was above him, at ground level. He had reflected at some length on the routes the tunnels took. He liked to monitor his position in relation to famous roads and landmarks.

It was the sensation of depth he enjoyed, imagining the foundations of the Opera House or the cathedral just yards from where he was standing. He even thought that he could locate, almost to the second, the spot on the line where it passed beneath his office. He would wonder if the desks jogged at all as he drove underneath them. Sometimes he would walk between stations just to check what lay en route, and as he jostled among the other passengers a hundred feet below the surface of the earth he would recite the names of stores under his breath: McDonalds and Seven-Eleven, then Benetton, then the Star newsagent on the corner, crossing the road now, the hospital, probably a queue at the bus stop just there, that supermarket – what was its name? Open all night – the bank . . . and so on.

It all made Luke feel like an expert, and when he stood on a moving train, swaying in the flickering light, his feet staggering under him as the carriages lurched over some snaggle in the line or braked without warning, holding on tight with just one hand, he tried to adopt the practised pose of a seasoned traveller. It was always novices – tourists and so on – who went for the seats. Wanting to sit down just gave you something to worry about every time you got on to a train, and it was part of Luke's attempt to refine the perfect urban lifestyle that all unnecessary stresses should be avoided.

Well, things had certainly changed. These days he went crazy if he didn't get a seat. And as for stress: well, it had been quite a long morning, and it wasn't finished yet.

It was shortly before Easter that Luke's parents, worried that he hadn't answered the phone for weeks, paid him a surprise visit. They found him playing a computer game in a room dominated by a large pyramid built out of empty dishes of takeaway food. The pile of silver foil threw a weird, fractured light around the room. His parents took it all in, the smell, the dirt. They spent the rest of the day cleaning, and then fixed Luke up with a psychiatrist recommended by one of their doctor friends. Bit by bit, he pulled himself together.

It crossed Luke's mind, as the taxi accelerated down a broad avenue, that while he thought part of his life was buried for good, he might still be at risk. He frowned.

But then he noticed that they'd turned off the main road and were nudging along a residential street. They must be nearly there. The driver was slowing down and peering at the names. Time to wake up.

He was perplexed by how calm he was. He would almost certainly miss his flight, but here he was, shrugging and staying cool.

They were right: meditation could do you the world of good.

All the same. He'd better snap out of it now.

It was common to read that people pinched themselves as a way of coming to grips with reality, but where did they pinch? Luke tried his earlobe, but no matter how hard he squeezed it didn't hurt. He tried his waist, but there was too much jacket and coat in the way. Eventually he found a place just under his arm where – ouch!

Was it really the case that in deciding whether to marry Carmen or not Luke was choosing between two different personalities?

He sighed. Would he never stop thinking about himself? He hadn't been to very many Italian classes yet, but he had discovered that personality came from the Latin *per sona* – through sound.

Personalities, he discovered when he looked them up, were masks, superficial things. There was no reason why you shouldn't have several.

How many bits are there? Carmen had asked. Well, at least two. And Luke was going to have to decide which of them he wanted to gain the upper hand.

A good clean break, she had said.

He shouldn't have let himself dream away like that; he should have spent the time preparing his speech, or having a proper think about the idea of marriage. Did he have anything more to say to himself on that subject? Hell, he'd hardly scratched the surface, that was the whole problem.

No such thing as marriage in general. It was odd: if he were to describe his thought-habits to a complete stranger he would say that he concentrated on small things. He had a private rule which said that the differences between things were almost always more interesting than the similarities. He lived in categorical times, when people loved to lump things together as if they were all the same – city life made it virtually compulsory, forcing you to come to fast conclusions all the time. People even linked arguments – saying that if you said this then you had to say that as well, or if you said that then you might as well say this – which often wasn't the case at all.

At some point during that blackout in his flat, he'd hit on something to do with taking marriage out of the equation rather than Carmen. Let's run that one by again.

Oh sod it, let's not. He didn't have the energy.

I agree we've been drifting a bit lately . . . She could say that again.

The thought of Carmen's letter sent the warmth rushing to his face; and there were goose pimples on the back of his shoulders. It was . . . I mean, there she was, moving about the flat, coffee, eggs, bacon, saying one thing when she'd been writing completely the opposite. Was there such a fine line between wanting to get married and wanting a good, clean break?

And oh my God, when she got back she'd see that he'd eaten the leftovers. What kind of a person would she think he was?

Carmen. Every time he thought of her moving close to him, her forehead coming up against his cheek so that he could feel hair against his face . . .

I've been wondering what it means, your going away like this . . .

He saw an empty glass, a few streaks of whisky on the side, a detectable pink kiss on the lip.

He nibbled at a fingernail.

The whole idea was such a bolt from the blue. Or was it? Even the man who couldn't say no couldn't get married simply to please someone else. But should he have been so taken aback? Had he kept his eyes shut, not noticed what was going on?

He checked his watch. Ten forty-five. Miraculous: this whole trip had taken only ten minutes. Felt like a lifetime.

There was her car!

Here we are, mate. Here.

Great. Luke thrust a couple of notes through the glass partition, reached for the door handle, and stepped outside. A few glimmers of sunlight fell through the clouds. There was honeysuckle along the railings by the pavement, and daffodils nodded in the front gardens. A blackbird waved its yellow beak from the low branch of a magnolia.

The door was open, but Luke lifted the knocker, a large brass dolphin, and let it fall twice. He stepped inside and put his cases down.

Hello? he called. He could hear voices upstairs, and feet scraping against what sounded like bare floorboards.

He went on up, and stopped on the landing.

A lot of people knock that wall down, he heard Carmen saying, to make one big space. But here you've still got the original features. It'd make a sweet little children's room. These are all on dimmers, by the way.

Certainly is quiet. A man's voice.

Yes, it's a popular road for families. Hardly any traffic. You see boys and girls playing out in the street on their bikes.

Luke held his breath and tried to think of a way in. Stupid, stupid, stupid. He hadn't budgeted for other people.

Was that a garage we saw on the way in? the man said.

Well, yes and no. Most of the houses in the road do have them, but this one's been converted. I'll show you.

His mind flew back to the time they met, Carmen moving around his flat, telling him how comfortable it was. They had gone round in a circle, and here they were again.

Hello? he said, giving the floor a scrape with his feet.

Who's there? Carmen's head leaned round the door, and they were face to face. Luke smiled and took a step forward.

A woman came through as well. She looked pregnant: that explained Carmen's kiddy references. The man was right behind her. He was very short: he only came up to Luke's shoulders.

What are you . . . ? Carmen began.

They said at the office you were here, so I came under my own steam. Seemed easier than fixing up to see it another time. He looked down at the man. You don't mind, do you? Only it sounded exactly the kind of place I'm looking for. He turned towards Carmen. Are you sure you've got the price right? Most of the ones this size are practically double. What's the catch?

Er, no, we don't mind, the woman said. Do we, darling?

I'm sorry about this, Carmen said, keeping her eyes on Luke. Tell you what, take these keys. One of them'll get you into the annexe. Have a good explore. I'll come and join you in a minute. She stepped back to let them past.

Luke watched them go: two newly-weds with a baby on the way, house-hunting out by the airport.

Then Carmen said: So.

So?

What are you doing here?

I had to come, Luke said. Sorry about that, I was only trying to help. You know, make them think someone else is interested.

Yes, well, they're interested already.

Carmen, I'm sorry about this morning. What I should have said . . .

I'm sorry too. About your face.

Oh, I deserved it. Though my lawyer says it could be worth a fortune.

Ho. We're at the lawyer stage, are we?

Listen, Carmen, what I should have said was . . .

Who cares what you should have said? What are you saying now?

I just had to see you before I went. To apologise, to explain.

What do you want to do, Luke?

What Luke wanted to do was put his hands into her hair and kiss her, and not let go.

God, if I only had another day, he said. He hadn't meant it to come out in words, though it was what he was thinking.

Carmen shrugged. Get high, she said. You're always going on about how time slows down up there. Go to Tibet.

Carmen . . .

Whenever you hear about people who are two hundred years old, it's always Tibet, isn't it?

Carmen, wait . . .

Or maybe it's not the height, maybe it's the roots and goat droppings.

Carmen, I had to see you. I couldn't leave . . . like that. He put his hand in his pocket and fondled the trophies he had gathered this morning: watch, bus, letter. I saw this church today, he said. After I came out of the supermarket. It looked so small. The priest was standing out in the . . .

You've got quite a nerve raising the subject of churches.

I know. It was sad, all the same.

Are you building up to something? Because if not . . .

Carmen, I read your letter.

You what?

I read your letter.

You can't have. It's in my . . .

Excuse me? Excuse me? We can't seem to get the key . . .

Jesus, Carmen whispered. Okay, I'm coming, she called. She glared at Luke and went down the stairs.

Luke followed.

Just go, Carmen muttered. This is hopeless. If you're going, go.

They went into the kitchen.

Sorry, there's a latch, Carmen said. Here we are. She opened the door into the garage conversion. It had a stone floor with mats, and glass at one end. Pot plants everywhere.

Luke took Carmen's hand as she walked in, and drew her back. The others went on ahead.

I don't suppose you happen to know, he said. Have you ever seen those bottles of brandy with an apple inside? I saw one earlier.

Actually, I do know, Carmen said. It's lovely. They tie the bottles on the tree; the fruit grows in the glass.

She twisted her head. There, she said. They've gone, now. You were saying . . .

What you told me this morning, he told her. I've been thinking. There's a famous line. I used to have the lines taped to my terminal. He squeezed Carmen's hand.

Let me go. What is this?

The things that people think are hard are easy. The things that people think are easy are hard.

Oh, great. The things that people think are simple are expensive. So what?

I've been a complete idiot. I don't know what got into me this morning.

Come on, he urged himself. Say something, for God's sake. He reached out his hand again.

Luke. Honestly, I swear to God.

She pulled free and turned away.

Mind if we go into the garden? The pregnant woman's head appeared through the doorway.

Feel free. Carmen gave a tight smile. Through the French windows.

Luke watched the small man step onto the patio and look up at the sky. There was a roaring noise. He nudged Carmen.

This is where they find out about the aeroplanes, eh?

Carmen said nothing. She walked across the kitchen and stood over the sink, looking out. On the lawn, the man walked up behind the pregnant woman and put his arms round her shoulders. Luke could tell they were imagining living here.

I wish I could say it was nice to see you, Luke.

You what?

Carmen turned to face him. So, you're down to rummaging through dustbins now.

188

Yes, Luke said.

And?

Luke wanted a speech to spring to his lips, but nothing came. There were things you couldn't say in a strange kitchen, with all this uncertainty in the air. He shouldn't have come.

I see.

No. I'm sorry. Your letter was . . . superb. Superb. It gave me quite a shake, I can tell you. And it made me realise . . .

Sssshhhh, they're coming. Luke, you'd better go. I've got to drive them back. Give me a ring later, if you want.

Luke frowned. That wasn't a bad idea. He'd been right all along: this could wait. He could get her a ring in Italy and give it to her, hell, he could fly back next weekend if he wanted.

The woman joined them in the kitchen. Luke could hear the sound of the bolts on the French windows next door.

What do you think? he said.

She seemed surprised. She looked at Carmen, who shrugged, as if it was nothing to do with her.

Because the thing is, I'd like to put in an offer, Luke said.

What? Carmen stared at him.

I said I'd like to put in an offer. Luke smiled. He put a finger to his lips and was surprised by how dry and still it was, not trembling at all. He looked at Carmen, and could see from the way her eyes gazed that she knew what he was saying.

But of course, I don't want to get in anyone's way.

Philip? the woman called. Here, quick! This man says he wants to put in an offer.

At the full asking price? Carmen said.

Of course. Well, you know, assuming the survey's okay.

Ah, the survey. She looked down and smiled.

Well, I must say. Philip joined them. This all sounds highly . . .

Is it freehold, by the way?

Yes, said Carmen. Yours in perpetuity.

Hey, wait. You can't just . . .

Have you actually put in an offer? Luke said.

Well, not in black and white. But this is the third time we've been round. You shouldn't even be here.

I know I shouldn't. Look, I'm not trying to pull anything. If you're saying you want the house, fine.

What do you think, darling? The woman took her husband's arm.

I don't know. This is all most . . .

Luke tried to catch Carmen's eye, but her hair had fallen over the top of her face, and she was looking the other way.

I'll leave you to talk about it among yourselves, Luke said. If you back out, my offer stands. We'll talk on the phone, right? I'll need to know about fixtures and fittings. You know, carpets and everything.

The carpets are included. Carmen looked up. But they're taking the blinds. She hesitated. So, that's agreed, she said. You have first refusal. I'll see you out.

Luke felt her hands on his back as he went down the passage towards the front door.

What do you mean, first refusal? he said.

The house is still on the market, Carmen said. Who can say what'll happen?

He picked up his cases, one in each hand.

She reached past him and opened the front door.

Bye, Luke. She put out her hand. Thanks for that.

Least I could do. Goodbye, Carmen.

He bent his head to kiss her, but she stepped back.

You shouldn't have read that letter, Luke. She gave him a little push in the stomach. And then the door closed.

The breath came out of Luke's lungs in a rush. He didn't know how long he had been in there, and he didn't care.

He looked around for a souvenir: this moment was worth commemorating. He tugged at the three numbers attached to the bricks beside the door, and the middle one, the O, came away in his hand. He tapped the dirt off on a tree trunk and put it in his pocket. It was large for a ring, but it would do.

On the pavement he couldn't resist avoiding the cracks between the paving stones. As a boy he would go for miles without stepping on a single one. It was a bit more difficult with these suitcases: he had to take uneven strides. But he kept it up all the way to the main road.

He turned left and started keeping an eye out for the station. Only two minutes, according to the particulars. He'd believe that when he saw it. But he was in no hurry – in fact he didn't mind any more whether he caught the plane or not.

As he crossed the corner of a grass verge, he noticed that the grass was sprinkled with primroses. For some reason they reminded him of something, of some ancient dread that still stirred in his dreams. He was careful not to tread on any of the flowers as he paced across the green turf.

But there were blue and white hyacinths in a window box over there; tulips were breaking out of their buds in pink flashes, and the willow at the end of the road was just coming into leaf.

He might as well give it a go. He had nothing else to do, after all.

Once upon a time there was a man who lived in the middle of a minefield. There was nothing sinister about this: he was not the victim of any discarded military initiative, and he had no enemies, so far as he knew. On the contrary, he had planted the mines himself, long ago, in response to some fear to which he had not been able to give a name even then.

He wanted to live an artificial life, a life he could pretend might last for ever. In an earlier time, he might have become a monk, though even a monastery might have seemed crowded to him. So he withdrew to a remote part of the country, not far from the sea. He never received visitors. But the last thing he wanted was to hurt anyone, so he put up signs on the boundaries of his land to warn people of the danger. The signs were old now, and the wind and rain had pulled the red paint off in large flakes, but the words were still visible.

At first it was easy: the mines stuck out above the surface of the ground and the man could see where they were. But as time passed it began to seem to him that the devices were not sufficiently discreet – and what was the point of a trap that anyone could avoid if they took the slightest trouble? What his charges needed, he decided, was depth.

This feeling coincided with a natural desire to develop the landscape, and one winter the man sat up late almost every night, with only a candle to see by, and composed elaborate drawings of lawns, borders, pathways, steps, a lake, clusters of trees, even a maze.

It took years to build. The man started by planting four cedars, which he christened Matthew, Mark, Luke and John; then he raked tons of new soil into a series of level areas, and scattered grass seed onto the earth through a child's fishing net.

He took care to mark each mine with a slender stick, and beside each stick he planted a yellow primrose. There were so many mines that, after only a season or two, the primroses had seeded and scattered themselves at random.

Digging out the lake was a big job, but after a couple of years a depression a few feet deep curled among the lawns and trees. It was a small matter to divert one of the streams that fell from a nearby hillside; and it didn't take long for various birds to find it. Mallard, gulls, swans, geese and even a pair of herons made it their home. In the quiet warm evenings of late summer the man would sit outside and watch the birds moving across the water. He would listen to their soft evening songs and light a pipe, and sit there hardly moving until it was so dark he could no longer see a thing.

By now the man knew where all the mines were without thinking. He didn't even need to keep his eye out for the primroses.

Wherever he looked there were drifts of poppies and wild rose, clumps of azalea and rhododendron. Foxgloves flourished in the shady spots, slipping their roots around canisters of high explosive and sucking fuel for their pale flowers from the dangerous earth. If anyone had come to see it, they would have been astonished to find such grounds around a mere one-roomed barn with a roof made of moss and corrugated iron. But no one ever came up this far.

He had no modern conveniences, not even a clock. He had no call for time, since he never had any appointments. And the plants and animals told him as much as he needed to know about the progress of the year. But an old habit prompted him to build a sundial on an open piece of ground. Each morning he would carve a notch in the largest of the cedar trees. Each week, he would carve a notch in another; each month, in another. At the end of the year he sank his blade into the last and smallest. Occasionally he would consult his four gospels to find out how old he was.

Sometimes, at night, he would drink as much as he could and then wander through the unlit garden, moving among the green things with hardly controlled lurches. It was a kind of pastoral roulette, and he never lost. His feet seemed to know where the hazards lay better than his head. He could walk for hours unconscious of the dangers, which he no longer thought about at all.

On his trips down the rough track into the world outside, the man *would see other people in the distance. They seemed so small and so ignorant.*

One summer, after they had flowered, he took a hoe to the primroses, which by now had spread into sizeable pools. It took a year or two, but soon it was impossible to tell where the new grass ended and the old grass began.

The maze matured, too. It was made of yew hedges and formed a circle, in a wooded hollow near the lake. The green alleys were strewn with grim canisters hidden beneath the turf.

Things changed the day he realised that he could no longer remember where the mines were. He pored over his charts, but he had not marked them. And with the primroses gone it was hard to be sure. For the first time since he had embarked on this unusual life, he grew afraid. He avoided his own gardens. Weeds began to clamber over the roses and drowned the poppies. The grass grew tall and was full of thistles and beds of nettle.

It struck him that the old rusty cans had not really been mines until now. If you knew where they were, they were just harmless tins. But at last they had assumed their true nature, and he feared them.

One day he took a risk, guessed a path out of his grounds and went for a walk in the world outside. Hours later, walking high on the hills far from his home, he came across a couple sitting on a clifftop, staring out to sea. The woman had her arm round the man's shoulder, but they weren't doing anything – just sitting there. They were very close to the edge, and the man could see that the cliff face curved back beneath their feet. They were sitting on a lip of loose soil suspended above a hundred yards of salty air.

But they didn't seem to mind. They were so wrapped up in each other they seemed indifferent to the danger they were in – the deep sea swishing a hundred yards below their feet, the precarious ledge above nothing.

For some reason the sight cracked the man's resolve. For years he had taken immense precautions against hidden perils – now he could see that the only traps he knew how to avoid were those he had planted himself. He went home and for several days found himself unable to sleep. At night he would drink a bottle of whisky, light his pipe and sway through the scented groves. Sometimes he would stand still and think of that exposed shelf above the sea. The slightest noise – a startled

194

fox, a badger pushing against a low branch, a bird moving its neck – made him twist and tremble.

One day he wondered whether the people he had seen were married. That night he pulled at an eyebrow, came up with a grey hair and realised that though he lived a timeless life, he was getting old.

Something had to give, he told himself. Something had to change.

He started by removing the signs. Then he took a slim metal rod and began to walk his wild garden, poking and testing. He had a delicate touch. He was able to sense the kiss of metal on metal almost before it happened. He fetched spades and a wheelbarrow and began to dig up the mines. One by one he took them to the lake, wading out to the centre and laying them on the sandy bottom. It was hard work: the weeks passed and winter came. But in the heat of his determination the man seemed not to notice the weather. Every day he levered and lifted and tiptoed down to the water.

One day a loud explosion sent birds flying into the air. The herons were the slowest of all, but even they were moving away towards the hills by the time the blast faded.

The man wasn't dead, though he had lost both his hands. He pushed his endless arms into his stomach: apart from that he couldn't move.

But if anyone heard the thunderous clap of high explosive, they probably thought it was a wave booming against a rock, or someone out after pheasant. In this part of the coast, strange noises were quite common.

Eleven o'clock

The station smelt of hot chocolate, but Luke didn't even notice. He swung the larger bag across to his briefcase hand, staggered up the steps and hurried into the gangway that led to the platforms. He could hear a train arriving, but couldn't tell which direction it was going in. Three or four people broke into a run. If you missed a train at this time of day you might as well walk.

He was in luck. The information panel was displaying a bright aeroplane logo. He could step right on. But the nearest carriage was full, so he clambered into the last compartment of all, where there was plenty of room.

It wasn't easy to know where to sit, though.

Planes were fine – you were given a seat number and forced to take potluck on neighbours. Luke always enjoyed the eager look on people's faces when you walked in to the passenger cabin. Everybody glanced up, wondering whether you were the one planning to spoil their view out of the porthole; whether – oh, look at her: please, just this once, make this be the day she sits next to me; whether right, typical, that huge dandruffy guy is going to collapse right here and eat some snack out of a paper bag, the fried fat smell gushing all over your freshly laundered clothes.

But on the tube you had to decide for yourself, and with long journeys it could make quite a difference. You wanted to sit in the middle of those teenagers who glanced at you out of the corner of their eyes and burst out laughing? Or opposite the old guy snarling and cursing? You wanted to be the one to ask that hairy fellow with the tattoos and the can of beer to take his boots off that seat, or the one presumptuous enough to sit opposite that girl who looked like a model, as if you knew her or expected to? Go ahead. Be my guest. Luke just wanted somewhere quiet.

Eventually he picked a seat opposite an elderly man in a tweed jacket and a trilby. The train lurched off just before he sat down, so the edge of the seat nudged him behind the knees and plonked him down with a thud, but he soon found his footing again. After only a few seconds of vacillating over where to focus his eyes, Luke was able to let his mind roam.

He looked for the route map, and found it above his head. What a stroke of luck! Only four stops. He'd probably hit the airport not much after ten past. He might yet make it.

Not that it mattered.

The best part was that for the next few minutes – unless there was a delay, in which case he'd have to throw in the towel altogether – he wouldn't have to speak to a single person. The phone wouldn't ring. No one would ask him any difficult questions. Heaven.

He closed his eyes as the train gathered speed. It seemed to be going at a good gallop, almost as if it knew there was an emergency going on.

The house is still on the market, Carmen had said. Hmmm.

His heart was still racing from the walk to the station, but otherwise he felt placid and resigned. You would have thought that by now he'd have been sweating like mad, checking his watch every few seconds, standing up, sitting down again, computing the length of time the train took between stops and revising his estimated time of arrival. Or that he would be planning in meticulous detail what he would do when the train stopped, how he would take off up the escalator, find a trolley, cruise along those long travelling pathways into the terminal, and glide down to the check-in desk.

But he just sat there, his head nodding, as if he didn't have a care in the world. He'd said yes, hadn't he? Not in so many words, but Carmen knew what he was on about.

At the first stop a guitarist joined the party. A tall girl with dark hair, she welcomed everyone on board, told them they'd be driving at a height of about six feet, and hoped they would have a pleasant journey. Then she sang a folk song in a broad Irish accent she hadn't had a minute ago.

Hold on a minute. Which terminal was it for Italy? Luke wasn't much of a swearer, but shit: he'd have to guess.

The train was slowing again and this time – yep – here they were. He jumped up to his feet too fast, just as the train braked, and because he was facing forward he toppled into the man with the hat. His hand, the bad one, crashed against the glass panel behind the man's head.

Sorry, he said.

The man said something in French.

These damn trains, Luke said, trying to smile.

The doors thumped open and Luke tried to push his way in front of the crowd, knocking a couple of elbows as he passed. It was impossible to make much headway on the escalator. People had put their luggage down and although one side was clear it was too narrow. So he put his suitcase down like everyone else, and waited for the stairs to grind their way to the top.

Up ahead of him two men in suits were talking about cars.

Cost me six hundred quid.

What, third party?

Would have been seven if I'd gone for the turbo.

Luke could sense a familiar worried expression attaching itself to his features. It had all seemed so simple a moment ago, but now the old doubts were stirring once more. The way Carmen pushed the door closed. The way she leaned away from his kiss. First refusal. The story wasn't over yet, not by a long chalk.

The first thing he saw when he finally made it to the top was a yellow arrow pointing to a phone box. But the plane was due to leave in – blimey – five minutes. For all he knew the engines were turning faster even now, flexing their muscles, rising to their crushing pitch of howl and whine. Stewardesses might be walking up and down the central aisle, glancing to right and left, making sure people had their seat belts on. Shrill, ice-rink music was probably spilling out of the invisible speakers above the seats.

If they'd just let him check in, he'd be home and dry.

Always assuming he was in the right place. If he wasn't, then, well, he could phone anyone he liked.

A voice filled the air. Would Karen somebody, who's meeting Michael something, please go to second-floor Information. The voice sounded as if it had been a long day.

There weren't as many people around as Luke had expected. A few floor cleaners drove in circles leaving a broad damp trail behind them. Knots of uniformed aircrew cut diagonally across the clean tiles.

What would Carmen be doing? Driving those people back to the office? Sitting at her desk already, sipping juice and wondering what had happened back there at the house? Shaking her head with that slight hasty flick to keep the hair out of her eyes, noticing the time and conjuring up a vision of Luke, strapped in and waiting to be catapulted into the skies above her?

Perhaps, Luke thought, she would have dropped the house-hunters off and headed for the swimming pool (she liked going in the middle of the day). By now she could be pushing water up in front of her face as she dragged herself from end to end, eyes going red from the chlorine.

He had his eye out for a trolley: he could push faster than he could lug. Those men from the escalator were arguing with the ticket collector, but he was being strict: no tickets, no entry.

Over there! Luke got in just ahead of a lady with a child on her hip. He grabbed the handle and swung it round fast, almost catching a boy in an anorak who was hanging around, sucking something on a stick.

Now, which way?

Excuse me, he said to the ticket collector. Which way for Italy?

That way. The man raised an arm towards several tunnels.

On the left?

No, straight on. He jerked his head.

Luke picked the centre tunnel.

These travelators: in theory they speeded things up, but usually a clump of people spread themselves out across the rubber belt and blocked the way, and you ended up wishing you had stayed on the polished tile floor. Luke needed all the help he could get, so he pushed the trolley through the silver teeth and onto the sliding tongue of the walkway, trying not to break stride, trying to stick to the steady trotting rhythm he had found, a rhythm he felt he could keep up for ever.

The air was full of announcements about flights and gates. Luke listened out for Rome but could hear only Frankfurt, Paris, Athens, Zurich, Glasgow and a few other places. It looked as though he was in the right terminal, at least.

On either side brightly-lit advertisements overlooked the passengers. Some of them, Luke couldn't help noticing, were for airlines. Did people say, Oh look, America's first, let's give it a go! or: All these destinations – Malta, Israel, Florida, Korea! Did holidaymakers turn up at the airport and say to themselves, Hmmm, that looks nice? Did they ever change their minds at the last minute and decide to go somewhere else?

One of the adverts was for a book. It said: Relieve terminal boredom.

If only . . . Luke wouldn't have minded a few hours with his head in a novel. Or boredom – that was fine by him as well, it would be better than this. But he was talking minutes . . .

Over the loudspeakers he heard the last call for Rome. Don't go without me, he muttered. A couple of moments is all I need.

Up another escalator, into the huge departure hall. Kiosks everywhere with colourful corporate insignia lit with neon. Men in short-sleeved white shirts with identity passes clipped to their breast pocket. The smell of talcum powder and air-conditioning. People sitting around just waiting, waiting. They weren't from here, and weren't coming here. They'd touched down for a few hours and didn't know what to do except sit.

Maybe this is what people were really after, this odd dislocation – they could be anywhere, after all. It didn't matter where you were heading, if you passed through an airport you suffered that stomach-tightening feeling of being in a place at once strange and familiar. Long journeys demanded sharp concentration, so it was always distressing to see how many other people were embarking on the same routine adventure.

Forget all that: Luke saw the sign he was looking for, up past the coffee shop that showed how raw and natural it was by painting a little sombrero over the O of coffee, and scurried towards it. That jaunty hat reminded him of – oh yes,

Mexican Orange Blossom. Honey's about the only thing they can't fake . . .

Jesus! He hurried along the booths looking for the shortest queue. He ran through a cloud of perfume from a one hundred per cent natural cosmetics chain, and breathed in as deeply as he could the essences of ginger, cherries, mint and rose. There were television screens all over the place, filling the air with the grey flicker of faraway places.

I fondly hope that you'll miss me a bit, too . . .

Quick! Up ahead there was just a single man with a deerstalker, leaning on the desk, chatting to the hostess.

Damn. Executive Superclub. But maybe they wouldn't mind. He tried to catch the ticket clerk's eye, but she was talking. Then a voice behind him said:

Well, if it isn't Luke.

Luke turned.

Brian! Gosh. Hello.

Well, that's a bit of luck.

They shook hands. Brian was wearing a dark blue blazer with polished brass buttons and a yellow tie. His ticket poked handily out of his top pocket. He had a snazzy raincoat over his shoulders, gangster-style.

What's a bit of luck?

Just the man. Got a little job for you.

A job?

Sort of. Tell you later. Let's check in first, then have a snifter.

I haven't got much . . . I'm running a bit . . .

Of course! The big day, eh? Rome, isn't it?

Er, yuh. Gate seventeen. Any minute . . .

Say no more. Behind the clock as usual. Still, they're flying you Club, I see. He made a mock-impressed movement with his mouth.

Well . . .

No last-minute second thoughts? Never too late to change your mind . . . He grinned.

Luke felt faint. This couldn't be happening. He couldn't do all this in front of Brian, of all people. The back of his neck was damp and he tried to keep his arms in tight to his sides to keep the heat in. Maybe he should just dash to the gate and see what happened. But the man in front had gathered up his ticket and passport and was getting out of the way. And anyway they probably wouldn't let him through. Still, anything to get away from Brian . . .

Go right ahead, Brian said, smiling. Age before beauty.

Er, actually, I don't think I've got time. I'll do it at the gate. Er, where are you going?

Nice. Some convention or other, you know, ha-ha-ha. Usual sort of thing. Here, hold your horses and I'll give you a hand with that.

It was only a few days since he had left the office for the last time, but Luke had already forgotten Brian's enthusiasm for scattering well-worn phrases as if he'd just thought of them.

Er, thanks. No, it's fine. Listen, I've really got to . . . How is everything?

Oh, you know. Swings and roundabouts.

Yeah. Luke wondered how he could get out of this. But he couldn't resist the urge to apologise for something.

I don't know, he said. About leaving and everything. It seemed a good idea at the time. After a few days I'll probably be dreaming about that old coffee machine.

Oh never mind all that. Actually, truth is, the way things are going we might have had to let you go anyway. I can tell you now. With this big reorganisation coming up, you know. Anyway, all water under the bridge.

It was as if someone had cut one of the strings that held Luke up. What are you saying? he said. And there must have been something in his voice to make Brian pause.

Yes, well, sorry, he said. Mister tactless. Didn't mean it like that. I thought the old office grapevine would have already turned that one into champagne. Nothing to do with me, I hasten to add. But yes, the word coming down from on high is that changes are afoot.

On high? Afoot?

Cutbacks all round, I'm afraid, Brian said. But bugger that for a lark, you've made your own bed now, and good luck to you, that's what I say. He leaned forward and propped his briefcase against a pillar. Suddenly he seemed, to Luke, old. His stomach, when he leaned forward, sagged over his belt in a white bulge. No, he said when he straightened, and the effort of bending added a breathy edge to his voice. Go for it, that's my advice. See the world. Christ, if I was your age . . .

Luke couldn't afford to start feeling sorry for the guy. He cleared his throat and turned his head, hoping to catch the eye of the ticket clerk.

Brian noticed. His voice, when he spoke again, had changed, into something brighter.

Now about this job. When's your flight, exactly? Got time for a stiffener?

No, it's any minute. Eleven fifteen.

Good, good. Like a man who cuts it fine. Best get your skates on, though.

Yes, I think I had. Luke put his hand out.

Wait, though. Check in here. Once they've got your luggage you're quids in.

He had a point there. But, oh . . . Luke swallowed.

Well, but I'm not actually Club. I was just hoping . . .

Brian was pushing past him.

Morning, he said, with all the accent and a bit of upwards stress on the *ing*. He laid a pile of documents on the desk. Luke could see American Express badges, frequent flyer cards, most favoured customer status printed all over the place. The 203 to Nice, please. Aisle, smoking. But first, my colleague here's late for his Rome flight. We'll check him in here, please.

Certainly, sir. The girl put out a hand for the ticket. Luke caught a flash of floral perfume and bright red fingernails like rosehips. He gave her his papers and held his breath. There was bound to be a problem: she'd notice that he wasn't in Club, the flight would be closed, he was too late. He realised now that the reason he hadn't wanted to check in was that he had wanted to postpone hearing the bad news.

But the girl was tapping things into her computer. You're lucky, sir. There's a delay on the flight.

Delay?

Only ten minutes. Don't worry, you're still late.

Hah. Thank God for that.

Hand luggage?

Luke held up his briefcase.

Did you pack all your bags yourself, sir?

What? Yes.

Did you leave your bags unattended at any time?

Yes, yes. And no electronic goods, nothing.

Only smoking left, sir.

No problem.

Smoking, or passive smoking? Brian said. Ha, ha, ha.

There we are, sir. Please go directly to gate forty-six, they're on last call.

A boarding pass came lurching out of the slit in her desk.

Thank you, thank you. Luke picked up his briefcase.

Enjoy your flight, sir.

I will. Thank you. Luke turned to Brian. Brian . . . that was . . . thanks. He gave a little splutter to show he was relieved. Thought I was done for.

Hang on. This won't take a mo. The girl was already running her fingers over the keys, hardly looking at what she was doing.

Did you say smoking, sir?

Yes indeedy.

Another boarding card came jumping out of the computer with that familiar dzzz-dzzz-dzzz printing noise.

Now, where were we? Brian rubbed his hands together. Gate what, did you say?

Forty-six.

Okey-dokey. I'm in the same direction.

Where did you say you were going?

Nice. Well, Monaco actually. Christ, look at that. Ten o'clock.

What?

Ten o'clock. The one in black. Mmmm, feast your eyes on those. God, if I were ten years younger . . .

They joined a queue of people waiting to have their passports checked. No one seemed to be moving. Up ahead, and a bit to the left, a girl stood smoking. It made Luke feel like one himself. She wore a low-cut halter and a pair of cut-off jeans. Her head nodded in time to some music no one else could hear.

Yeah, Luke said. What was Brian on about?

He thought of Carmen. So, that's agreed. Hardly the most romantic thing you'd ever heard. At the time it seemed exhilarating. In here, well, it was all getting confused again.

You married yet, Luke?

Sorry?

Married. You know, spliced.

Er, no. Luke looked the other way.

Lucky man. Footloose and fancy-free. That's the way to be.

Oh? Would this queue never move? What were they doing up there?

Me, I tied the old knot years ago. Well, you can probably guess. Two kids, two cars, two dogs, two tellies, you name it. Too bloody much. If it weren't for the odd spring jaunt, the odd, you know, business trip . . . Any idea what the French are like? He poked Luke in the ribs with his elbow.

Like?

Well, it's all right for you. Italy, my God. Have a job to keep your powder dry over there, old man. Absolutely begging for it. All over the place.

Oh well, you never know. For some reason, Luke forced himself to give a modest smirk, which died on his lips as soon as he found himself thinking of a single empty glass on a mantelpiece, a cluster of amber tears at the bottom.

Well, just in case, Brian said. Here, have you got a pen? I know this place in Rome, I'll give you the address.

Luke shook his head and started to mumble something about the time. But there was no stopping Brian. He had a pen out and was writing something on the back of a business card.

Here you go. It's called Carla's. Absolutely amazing. Private club, but you pay at the door. And the waitresses, you've never seen anything like it. They put one each side of your face when they bring you a drink. I'm not joking: literally one each side. Fanbloodytastic. He paused. Pretty pricey, of course, he said. Only really works if you're on exes . . .

Brian, Luke said. I really think I'm going to have to run, okay. It was awfully nice . . .

Keep your trousers on. They won't go without you, not with

your case checked. Besides, there's something you could do for me. Let's just get through this, okay.

He slipped off to one side, Luke following, and marched up the side of the queue towards an empty desk. Excuse me, he said in a loud voice. Excuse me. He held his passport up high, and gestured to Luke to do the same. We're dreadfully late, he called. Thank you so much.

And they were through!

Luke couldn't say that he liked Brian much, but he was impressed. He couldn't have done anything like that on his own, not in a million years.

As I was saying, Brian said as they walked through the bars, past the chairs with people curled up sleeping, past the blazing duty-free shop. There's this little thing I need you to do.

Ah, this was the bit of luck. The duty-free, Luke thought. He's going to ask me to go shopping.

It's nothing really. It's . . . well.

Well?

I wonder, I mean. It's a bit tricky to explain. Without stopping, he snapped open his briefcase and took out a small paper bag. Postcards, he said.

Luke took them in his free hand, pushed the paper up into the cut on his thumb, and winced.

What's the matter?

Oh, nothing, Cut my hand.

Well, be bloody careful, all right.

What do you want me to do with them?

What do you think? Post them. Do I have to spell it out? Christ almighty, cop a load of that. Three o'clock, in the fur hat. Hold me back, hold me back.

Luke put the postcards in his pocket.

Okay, he said. I'll post them. But he was curious. What would you have done, he said, if you hadn't run into me?

I was going to catch a train down to Rome. Only takes a day, there and back.

Luke remembered something. Are you on your own? he asked.

What's it look like? Brian gave him a funny look.

So why Rome?

There's a conference going on, believe it or not. No one will be any the wiser.

And meanwhile . . .

Ah, meanwhile . . . Suffice it to say this particular hard-working pillar of the family is off for a little rest and recreation. Mum's the word, old man, mum's the word. Just be sure and post the cards, there's a good chap. I go left here.

And he did. He peeled away without a word; and without a backward glance he strode, swinging his briefcase ever so slightly, right down the centre of the corridor. A large group of young people, students, were coming the other way, pushing trolleys loaded high with bags and tennis racquets. Brian didn't change his course for a second. The students had to swerve aside, and the group split into two parties which separated and wheeled on either side of him. Then they came together again, and Brian vanished into a black hole made of other people, for ever.

Luke took a deep breath. It was easy enough to say they wouldn't leave without him, but who knew? He looked around. He was standing by a sales stand full of shirts that changed colour according to your body temperature.

He broke into a run. Someone heard him coming up behind and tried to move out of the way, but only succeeded in straying smack into his path.

He heard his name booming over the loudspeakers.

God, everyone could hear. He tried to speed up without making it look as though he were responding to the tannoy. It's not me, he tried to tell the passengers coming the other way. I don't know anyone of that name.

Sorry, he breathed. Sorry.

When he ran into the boarding lounge no one was there except for a couple of stewardesses. They were closing the big double doors at the far end. On the left, plate-glass windows looked out over the apron where the aircraft stood. He could see a wing and a tailplane, but they were blurred by quivering fumes. They were ready to push off.

Come on, sir, the women called. They're closing the door.

The phones, Luke thought. He wanted to give her a ring right now, goddamnit. To make sure. What had she said? I'll be happy to refer your offer to the vendor? First refusal? That didn't sound very . . .

And these phones were just begging to be used, crying out for someone to pick them up. All you had to do was push a few coins in or use one of those cards, and within seconds Carmen would be there, saying Luke, oh Luke, I'm so glad . . .

But it was impossible. The stewardesses were smiling, as if they enjoyed the sweaty comedy of the last-minute dash, even though they must have seen it a million times. He couldn't possibly hold them up any longer.

Besides, he was in mental disarray. He felt as though he had finally made it up the long steps to the top board, but now it was time to dive off, and he wasn't so sure. For a moment he wished himself back in Carmen's flat, a plate of bacon and eggs on the table, the morning stretching out so far ahead of him that it seemed like a whole lifetime.

What was she doing this minute? Tying a knot in a strand of hair, rolling it round her fingers the way she did when she was concentrating? Crossing her legs, with one foot twisted all the way round behind the other? Squinting at the phone, wondering if there was still time?

But there wasn't. Even a snatched call on a payphone, in a mass-produced waiting room that smelled, just faintly, of petrol fumes and electricity, struck Luke at this moment as passionate in the extreme. But it wasn't possible.

He could feel the packet of postcards in his pocket. For a moment he felt like tipping them out, letting them drop to the floor of the lounge so that everyone could see them. But he didn't do it.

As he paced across the boarding lounge he could not resist the feeling that the ground was unstable, that any one of his steps might trigger an explosion. He didn't know where to put his feet, and his hands itched.

One of the stewardesses looked at his ticket and tore it in half. As he passed down the dark corridor towards the cabin he could hear the roar of the engines and the hiss of compressed air. He tried to steady his breathing, but it was difficult. His heart was beating too fast. He could almost feel it swelling and shrinking, swelling and shrinking as the blood rushed through in big waves.

Forty-three-A, he said to the man at the door. The man held out a hand, this side, sir. On the right. You're just in time.

Yuh, Luke couldn't quite manage a smile. Thanks.

People looked up as he ambled down the aisle, his seat, worst luck, was at the back. The passengers up here in the expensive seats seemed well dressed and calm which only made him feel even more hot and awkward. He was aware that his freshly-ironed collar was grimy, that his jacket was creased and his shoes scuffed. But it would be okay as soon as he sat down. Everyone looked the same then. The pitch of the engines rose several degrees and Luke heard the door thump shut behind him.

It made an awful noise. Luke felt the blood drain from his face. Suddenly he could see how eloquent his silence must appear to Carmen. Sod the ring he was going to give her later. He couldn't leave without phoning her. He simply couldn't.

He turned and hurried back to the door. A man wearing a smart cap was just putting his weight against a red lever.

Excuse me, Luke said. I'm really sorry, but . . .

The man straightened.

My wallet, Luke said. I've left it in the boarding lounge. Can I just . . . It won't take a minute.

The man looked suspicious.

Sorry, sir. I can't let you off.

But it's got everything . . . it's only just over there. I know exactly where I must have left it.

The man seemed to take a decision. He unhooked a phone from the cabin wall.

I'll call the desk, he said. They'll bring it through.

But Luke was pulling at the lever, pushing at the door. Really, he said. It'll only take . . .

The door sprang open.

Luke was aware of a hand on his arm and then he was running. Running as if against the clock, running as if his whole life were in the balance, running for all the world as if some remote force had taken possession of him. The floor beneath his feet felt as thin as the skin of a drum and he ran as if he might fall through it at any moment, as if he were only one step away from catastrophe. As his feet bounced on the rubber mats, in his mind the same things tumbled into a combination that seemed to open all the locks. The chauffeur holding open the door of that big black car . . . a whisky tumbler on a white mantelpiece . . . a plate of cold bacon and fried eggs . . . the warm surface of a brown river, with Carmen's slim shoulders . . . his empty, empty flat . . . the racks and piles of glinting tins and bags of preserved food on disinfected shelves . . . He hurtled upwards and threw his shoulder at the double doors into the boarding lounge.

There was no one there. At the far end, a phone rang on one of the desks.

Luke ran to the hooded perspex booths and, his hands shaking, pushed his credit card through the slot. Then he dialled the number. He could hear feet hurrying up the passageway, and voices.

Hello? Carmen?

Hello?

It's Luke. He couldn't believe it. She was there. Listen, the plane's about to leave. I just wanted to say . . . well, oh God, yes. Hello?

Hello?

Christ Almighty. Can you hear me?

Hello?

Yes, for Christ's sake. I'm saying yes, basically. Yes. I meant what I said. I'll top any offer that's going. Can you hear?

The phone went down.

Luke felt a hand on his shoulder and heard a voice saying, Come along, sir.

I'll call again, he shouted. Listen, can you hear . . . ?

Someone clutched his wrist and took the phone from his hand. I'm sorry, he said. I just had to make that call.

All right, sir. Easy does it.

What, did they think he had lost his wits or something? Luke gripped the credit card in his hand until he felt the blood coming through again. Years of forms and letters and interest charges and he still didn't have enough credit to buy himself a few seconds of telephone time. He shook his head.

Then he realised: it wasn't Carmen. She didn't say Hello like that. She said Hi, Carmen speaking. It must have been Jenny. Or Fiona, or whatever her name was.

Thank God she hadn't heard him.

I'm okay, he said. I'll come back now. I didn't mean . . .

And they led him back to the aircraft.

I know, sir, one of the men said. Our slot's in five minutes.

Four or five members of the cabin crew had gathered in the doorway and watched Luke being led back on board. One of them wanted another look at Luke's passport.

It's okay, the man said, still holding Luke's arm. Idiot wanted to make a phone call, that was all.

Quite a few heads craned up to look at Luke. The people in the front seats had seen the disturbance. But Luke didn't care. He looked straight ahead as he walked down the aisle, tapping his fingers on the headrests as he passed by: 40, 41, 42 – hello, what was this?

Seat 43A was next to the window, and look – someone was already sitting there. An Indian woman, or maybe Pakistani, quite smart, lots of bright make-up and a pink headscarf. Luke didn't want to make a fuss, but he liked the idea of sitting by the little porthole. You could get a grandstand view of the reservoirs when the plane took off, and then there were the Alps, and the towns along the Mediterranean coast. It'd be panoramic all the way, and even if you couldn't see anything, Luke would be happy to stare at the tops of the clouds. They seemed so solid from above, as if they would catch you if you fell. Anyway, he was damned if he was going to let someone else sit there. Hell, she was probably off to meet the husband her parents had chosen for her, a nice boy, you'll get on well, sign here. Who cared what she was up to, so long as she moved?

He began to peer up at the numbers above the seats and then down at his boarding pass, so that the woman would realise that there'd been a mistake and he wouldn't have to say anything. But then she spoke.

Would you mind terribly, she said, if I stayed in the window seat? I'd be so grateful.

Oh, right, Luke said. Fine. His knees felt a bit soft – to be honest he didn't care which seat he had. That's fine. I'll just – he

211

pushed his bag into the overhead locker – get rid of this . . .

And he sat down.

The sweat on his back started to cool in the controlled atmosphere. He pulled out the in-flight magazine and turned the pages. Golfing paradises, culinary delights . . . the usual. There was a special feature about the joys of icebergs: apparently you could go hot-air ballooning over the Arctic Ocean, and enjoy a bird's-eye view of the shadowy green depths that supported the pale ice-slivers above. Luke thought of the vast frozen reservoirs down there, shivered, and turned the pages fast. His attention snagged, though, on a photograph of a huge fish – the first 100lb salmon ever caught, according to the caption. It was tempting to imagine someone wrestling the giant fish down some fast-flowing river, the water turning white as the salmon twisted and flapped. But it had been caught in a reservoir; probably it had been fattened in a tank and stocked in the lake only a few days before. Luke sighed.

I do appreciate it, the woman said, turning to him with a smile. It was so late, I thought no one was coming.

She was rather well-spoken, Luke registered. Almost posh.

Yes, it's a bit of a miracle, he said. I got stuck. You know, the tube . . .

He looked at her. Underneath her scarf was a lot of very dark hair. She'd be, oh, about thirty – but it was hard to tell. She could have been much older. Her teeth seemed very white. There was a magazine on her lap.

Did you see . . . ? I mean . . .

See what?

Well, there was a bit of a scuffle . . .

A scuffle?

She must have been reading, or something.

Nothing serious, Luke forced himself to smile. They were just shutting the door. It was a close thing.

Anyway, you made it.

Just, yes.

And you're going to Italy?

Er, yes. I suppose we all are. He turned his head a couple of times to include everyone. He couldn't help feeling that they were all still staring at him, but it didn't seem to bother him that much. Who cared?

A holiday?

Work, I'm afraid. How about you?

Oh, just a tourist.

Luke didn't know what to say next. His heart had started to race again. It was as if, now that he at last had time to just sit back and think about things, it was too late. He could still hear the thump of the door that had just closed again, and it made him feel cut loose, cast off. It had been a bad morning for doors closing. This one made him feel that he had taken a step he might never retrace.

Where are you from? he heard the woman ask.

London, he said. It was usually easier just to say that. How about you? Where are you from?

Well, you had to be polite.

Me? Canterbury. You know Canterbury?

Well, I know where it is. But where are you really from?

Her eyelids fell just a fraction and there was a slight, patient pause.

Canterbury, she said. She looked at Luke in a kind way.

How *could* he have? If there had been such a thing as a delete character button to hand, Luke would have pressed it. How *could* he?

A lot of people ask that, she said.

That only made it worse.

No, I only ask, he said. Because I'm from Ceylon, actually.

She laughed, and patted him on the arm.

Well, I forgive you, she said.

Luke smiled. What else was he supposed to do?

He hunted in the bag at his feet, came out with the guidebook, and began to turn the pages. Lots of paintings and churches, pillars and columns, frescoes and friezes and fountains, even some things that were probably pilasters. Luke flicked past the art treasures and stopped when he came to a section called Driving in Rome. It was not very informative: there were exclamation marks and a picture of a traffic jam wrapped round the Colosseum. But there was this one detail. At night, Luke read, they switched the lights to flashing amber and let the traffic do all the work itself.

Luke winced. Flashing amber! My God, he was going to have his work cut out.

But when he thought about it some more, he was surprised to discover that he didn't mind at all.

And then he closed his eyes.

It was as if he was falling through space, plummeting down through some crack in the pavement. From far away he heard a voice. Oh, no, they were calling his name. Would he please report to the steward.

He unsnapped his seat belt and lurched back towards the front. Someone was coming to meet him.

Message for you, sir. Important, sounds like.

Carmen! It could only be Carmen! That wasn't her on the phone, how could it have been? At that very moment she was sprinting along the endless travelators towards the information desk . . .

Where?

Just step outside, sir.

Thank you.

He was off the plane again. Would it leave . . . ?

Oh, who cared?

A stewardess was waiting, or maybe she wasn't a stewardess, what did it matter? She led him back into the boarding lounge and handed him one of the utility phones that was lying on the desk by the computer.

Luke?

Carmen! Where are you?

I'm upstairs. No, downstairs. I'm here, at the airport.

I'm coming. Stay there.

You don't know where I am . . .

I'll find you . . .

He put the phone down and said, I've got to go and meet her downstairs. Don't worry about the flight, I can take a later . . .

But your baggage, sir, we can't . . .

Take it with you, that's fine by me. I'll catch up with it. Don't worry.

And he set off.

The corridors seemed even longer this time. They seemed to go on for ever. Luke wasn't aware of the slightest physical sensation as he walked – forget about running, he didn't want to be all sweaty and breathless – back past the boarding lounges towards the departure lounge, and then back through into the main hall. He showed his passport to a man who said, Welcome back, sir.

He couldn't believe that a happy ending was happening to him, him of all people.

There she was! Running! Luke put his arms out to catch her and she almost threw herself into them. He nearly fell over, but managed to wheel round just in time, and Carmen's feet described a perfect circle in the air before they landed on the slippery linoleum floor.

I can't believe I made it. I can't believe . . .

Believe it, said Luke. It's all true. He pushed his face down into her soft, soft hair and . . .

And then he opened his eyes, and what the hell was that . . . ?

The plane gave a little jolt, and began to move backwards.

What in Christ's name? He couldn't have been . . . It was so . . .

The Indian woman put her arm on one of the handrests as if she thought she might be about to lose her balance.

This is it, she said.

Sorry?

Nothing. We're off. Are you all right?

Yes, fine. A bit . . . but fine.

Me too, I'm nervous.

Oh, it's not that. I've just had . . . it's been a long day. Luke let his head settle back into the rest.

I'd have been awfully cross if you hadn't turned up, you know.

What?

If you hadn't come. My husband had to take a different flight. There weren't enough seats.

Your husband?

Yes, we're meeting there.

Luke rubbed his forehead. I'm sorry, he said. I don't understand.

It doesn't matter. You're here now.

You mean, because of me your husband had to go on another plane?

The woman nodded.

An earlier one?

No. It leaves in an hour.

Let me get this straight . . . Luke tried to see what it all meant, but could only make out dim outlines. He had a general sense that modern timetables were too stiff to accommodate the ancient vagaries of human conduct, and as for the idea that other people would have been delighted if he had delayed by an hour – it was an irony almost too painful to contemplate.

I wish I'd known, he said in a quiet voice. I'd have been perfectly happy to take a later flight.

Oh well, we'll all get there in the end.

Actually, I'd have done anything for another hour.

How so?

Can I ask you something, Luke said. How long have you been married?

The woman looked surprised, but smiled.

Three months, she said. We didn't have time for a honeymoon, so this is it.

I feel awful, Luke said. You should have travelled together, with your husband. Maybe it's not too late. I don't mind getting off.

The woman patted his arm once more. It's all right. I'm happy on my own. Anyway, I've got you now.

Luke didn't answer. It was rude, but he couldn't help that. He didn't even know the woman. The whole morning had been spent talking, for the most part, to people he didn't know or didn't like. The one person he wanted to be with was . . .

This was no time to be having sinking feelings, but that seemed to be the size of it. He was still on the plane. Carmen wasn't. And that was that.

What was it, though? What had this morning been all about?

He wasn't at all certain that he would be able to stand the strain of not knowing . . . How long was this flight going to take? What would Carmen say when he got there?

God, all these questions. It was about time someone came up with some answers. But who?

He started to rewind his morning. Two clocks that told different times. Carmen's proposal. I realise it's unconventional. I hope that hasn't bothered you. The lie. The slap. His father on the phone about the shopping. The toy bus. The wrong letter out of the swing bin. The five-item queue. The house-buying deception – Philip, quick! This man says he wants to put in an offer – it was practically fraud! Brian. Fanbloodytastic. The ludicrous dash off the plane. The woman sitting in his seat. The vicar standing outside his church, waiting and praying for someone, anyone, to turn up.

Conventions were . . . convenient.

Was that all?

He knew the bus had been trying to tell him something when it knocked him down. Life, let's face it, was too big to see. That's all there was to it. You couldn't hope to see everything, calculate everything. You just had to follow the rules and hope for the best.

But which rules?

Suddenly, Luke had a brainwave. What if the computer didn't bother to count all the cars and work out how fast they were going? What if it looked, instead, for gaps. Any space longer than ten seconds would trigger the lights. And you could domino that data through the whole network in a flash . . .

It was a thought: he could investigate it further once he got to Rome. It would mean giving the computer different ground rules, starting from scratch . . .

Ground rules: they were what stopped people taking those wrong steps that made life blow up in your face. They were to do with coming together, to do with getting married. Take a conventional emotion like . . . he shuddered.

No such thing as marriage in general? Perhaps Carmen was dead-on. Only this morning he'd been offered a range of different versions: Brian, Jonathan, Mrs Granville, his father, the house-hunters, this civilised woman next to him – they didn't seem to have anything in common at all.

It struck Luke that the time he lived in was teetering between conventions. It had pretty much sacrificed the old ones, and no one had programmed in the new ones. So it was every man for himself. And every woman. Oh, you could follow any convention you pleased, but you could never tell if other people were using the same one. You could talk up your hearts all you wanted, but your partner might carry on thinking about diamonds. And there was nothing – nothing! – you could do about it.

God, he'd been stupid. Stupid, stupid, stupid. But it wasn't too late. His offer was on the table. All it would take was a ring.

He felt in his pocket for the O, and heard the crunch of paper as he leaned against the postcards in his pocket.

Running into Brian had been just about the last straw, but still . . . he was curious . . .

To take the cards out of his pocket he had to lean out over the aisle. These seats were damn narrow.

Yes, he'd said. Basically yes. He'd top any offer that was going. Though if Carmen hadn't heard, a mischievous voice butted in, he could still change his mind. It was a free country.

Don't start, don't start.

They all showed the same view, he could see that at once: a wide-angle shot of Rome from the air. Flicking through, Luke could see that they all had the same message, except one.

Darling, he read. No alarms so far – usual sort of thing. And no time for any sightseeing, so far. Rome looks hot and full from here, though. Tried to ring a couple of times. Hope all's well. Give Horace a pat from me. Love, Brian.

Hell's bells. Is this what happened to people who got married? Did they all end up with deceitful postcards? No wonder they called it adultery. It was so . . . grown up.

They were swinging round and speeding up. The music stopped and videos unwound onto the screens moulded into the plastic ceiling, by the individual air vents and reading lights. A girl was showing you how to blow a whistle in the unlikely event of a landing on water. Luke had seen it plenty of times before, but if he looked away he started to feel guilty, so he kept one eye on the pictures of oxygen masks and escape chutes.

He wondered who Brian would be meeting in Monaco. Would she know he had given someone a bunch of cards to send from

Rome to fool his family? Hell, maybe he'd got the wrong end of the stick completely. Maybe Brian was meeting up with some mates for a few days of golf by the seaside. It would have been typical of him to pretend it was something else.

He shoved the cards into the elastic net on the seat in front and sat back. The captain was apologising for the slight delay, but saying that they had a good wind behind them so they ought to be able to make up for the lost time. Weather in Rome – a very pleasant twenty degrees, he told them. The plane was stationary, and the atmosphere had turned tense. Any minute now . . .

You've written your postcards already? How British.

Luke turned his head.

No, they're from someone else.

How could he explain it?

He felt like an arrow in a bow, the string pulled back in a tight angle behind him. But where was he being fired? Towards something, or away? He thought of that list he had made, all the things he hadn't done. The bank, the envelope . . . it didn't seem to matter now. And then he thought of the other list, the one with the big questions.

It sounds like a plot, the woman said.

Yes, Luke said. That's what I'm starting to think.

You know, you forget to post the cards, so someone doesn't get an important message, so they don't know something they were supposed to know, so life gets turned upside down . . .

Hey, this was pretty good.

That's not bad, Luke said. Or you deliberately don't post them, knowing that you can mess up . . .

Or you could write new ones with different messages, imitating the handwriting . . .

Or you could just change the addresses, so everyone gets the wrong version . . .

There was a pause.

The wrong version of what?

Oh, I don't know. Events.

And before either of them could say another thing, they were away. Luke felt himself being pushed back into his seat and the plane surged down the runway. He imagined the headwind curling under the flaps, struggling to lift the great wings. He glanced across and through the window; he could see the steel tips shaking as the damp, oily air skidded past the leading edge.

And then came that moment of miraculous release as the juddering from the wheels stopped, just like that, and the tyres sailed away from the concrete airstrip.

Luke had expected to feel something crystal, something clear – but instead he felt dizzy; and he gripped the armrests hard with his two hands. His thumb still hurt.

For a minute he let the force of the take-off push him back into his seat and then, as soon as the plane began to climb less steeply, he felt that strange sensation of weightless comfort. He was sitting on a velcro-cushion with a corporate motif stitched into it, and he was moving at high speed. He was sitting in a seat that had been held and prepared for him over a month ago. He was sitting beside someone pleasant, and soon one of those nice women would bring him a drink. For the first time since he had woken up, a gentle shower of blessed calm passed over him.

He looked out of the window, past the pink scarf and that exotic profile, and saw the sky turning blue as the plane shrugged off the last of the clouds. Then he closed his eyes.

There was this one moment in his youth. He'd travelled to the Alps with a school group. They'd been practising on small rocks at home, but this was their first taste of the real thing.

He was still only a beginner. But one day he found himself high up and alone. Everyone else had made it to the top; he was the last. The orange rope snaked up in front of his face and then disappeared. Because of the curve of the rock he could see nothing of the people above him on the ledge. The sun had been shining all day, but suddenly it was cold. There was moisture on the rock, and when Luke looked off to his right he could see skeins of mist coming in fast. Higher up and all around, it seemed, great drifts of snow and ice turned suddenly blue.

And he couldn't move. He had a firm grip on the rock, but could not force himself to make the smallest movement. His hands, stretched out above him, the arms almost vertical, refused to let go. He didn't even seem to be breathing, and for a while he didn't know how long he was hanging there.

And then, all at once, he seemed to fall through this freezing fear and began, for the first time in his life, to climb with the kind of magical rhythm he had until then only read about. His hands and fingers seemed never to be still, his toes and knees were sensitive to the faintest alterations in the granite. He seemed to weigh nothing: it cost the muscles in his arms and his legs no effort at all. He floated up like a fly on the stalk of a daisy.

It was as if his hands and feet and hips became part of the rock; they seemed tailored to these minute fissures and creases and knuckles of granite. For a few moments he belonged to the mountain, and the mountain belonged to him. And for a few moments he was inspired by a precious sort of self-knowledge, the sort that knows it is doing something remarkable and is happy. He clutched on to a knob of stone and it struck him that his might be the first hand ever to touch it. Maybe it would be the last, too. A million-year-old geological shift had thrown up this one chance encounter.

He knew that if he were to think about this for even an instant he would lose his footing. So he looked the other way as he climbed, and felt himself dissolving into the blue ice, into the white sky. And he felt his heart turn cold as he danced up the rock.

What had he gained up there on the mountain? What had he lost? Something decisive had happened to him, that was all he knew, something to do with solitude, something to do with happiness. Afterwards, when he made it to the ledge, he was almost bursting with excitement. But then someone said, What kept you? and he couldn't think of a single thing to say.

Did this have any bearing on Carmen? Up here in mid-air, the skies in his mind seemed to clear. Wherever he looked he could see her – walking up the stairs ahead of him that first time, smooth legs covered in silk, kicking her shoes under the sofa after they'd had dinner, pushing that amazing hair away from her eyes, rolling around and around in the centre of the river, her hands clasped tight round his neck. It took almost no effort to imagine her sitting right here beside him, on the plane. He took the letter from his jacket pocket, started to read it again, smiled, and decided not to bother. He folded the letter into a small square and wedged it into the elastic basket on the back of the seat in front.

Even in that moment of inspiring solitude he had been grateful for the nylon rope that tied him to the other people higher up. You had to know the difference between life on the surface and life in the depths. But you couldn't allow yourself to live in either place. You had to throw ropes, frail threads, from one to the other. And then you had to hang on for dear life.

For some reason the thing he couldn't shake from his mind was the image of those big black cars and the people standing around, being gentle with each other.

Basically yes, he'd said. He smiled. He'd give her a ring when he landed.

Anything to drink at all, sir?

Luke opened his eyes.

Beer, wine, soft drinks?

Er, beer. Beer would be great. Out of the corner of his eye he saw the Indian woman lean forward in a flash of pink.

Actually, make that orange juice, he said.

Ice?

Sorry?

Ice in your orange juice, sir?

Oh, no thank you.

He looked over his shoulder. His view was blocked by the big aluminium drinks cart, but he could see the tops of people's heads, and a few plumes of cigarette smoke.

Will you be having the beef or the vegetarian, sir? he heard a voice say. But it sounded a long way away, and he just shook his head and felt something damp in his eyes, and when he went to speak, not a single word came out. Not a word.

It was eleven thirty-eight, but he wasn't to know that.

THE END

About an hour later, somewhere over the Alps, Luke put down his plastic cup of coffee — black, no sugar: he was trying to get into the mood — and took a notebook out of his briefcase. It had a black cover, a red spine and unruled sheets of white paper. Luke read the solitary line he had written earlier: Friday. Ten Thirty. Dear Carmen, what I should have said was . . .

He put his pen between his teeth for a moment and stared ahead, past the row of heads in front of him, past the grey curtains that screened off the expensive seats and the cockpit, past the high clouds that lay in the path of the aircraft, far out into the future. He thought for a moment longer, and then wrote: Actually, it wasn't the clocks that woke Luke.

He looked at the words, then drew a line through them. He'd have to go further back, all the way to the beginning. It wasn't easy to say where things started and ended, perched as he was on the fragile ledge of the present, suspended over a mile of empty air. But he had to try.

Luke must have been dreaming, he wrote, because one minute he was leaving the office at the usual time and in the usual way, and the next he was lying in the road in front of a large red bus.

He hesitated, then smiled. Even just writing about his extraordinary morning he was still faced with a choice; he still had to be selective.

There was a time — it seemed an age ago — when Luke wanted to be like a second hand. But there was no way to prevent the past from stealing up behind his back: the hour hand always caught up in the end. And the future always beckoned, no matter how fast you erased it.

He was flying at six hundred miles an hour, 28,000 feet above the surface of the earth. His pen was poised above the pure white space below.

For ever and ever, he whispered, Amen.